PRAISE FOR *CRECHELING*

"Vibrant and dangerous."

—Attack of the Books

"*Crecheling* is an exciting, somber, exuberant, measured coming-of-age story on multiple levels, not the least being incorporating readers as well as characters into its meaning. And it is a perfect opening to more stories … and more."

—Dr. Michael R. Collings

"The action-packed plot is full of twists that will keep you on the edge of your seat."

—Sarah E. Seeley

URBANE

A DYSTOPIA

BUZA SYSTEM #2

A DYSTOPIA

URBANE

BUZA SYSTEM #2

D.J. BUTLER

WordFire Press
Colorado Springs, Colorado

URBANE: THE BUZA SYSTEM, BOOK 2
Copyright © 2016 D.J. Butler

ISBN: 978-1-61475-426-8

Cover design by Janet McDonald

Art Director Kevin J. Anderson

Cover artwork images by Dollar Photo Club

Edited by Bryan Thomas Schmidt

Book Design by RuneWright, LLC
www.RuneWright.com

Published by
WordFire Press, an imprint of
WordFire, Inc.
PO Box 1840
Monument CO 80132

Kevin J. Anderson & Rebecca Moesta, Publishers

WordFire Press Trade Paperback Edition August 2016
Printed in the USA
wordfirepress.com

DEDICATION

For Grace Shelby Perry,

an early reader,

who is awesome.

PROLOGUE

The Wahai

J ak sat on the back of the stolen horse and looked down into the Treasure Valley. The valley's name was ancient, at least as old as the settlement where Jak had grown up—Ratsnay Station, a stockade village of farmers and herders to the east and south of where Jak was now, and not far from the ruins of Farkill. Jak could not go home for fear that his mere presence would endanger the life of his only remaining family, his mother, Rosyn.

His sister Aleena had been taken from his family five years ago in what Magister Stanton and the other people of the System had called the Selection, but which had turned out also to be called, by Systemoids in the know, the *Cull*. Aleena and the four taken from Ratsnay Station with her, ostensibly to be brought into the System, were instead marked for ritual slaughter. In this way, inhabitants of the System were made; every Systemoid was a murderer. But Aleena, somehow, had survived and had taken to a life under a false name on the edges of the mountainous Wahai only to be killed as an outlaw in front of Jak just a few days ago, sliced to pieces by a young woman, a Creche-leaver of Buza System.

Murdering Aleena had made the Creche-leaver advance to the status of an Outrider, one of the mounted and far-riding enforcers of the Buza System. With their monofilament whips and bolas and their vibro-blade knives, the Outriders brought outlaws and renegades to the justice of the System, and kept the Basku and the Shoshan of the Wahai, as well as the people in the various settlements around Treasure Valley, in line.

Jak refused to be kept in line.

The savage events of recent weeks had separated Jak from his family and his home. They had also stripped him of his best friend, a fellow Landsman youth of Ratsnay Station named Eirig. Orphaned Eirig had grown up as Jak's brother, and to save Jak he had first given up to the vengeful servants of the System one arm, and then his life.

But Jak was not alone.

Warm autumn breeze riffling his short hair, he turned to look at his companion. Dyan was short and slight, almost boyish in her figure. She was naturally fair, so the recent days of sun had spattered thick clouds of freckles on both cheeks and onto her forearms, when they showed from beneath the black Magister's cloak she had taken from one of her defeated enemies.

He had called her *Systemoid* when they'd met because Dyan had been a Crecheling, a child raised in the nurseries of the System. Dyan had further been a Magister-designate, intended to become one of the teachers and supervisors of the young in the System's twisted structure, and Jak had taken her prisoner and used her as a hostage. As bad luck and misunderstanding and rivalry had turned Dyan's Crechemates against her, Jak had come to see her as a fellow refugee, and then a friend, and then, finally, as something more than a friend.

He had offered to be her Goodman.

They couldn't go back to his home, or to hers, but Jak offered to travel with Dyan into the wilderness and take up farming or sheep. She had accepted, and her acceptance had given Jak a thrill he was too weary to describe. So close on the heels of Eirig's self-sacrifice, muted by exhaustion, and all but snuffed out by fear, the joy of her "yes" had flowed through him like a spring gushing water onto sunbaked desert clay.

But then she had shared with him a revelation.

Magister Zarah, the woman who, as Dyan's final Magister, had brought her to Ratsnay Station to carry out her part in the Cull and thereby become herself a Magister and an Urbane, a full adult participant in the System; the woman whose words had assigned Dyan to kill Jak by her own hand, was Dyan's mother. Dyan had learned it from Zarah herself, in a midnight conversation during their flight, and had it confirmed by Shad and Cheela, her former Crechemates and now both Outriders on their trail.

Zarah, Dyan's mother, had let Dyan and Jak escape. And for that crime, she was now imprisoned somewhere within the System, awaiting execution.

Jak turned to look again at the System itself.

He was Redcap Rider, he told himself, on his flying horse and charging the Sea Ogre to rescue the Chained Maiden. He tightened the muscles of his stomach and raised his chin.

The Buza System, another in the constellation of ancient names, lay along the Buza River. The buildings of the System were all of white stone and the river fed lush parks and gardens. The band of white, green, and late-autumn red cut across a desert that was otherwise a bleached yellow sea of tall dry grasses beneath the watchful stare of the Jawtooth Mountains. Only now were the snowpack's on the highest peaks of the Jawtooths beginning to disappear.

The System filled the valley of the Buza River at the eastern edge of the Treasure Valley, with the foothills of the Jawtooths along one side and a bluff and plateau on the other. Jak stood at the edge of the Wahai, a mountain wilderness on the far western edge of the Treasure Valley. Between him and the System lay the Lull Sea, with Nemap on one shore and Cowell on the other and the Dam at its far northern and western corner, and many miles of desert grass.

"I don't know how to do this," Dyan said. She looked at the System. Jak wanted to remind her they could still walk away. They could risk the ancient spirits Pistols and Guns and make their home in the ruins of Farkill. Or they could pass Farkill and keep going to far Satulak in the south. But he didn't.

"I think," he said instead, "we need to get me something more appropriate to wear."

CHAPTER ONE

s the ship carrying them across the Lull Sea neared Nemap on the far side, Dyan started to express reservations.

It was not the same ship that had carried them across in the other direction a few days earlier. This was a good thing. Jake had no interest in attracting any more attention than he needed. They'd traded their horses for passage rather than paying with anything more distinctive—like the System's square metal Scrip tokens, or a pair of monofilament bolas—in order to avoid standing out.

Even the horses were distinctive enough, being the muscular steeds of the System's Outriders, rather than the Shoshan ponies more common in Nemap.

"You probably already realize this," Dyan said to him over the call of water birds and the slap of waves against the ship's hull, "but the penalty for most crimes in the System is death."

"You're nervous," Jak said.

"No. I'm scared. I don't want to be hanged."

The ship's captain, a heavyset Basku in a green cap, shouted instructions to his Basku crew. Jak liked the fact that they all spoke to each other in Basku. It made him worry less about the crew being interrogated by the Outriders, who were a day or two behind him at most. Cheela and Shad were their names; they had been Dyan's Crechemates, had tried to kill her and Jak, and Jak and Dyan had taken their horses and left them in the middle of the Wahai. They hadn't killed Cheela and Shad, which might have been a mistake.

Of course, for all Jak knew, Outriders learned Basku. It certainly might be useful to the two who were trying to make their way out of the mountains.

Would the Basku eat the horses Dyan and Jak had given them?

Jak held Dyan's hand. "I'm scared, too." He didn't need to offer to turn around and run with Dyan; he had already made that offer. She knew it was still good, and he knew she'd never accept it.

"I don't feel like I have any choice in this."

"You do, though," Jak said. "It's the same choice we had with Aleena."

"We could walk away and let Zarah die."

"But we won't." He squeezed her hand. "*You* won't."

"Why won't I?"

The slouching Nemap docks grew nearer. A three-legged dog sniffed the air and then got up and limped away. Probably disappointed that he didn't smell meat in their cargo.

"Because you're good." Jak squeezed her hand again.

Dyan shook her head, fair hair falling around her face. "That isn't it."

"Then tell me why you think you're doing it."

"I think it's because I understand her," Dyan suggested.

Jak's eyes met hers as he raised a brow in question.

"I think in her place I would have done the same thing. If I knew I had a child, and I had the possibility of watching over the child and seeing her to maturity, I think I'd do it. I'd take any risk."

"That can't be everything," Jak said.

"Why not?"

"I think you understand your friends the Outriders, too."

"Shad and Cheela."

"I saw you with that bola at Cheela's throat. If you'd had to I think you would have taken her head off, understanding or no."

"She had just killed Eirig."

The force of her words hit Jak in the chest like a hammer. "Yes," he managed to squeak out. "But I think there's something else, too. Another reason we're going in after your Magister."

Dyan nodded. "I want to know what else Zarah can tell me."

"You want to know who your father is."

The ship bumped against the dock, and two Basku sailors jumped ashore to begin tying lines to metal cleats to hold the vessel in place.

"If you had asked me when we met," Dyan said, "I'd have said I didn't care who my father and mother were. I mean, who provided the basic biological material. I'd have said it didn't matter, and I'd have meant it."

"Everything's changed though, hasn't it?" Jak said. He arced a finger in the direction of Nemap to point beyond the seaside town and in the general direction of the System. "You had a family."

"It was the System," Dyan agreed. "Buza System was my family."

"Your family—the System—cast you out," Jak said. Shouldering his pack, he stepped onto the dock and helped Dyan follow him. "But that doesn't mean you don't have any family left."

"I have Zarah," Dyan said. She wasn't focusing on Jak, she was looking into the distance, thinking about something.

"You have *me*," Jak said.

"And I may have a father." Dyan looked into Jak's eyes. "I want to know. And I want to save Zarah, if I can."

"I'll help you. But it isn't for Zarah. She let me go, but not before she tried to have you kill me."

"But I didn't do it."

"But she tried."

"Did she have a choice? I mean, really?"

"Of course she did, Dyan. We all choose, all the time."

"You don't have to help me."

"I'll help. I'll do everything I possibly can. But I'm doing it for you."

"We might be hanged."

Jak laughed and started walking up the dock. "You need to act more like a Magister," he said, pointing at her black cloak. "Remember, I'm just your hired guide."

"Jass," she said.

"Magister Dana," he shot back.

"Hopefully no one realizes I'm not wearing the medallion that goes with the Calling."

"But don't you see? If I'm caught, I'm hanged already. Or chopped to bits, or stabbed, or whatever. I've been under a sentence of death since I was Selected for the Cull. There's just nothing more they can do to me. It's kind of liberating, actually."

"They could torture you," Dyan said.

Jak stopped at the end of the dock. A cart of baked goods wrapped in brown paper rolled by; the smell of cake made his empty belly grumble. "They do that?"

Dyan shrugged. "Not often. But the Cogitant Council sometimes orders it for really serious offenses."

"Like surviving the Cull?"

Dyan laughed, and the uptick in her spirits made Jak's step feel lighter. "I don't know for sure, because I never actually knew what the Selection really was until I saw it … but I don't think so. I think you get tortured if you do things that really threaten the System."

"Like lead a revolt."

"Yes."

"Like … rescue a condemned prisoner?"

Dyan hesitated. "Maybe," she finally said.

"Huh." Jak scratched the very light stubble on his chin. He wasn't much of a beard-grower. "Well, let's hope we don't find out."

"So I'm scared."

"Well, I'll stop when you tell me to. In the meantime, I don't hear you saying mere theft will get you tortured."

"Nope." Dyan shook her head. "Just hanged."

"Good." Jak rubbed his fingers together. "In that case, let's find someone from the System. I'd like an Outrider, but I'll take anyone in the right clothing."

"You want a vibro-blade or something? Why would you want an Outrider in particular?"

Jak shook his head. "I'm scared of cutting myself to pieces if I use any of those weapons. I just want the hat."

In the end, he rented a room at a small inn built of adobe bricks sagging at one end of the waterfront and left Dyan there. Dyan was a much better fighter than Jak because she was skilled in the use of the System's monofilament weapons, but in her Magister garb, and without the five-fingered medallion Magisters usually wore, she risked attracting attention.

Also, she was exhausted.

They'd need the right clothing to get them into the System, Jak thought. He thought it mostly an exercise in imagination since he'd never actually been to the System. But here in Nemap, he didn't want anyone asking inconvenient questions.

Dyan gave him a jingling purse full of Scrip. She'd taken it from the body of Haika, a Magister who'd come after them with Shad and Cheela, and whom Dyan had killed by bashing in her skull with a rock. In Ratsnay Station, Jak had never used Scrip, just bartered things for other things, and when the System's Collectors came to claim the System's share of the annual harvest, they also took crops and animals rather than trying to convert any of it into currency.

Still, Jak had an idea of what Scrip was, and he could read, and the values of the different pieces were printed right on the coins, so it only took a minute's explanation before the jingling purse felt right in his hand.

He also borrowed Dyan's black Magister cloak, which he folded up and tucked under his shirt to hide it.

Then he went looking for trouble.

He found a Magister with a group of young Systemoids. They stood at the open window of a butcher's shop, and the Magister narrated to his pupils as the butcher efficiently turned a whole hog into discrete cuts of meat, spinning the pig's carcass with his left hand while the cleaver in his right moved up and down with mechanical speed and precision.

The more the hog disintegrated into its component parts, the more it looked like a human being, and the more Jak wanted to vomit.

He avoided the Systemoids, keeping his face down.

He found several of the System's warrior types, Guardsmen, the men with the tabards and swords, and he avoided them, too. There were just too many of them. And besides, his comment about the hat had been a joke. There was a specific reason why he was looking for an Outrider, a different reason, and it, too, was based on an exercise of his imagination.

On the other hand, by her own account, Dyan had lived her life mostly in a sort of barracks called the Creche, and not among the adults of the System anyway, so to some extent *her* views were also driven by imagination.

What Jak knew about Outriders was this: they spent a lot of time outside the System. He knew this because he'd seen them, riding across the desert around Ratsnay Station on the trail of outlaws, or policing the Basku or the Shoshan. The Guardsmen were more rare and usually came in the company of a Collector; Outriders were the System's presence beyond the System's borders.

And if they spent a lot of time outside the System, then people who stayed in the System should expect to see Outriders and not recognize them. Or at least, not recognize them as much as they would recognize someone in one of the other roles. *Callings*, Dyan had said they were called.

That stood to reason, didn't it?

Jak found two Outriders eventually in a small tavern on the other side of Nemap. The signboard hanging over the door was painted with the image of a two-headed mountain lion, and Jak found the Outriders by the large, muscular roans munching hay in the attached stable. The Outriders sat in the back corner of the common room, hard to see in the greasy orange light of the candles lighting the place, and their boots were caked with dust.

Jak made a point of walking in off-balance. He banged his fists on the bar—a mere board resting on trestles—then he took the offered beer and drank a little, making sure to spill most of the mug on himself. That would give him the right smell.

Then he headed for the Outriders.

"Hey!" He slurred his words and staggered left as he approached them. They were a woman and a man, and for just a moment he feared he might have accidentally stumbled upon Shad and Cheela. That would put a quick end to his plan.

But no, they were older. The man had a ragged beard and a long scar running down the bridge of his nose, splitting one nostril open. The woman was thin as a stick and squinted.

"You're drunk," Squint said to him.

Jak shook his hand, letting the pair of bone dice he'd bought from one of the Basku sailors rattle loudly in it. "No, I'm not!"

"Go away, Landsy," Scar said, glowering.

"What?" Jak deliberately slurred his words. "My sh-shcrip isn't good for you?" He took out Haika's purse and shook it in his other hand.

He had their attention now, like a field mouse gets the attention of a pair of circling hawks. "Where'd you get that?" Squint asked. "Is it really Scrip?"

Jak made a show of very precisely taking out one rectangular bit, a fifty-piece, reaching forward to lay it on the table, and missing.

The coin rattled on the floor as it hit.

"Holy Mother," Jak wheezed. "I'm a shight."

Scar leaned back, and Jak noticed him loosening his vibroblade in its sheath. "You'd better answer the question, Landsy. Where'd the Scrip come from?"

"Right." Jak scratched his chin. "Haiku. No, Kayak. Hayek. Yak-yak." He shook his head and sighed. "One of youseh, but in the black, and with no hat."

"A Magister?" Squint asked.

"Yeah, thash it. Wanted directions out Marshick way a few days ago. Was willing to pay. You people. You Bu-Bu-Buza people. You're great." Jak shook the purse. "Haven't drunk it all yet."

Scar grinned, and from there it was easy.

Jak squeezed into an empty seat at their table. He made a point of sitting with his back to the bar. He was about to make a spectacle of himself, but he'd try to minimize the number of witnesses who could actually describe his face. "Alcohol!" he shouted. "What's your shtrongest?" Then he threw the dice on the table, and the purse next to it.

The Outriders were willing to drink, with Jak paying. Jak was careful to drink some of the distilled potato alcohol the bartender sent over, but not too much. He was relying on something Dyan had said—that the Systemoids didn't drink.

Because the people of Ratsnay Station drank a lot. Jak had been raised on small beer, and then on ordinary beer, and wine when he could get it. Beer was safer than water around Ratsnay Station, and sometimes easier to come by. As he continued playing drunk, it wasn't long before Jak saw signs that the two Outriders were actually starting to get inebriated. Their movements slowed, their speech became more halting.

He pushed them to throw dice with him too, and he lost. That was easy; he just bet big when the odds were against him, and bet small when they were in his favor, yelling obscene expressions of confidence either way. A string of good luck might have sunk him, but he had a very ordinary night from a dicing point of view. The Outriders were happy to take his Scrip, and celebrated their happiness by toasting him and Magister Kayak and the Buza System.

When the Scrip was gone, Jak made a show of looking disappointed, sighing, and then staggering out into the night. Once he was through the door, no one gave him a second look.

Then he waited.

He stood in a darkened doorway for twenty minutes, keeping an eye on the common room through its front window. As the Outriders went upstairs to their sleeping chamber, he watched the lights in the windows to see where they went.

He gave them twenty minutes after the lights were out. The night was far advanced.

Jak pulled the Magister's cloak from his shirt and shrouded himself with it. He walked into the inn's common room with his face down and the cloak pulled about him. No one bothered him, either because of the cloak or because of the hour, and the fact that the few people who were still awake were a little drunk.

He walked upstairs and counted doors until he got to the Outriders' room.

He listened and heard deep breathing.

He pulled their door out as far as he could, which made the metal rod of the latch peep out. Taking one of Dyan's mono-filament bolas from his pocket and pulling out the counterweight, it only took three slices to cut through enough of the door to expose and disconnect the latch.

He carefully pocketed the pieces he cut from the door. Then he entered the Outriders' room and shut the door behind him.

They were both snoring.

For a moment, Jak hesitated. Would this make him like one of them, like a Systemoid?

Stretching the bola again between his two hands, Jak sliced off the man's head first. He did it in one motion. The Outrider lay on his back, and as Jak severed his head he opened his eyes and mouth in a surprised expression. He seemed to be trying to say something, but with his lungs and vocal cords disconnected, no sound came out, and then the head rolled onto its side and was still.

The room smelled like iron as blood gushed into the straw tick mattress on which the Outrider lay.

Jak hesitated, standing over the woman. Some of Scar's blood was on his hands and the sight of it bothered him. But he thought of Aleena, his sister. And Eirig. And Jone and Yoel and his other friends, murdered by these people and their kind.

And Dyan and her mother Zarah.

He dropped the door fragments to the bed next to Scar.

Jak sliced Squint's head off in a single motion, too. She was lying on her side, so if her eyes and mouth opened, he didn't see it.

He didn't *have* to kill them.

It was his *choice*.

Fortunately, the Outriders had been sleeping in simple tunics and trousers, so their blood hadn't fouled any of the rest of their gear. Jak took his time carefully gathering all of it. After he'd loaded it onto their horses in the stables below, he splashed petrofuel all over their room, lit it with a sparker, and then walked back to rejoin Dyan in the early light just before dawn.

CHAPTER TWO

Y ou look very fetching as an Outrider," Jak told Dyan. "Maybe they got your Calling wrong."

They rode along a broad dirt track above the Buza River on its south side. This choice deprived them of the shade of the trees growing along the river but also meant they encountered fewer curious eyes. The river itself was big enough to have a fair amount of traffic, but the road directly beside the river to its north was positively busy with travelers going to and coming from the System.

Also, the road along the top of the bluff gave Jak better visibility, so he could see people approaching from further away. Moreover, from here, if he had to, he could turn and bolt across the desert.

And when they needed water, for themselves or for their mounts, it was easy enough to drop down to the river.

The choice of roads had been Jak's.

"I don't think the Lot Letters are written based on how attractive you'll be in the clothing of a given Calling," Dyan said.

"You don't *think*," Jak teased her. "But you don't *know*."

They traveled side by side on the Outriders' horses and wearing the Outriders' clothing. Dyan rode with the easy comfort of someone who'd spent many hours in a saddle. Jak bounced on the back of the horse, accidentally gave it too much rein, and felt stiff and sore. The people of Ratsnay Station had horses, but they mostly pulled plows, and Jak had never been a rider.

"That's true," Dyan said. "There are many things about the System I don't know."

Dyan's admission only made Jak more aware of the System drawing nearer, now hidden by the depression of the river valley ahead of them. He scanned the horizon to his right. The desert rose in a series of long, gentle slopes, coated with crackling yellow grass. Beyond the point where those slopes turned downward again lay the Lull Sea, now out of sight, but on the other side of the Lull rose the Wahai. They looked dusty and slightly unreal from this distance.

In the Wahai, Jak had nearly been killed by bandits. Then his best friend Eirig had been murdered. Jak himself had only narrowly escaped the same fate.

And yet, looking back at them now, the Wahai looked like safety to Jak. Compared to the System toward which he rode, they probably *were* a safe haven.

Dotting the grasslands above the System were ruins. They weren't the huge, solid ruins of Farkill, but they were spread wider. All of the Treasure Valley, it seemed, had once been a single city. Jak saw now a pair of crumbling walls rising to meet in a corner, a short ride from the road.

"You're a natural Magister, though," he said. "You taught me how to shoot a bow."

Dyan shrugged, the motion barely perceptible through the Outrider's coat she wore. "It isn't hard." She didn't look at him, focusing instead on the road ahead where it disappeared in the distance.

"The bolas and the whip aren't too much harder, are they?"

"They're not harder, really, but they're much more dangerous if you make a mistake." Dyan turned to look at him. "What are you thinking?"

"I'm hoping you trust me enough to teach me how to use them." Jak felt a little guilty as he said the words because he knew they were manipulative. Dyan would now feel she *had* to teach him.

On the other hand, it wasn't obvious that Dyan should trust him. He'd held her prisoner only a few days earlier, and had killed one of her Crechemates, a heavy, jovial Healer-designate named Wayland.

Also, Jak really wanted to learn how to use the whip and bola. He'd seen untrained people, fellow Landsmen from Ratsnay Station, slice themselves to pieces in the attempt. He understood *exactly* what Dyan meant by *dangerous if you make a mistake.*

"Now?" Dyan asked.

Jak pointed at the ruined wall. "We'll be hidden from the road over there. And I'd kind of like to know what I'm doing with these," he patted the whip on his belt, "*before* it becomes a matter of life and death."

"Of course." Without waiting for more discussion, Dyan turned her horse and headed across the grass.

They tethered the horses to the ruin itself. Against the far side of the long wall, opposite the road, a lattice of wood was bolted into the wall's brick, and the lattice made a natural place to hitch the horses. Moreover, it was within reach of a good patch of grass, and the horses soon set themselves to grazing.

Jak wondered what kind of building this had once been. It was bigger than anything in Ratsnay Station, and the brick suggested a permanence that many of Treasure Valley's ruins lacked—especially the smaller buildings, which tended to be nothing but a cement foundation, the building itself having long since rotted away. Where fragments remained, they were usually wood, or a crumbling cement composite wrapped in paper.

The Ancients had built strangely, and mostly not to last. Might that reflect a powerful spirituality and a detachment from material things?

Dyan took a bola in her hand. "We'll start with these."

"Ranged attack," Jak said. "I like it."

"The whip is inherently more dangerous to its user," Dyan said, "since by design it comes back to you."

"Oh. Right."

Dyan hesitated. "Really, if I were going to teach this to you as it was taught to me, the first lesson would be all about safety. I'd tell you never to take the bola or the whip from their holsters unless you intended to use them. I'd tell you that the filament inside each whip or bola is one molecule thick and extremely strong, making it impossibly sharp. I'd show you this by slicing through a gourd." She seemed almost to be in a trance. Was she remembering her own introduction to these weapons? "That would be impressive, but then I'd slice through a rock just as easily, and you'd be astonished."

"I see," Jak said.

"I sort of feel like you're past gourd-slicing. Don't you?"

Jak hefted the bola in his hand and tried not to remember the many deaths he'd seen by the instrument. He focused instead on the memory of Cheela, the Outrider-designate, showing off by slicing a dead tree in half with her bola on the hill above Ratsnay Station. "I don't know what a molecule is," he said, "but I have a pretty good feel for how dangerous these weapons are."

Dyan nodded. "So, on to lesson number two. Weight and balance are everything and you must *always* be clear where the counterweight end of the bola is."

Dyan taught Jak the basics of the bola. By the time the sun had crawled another hand's spread across the sky, Jak was throwing the weapon at a desiccated stump with confidence. Dyan chanted along with each throw, "Grip, angle, arm, swing, release," which made him feel a little childish. On the other hand, he'd rather have the constant reminder of good, safe form than lose an arm to a poor throw.

"Good." Jak exhaled with relief as he sent the bola through the target stump a final time, reducing it finally to ankle height. Pressing the locator button on his holster made the bola glow red so he could find it easily in the grass. "I feel much better now."

They camped in the ruin. Jak offered to light a fire in the angle of the two walls, but Dyan shook her head.

"I'd rather not be visible," she said, gesturing at the gently sloping grasslands above them. "With the coats and blankets, we'll be fine."

Jak led the horses down to the water one more time and then picketed them in taller grass. Then he and Dyan lay with their backs to the wall and its wood lattice, propped up against their saddles and covered with microfiber blankets. They watched the sun disappear and the stars come out, munching on dense ration bars and mostly not saying anything.

"You know, you can't really see the stars like this in the System," Dyan said eventually.

"All the light." Jak cleared his mouth with a swig of water. "Can't see them that well from Ratsnay Station for the same reason, when the fires are lit. Even from here, light from the System gets in the way. We'd see them better from further out. Farkill, for instance."

"The ruins?"

"Across the river from the ruins; there are some dunes around a little lake. Great place to see the stars, as long as you're careful about mountain lions. Or out past the Wahai."

"Dangerous places."

Jak laughed. "Yeah. Only I'm looking for a place that *isn't* dangerous, and I haven't found it yet."

"The stars are balls of plasma," Dyan said. "Matter heated up to incredibly high temperatures. And they're far away. Impossibly far away, unreachably far."

"Yeah?" Jak took another swig.

"The distance makes them useless," Dyan said. "Irrelevant. So we don't learn anything much about them in the Creche."

Jak didn't quite like her use of the present tense. "Well, if you didn't learn anything there," he said, "that doesn't mean you can't learn something about them now."

"Oh, yes?" Dyan laughed. It was a soft sound, and slightly merry. It was the most pleasant sound Jak had heard from her in a long time. Since they'd entered Marsick. "Will you teach me, Magister Jak?"

She didn't believe him. That was a challenge to which Jak could rise.

"It would be my pleasure," he said. "For starters, notice how the stars move across the sky in the same direction as the sun, from east to west."

"Only the sun doesn't really move."

"Of course it does. Everyone sees the sun move."

"Nope. The sun is still and the earth rotates, so it looks to us down here on earth as if the sun is moving across the sky." Dyan held up her two fists and rotated one to demonstrate what she meant.

"Right." Jak sort of wanted to argue the point, but he suspected he'd learn he was wrong. His effort to teach Dyan something was off to a bad start. "Okay, so I guess the stars must appear to go from east to west for the same reason. They're standing still and we're rotating."

"Yes, Magister."

"But they aren't useless, that's the point. For starters, there are mighty beings up there in the stars."

Dyan sat upright. "Really?"

"Yes." Jak pointed. "Look over there: that's west, where the sun went down over Cowell. You see a sort of square made of four bright stars?"

"Yes."

"And if you look—and you have to use your imagination here—there are more stars arranged in two long curving lines coming down from the box, and two jagged lines coming up from it."

"I see them."

"That's the Summer Son. *Son* as in *child*."

"Wait … you mean those stars make a sort of picture?"

"Exactly. The Summer Son is one of the two children of the Holy Mother. He's a tamer of beasts, and you're seeing him upside down right now because summer is almost over and he's starting to disappear. So those curved lines are his long wrestler's arms, not far above the horizon, at an angle, you see? And the jagged lines are his legs, which are bent because he's wrestling the Rattler, which stretches all across—"

"I'm sorry." Dyan was giggling. "I thought you meant there were actual people up there. Maybe watching us."

Jak nodded. "That's exactly what the Summer Son does. He's a performer of mighty tasks. He protects our cattle, he herds deer in our direction to be hunted, and we invoke him when we need to drive away evil. Especially snakes. Because, you know, the Rattler."

"Of course," Dyan said. "So you're right, in that sense, the stars are very useful. You said two children. Is there a Winter Son, also?"

"A Winter Daughter, actually. She brings fire and she can throw her spear very far, and with great accuracy. Kind of like you, actually."

"The Winter Daughter." Dyan said the words slowly, as if she were tasting them. "She brings fire and is armed with a spear. I kind of like that."

"If we stay awake late enough, you'll see her tonight. She's impossible to miss, she has a belt of three very bright stars, and she's followed by her hunting dogs."

"So these two children, they … bless the people?"

"Yes." She didn't believe him, but Jak continued anyway. "The Holy Mother is everywhere, and especially where there is life. In the sowing and in the harvest, in the brewing and in the drawing, in new births, in the union of Goodwife and Goodman. Her children bring us specific blessings and protect us. One of the Holy Mother's children watches over each half of the year, so we are never without a defender."

Dyan was quiet for a while. "And you … believe this?"

"What should I believe in? The System? The idea that the System is everything? That it's acceptable to murder people to keep them in line?" Jak thought of Scar's face staring up at him in the moonlight and felt sick to his stomach. He set down his half-eaten ration bar.

"I don't know," Dyan said softly. "I'm not sure what I believe in either, now. But it feels odd hearing you talk about giant people in the sky the way you do. As if they're real people and do real things."

Jak considered. "I don't *not* believe it," he said.

"That isn't quite the same thing as believing."

"Well … I believe in the Holy Mother. Her life has been inside me too many times to say I don't. As for the Winter Daughter and the Summer Son, well … they work. They work for me. They work for people."

"They're beautiful, anyway," Dyan said.

"They are beautiful," Jak agreed.

"I don't know why I said they're useless," Dyan said. "You can also tell directions by them. Anyway, I know the Compass star," she turned around and craned to look above the ruined wall, "always indicates north. Approximately. So in the Creche we learned to find it, by finding first that shape of stars over there, and then following the line of those front two stars to the Compass Star."

"The shape is the Big Bear," Jak said.

"In the Creche, we learned the basics of everything," Dyan said. "A Creche-leaver is ready to begin in-depth study in any Calling in the System, so no matter what her Lot Letter says, she's prepared. So maybe Outriders learn more about the stars once they've moved to the Camp. That's the Big Bear, and the Summer Son is starting to disappear ... what other shapes are there in the sky, then?"

Jak showed Dyan the Little Bear first, and the Rattler, facing off forever against the Summer Son. Telling her stories about the residents of the sky made Jak feel at home in a way he hadn't felt for weeks. These were the tales he'd grown up with and the stories he used to think about his own life.

When he had exhausted all the tales he could think of, Dyan was quiet.

"Are you asleep?" he whispered.

"I'm thinking," she said.

"Thinking what a strange bunch the Landsies are, and worrying what a huge mistake you made, casting your lot in with this one?"

"No," she said. "I'm thinking about an expression I've heard before. That I've used before, but I never knew what it meant. Not really. Star-crossed."

"Having bad luck, or fated for a bad end."

"Of course. But I'd never thought about why it meant that, and now I see it." Dyan gestured up at the night sky's glittering harness. "You see, your life as a child was different from mine. My life was always down here, on earth. But your life, in part at least, was up there."

"Yeah." Jak let the idea sink in. "I guess there's truth to that."

"So the stars always told you where you were. In more ways than one. So to be star-crossed is to have your stars mixed up. To be out of place. To be lost." Dyan laughed softly. "Like you and I are now."

Jak had nothing to add, and they lay in silence, watching the heavens turn above them.

Chapter Three

A white stone wall sealed the System off from the rest of the Treasure Valley. The sun was climbing toward noon when Jak first saw it, sparkling and massive, stretching across the entire river valley. The water of the Buza River itself flowed through a steel grate sunk into the stone, and a broad stretch of treeless gravel separated the trees from the wall.

A gate pierced the wall through a solid barbican tower. As he entered the gravel clearing, Jak saw Systemoids in tabards with the System's five-fingered fist icon on them standing guard in and around the gate. More such men stood on a walkway above the gate, pacing slowly back and forth.

Dyan noticed where Jak was looking. "Guardsmen," she said.

Jak knew what they were called because Guardsmen always accompanied the Collectors who came to Ratsnay Station. The swords at the Guardsmen's belts looked primitive and anticlimactic, but they were vibro-blade weapons. They weren't as thin as the cutting monofilaments in the System's whips and bolas, but their mechanisms caused them to vibrate at very high speeds, which had the same effect—reputedly, a vibro-blade could cut through anything.

This was how the System armed its warriors, with weapons that killed in a single touch.

A line of people and carts shuffled slowly toward the gate. Out of sheer reflex, Jak looked down to hide his face and put himself in the back of the line. The wagon in front of him looked like a Collector's, and it was piled high with sacks that must contain grain from the recent harvest.

Did any of the grain come from Ratsnay Station? Probably not, since Jak's home was south of the System and he and Dyan were entering on the System's west side.

On top of the Collector's wagon was a high bench from which a rider could see down clearly on all sides. A single Guardsman sat on the bench, hand on the hilt of his vibro-blade sword. He met Jak's gaze and they nodded at each other.

"Outrider Jass," Dyan said at his elbow. Her voice was tight with formality and strain. "Is there something about this Collection that troubles you?"

Jak looked again at the line ahead of him and realized his mistake. There were no Outriders standing in the line, only Collectors' wagons and people who looked like they were not Systemoids. Landsmen, like him.

He looked up at the Guardsman again. "Where are you bringing this from?" he called.

"Eyrie," the Guardsman shot back. "Oats, and of course eggs from the coops. We brought the foals in a few weeks ago."

"Eyrie." Jak nodded officiously. To Dyan he said, "this isn't the one we're looking for."

"Agreed." Dyan waved at the Guardsman on the wagon back to carry on and continued towards the gate. Jak followed.

"Sorry," he said to her out of the corner of his mouth.

"It's my fault," she said. "We should have talked earlier about expectations and how to carry ourselves."

"We've got a minute now, crossing this wasteland."

"It's defensive," Dyan said, nodding at the gravel under her horse's hooves. "Anyone attacking the walls would have to do it without any cover."

"Do you imagine that makes me feel better?"

Dyan laughed softly. "Only in the way that knowledge should always make you feel better. Wouldn't you rather know the truth, even if the truth was hard to take?"

Jak considered the question. He had been happier when he thought his sister Aleena had moved into the System and was happily working there, and before he'd realized she'd been murdered. "No," he said finally. "I'm not sure I *would* rather know the truth."

They drew near the walls. "Well, then I apologize for this hard truth I'm about to tell you. The fact is, I don't really know how the System works."

"You told me. You were raised in the Creche."

"Exactly. And after leaving the Creche, each of us would have been given more training in how her Calling works. But I haven't had the training. Which means I know how the Creche runs, basically, and I can find my way around the System, in general, but I don't really know what Outriders do when they're in the System."

"You mean do we have to report to someone, are there ranks, things like that?"

"Exactly." Dyan straightened her back as they entered the gate, passing Guardsmen on either side. "Is there a password for us to get into the Camp? Where do we put our horses, and can we trade them for fresh ones? And so on. So I think our best bet is just to always look as if we're on urgent business."

"Just act like we own the place," Jak said. "Like ... Outriders always do."

He'd almost said *like Systemoids always do*. But he caught himself in time, straightened his own posture to match Dyan's, and twisted his face into a scowl as they exited the gate on the System side.

The buildings within the wall were also made of white stone, but still they managed to avoid the taint of beauty. Jak saw long, narrow halls like barracks, laid out in straight rows with narrow roads between them. The roads were coated with a black, dimpled, tar-like substance, and he could look all the way up the roads to his left to where the foothills of the Jawtooth erupted upward.

The people moving among the long barracks didn't look like any Systemoids Jak had seen before. They wore very simple clothing, brown tunics and trousers, and they didn't carry the System's symbol anywhere on their persons.

"What do you call the ... that sign?" he asked Dyan. "The one Magisters and Outriders and Guardsmen wear. The symbol, does it have a name?"

Dyan hesitated. "Not that I know. Maybe that's something I would have learned if I hadn't run away."

"A secret, is it? Right." Jak pointed at the people in brown. "Whatever it is, they don't have one."

"Gardeners," Dyan said simply. She pushed her horse into a slightly brisker pace and Jak did the same.

"Somehow I imagined life here would be … fancier."

"System life isn't opulent," Dyan said. "Not for anyone. It is safe and predictable, mostly. It is … organized."

"Still," Jak said, "I imagine your Crechemates whose Lot Letters said *Gardener* were pretty disappointed."

"These people were never in the Creches," Dyan said. "At least … I don't think they were."

"Where did they come from, then?" Jak asked. He left unspoken between them the fact he and Dyan both knew: that the Gardeners didn't come from Ratsnay Station or the other settlements around the system. These people were not the Selected Landsmen youth, because the Selected all lay dead, sliced to pieces, and bleaching in the desert.

Dyan didn't answer.

They rode along the Buza River, ever so gently uphill, with the Jawtooths rising to their left and ahead of them. Jak followed Dyan's lead in nodding to anyone whose clothing identified him or her particularly with a Calling. He recognized Outriders, Guardsmen, Collectors, and Magisters.

"How about those?" he asked Dyan, pointing to a couple of women working on a pump mechanism in a weir on the river. They wore one-piece garments with the System's emblem on their chests, but in this case the emblem was superimposed over a toothed wheel, with the five arms merging into five of the cog's teeth.

"Mechanicals."

"So if we're looking for your friend Deek," he said, "we could follow them." Jak had met Deek at the Cull and knew he had been a Mechanical-designate. Following the ritual murder Deek had been willing to commit—Jak had seen Deek use his monofilament bolas to slice off first the hands, and then the head, of a girl he'd known all his life—he would be a full Mechanical now.

"We don't need to follow them. I don't know exactly what kind of Mechanical Deek is, but as long as they're in-System, the Mechanicals eat and sleep in the same place. It's called the Garage." She gestured up at the sun. "We should get there as the Mechanicals are coming out from their midday meal."

"I guess you took a tour of the Garage with your Crechemates."

"More than once."

"What's a *Garage?*" Jak asked.

"It's an old word. Pre-Cataclysm. It originally had something to do with machines, I think. Now it means the building complex where the Mechanicals live and eat. As I was saying."

"And the Outriders have a similar place they live and eat? A Garage?"

"They do, only it's called the Camp."

"Camp? That's funny. I know what a camp is."

"I think the name is intended to remind them not to get too attached to buildings. They're supposed to feel equally at home on a bedroll in the Wahai as on a cot in the System." Dyan looked away. "Everything is just a camp to them. There is no permanent attachment to a home. Or other people. Except to their Squad. People in other Callings can make Love-Matches, and when they do, they move into the Shackups for as long as the Love-Match lasts. Not Outriders. If you make a Love-Match with an Outrider, he stays in the Camp."

"You're thinking about Shad and Cheela," Jak said. "We left them on foot. If they survived, they're days behind us."

"They survived," Dyan said. "We left them armed. And a determined person on foot can travel as far in a day as a rider." She still looked away, at the river, and her voice sounded hollow.

"More hard truths," Jak joked, only it wasn't funny. "Anyway, I only meant maybe we ought to drop into the … Camp, I guess it's called … and get something to eat. The ration bars are fine, if your alternatives are carrion or starvation, but …"

Dyan snapped her head suddenly back to look at him. "Not a good idea," she said.

They were approaching the center of the System. The buildings here were larger, the avenues were broader, and there were open spaces, green-grass and trees blazed the red and gold of autumn, along the river as well as among many of the buildings. Everything was built of white stone.

"Fine," Jak said. "More rations it is."

Dyan sighed. "I think most people here won't know our faces. Even if I happen to meet someone I know from the Creche, a Crecheling or a former Crechemate, I think they won't necessarily know that I … that we …"

"That we're outlaws," Jak said.

"That we're outlaws. But I think the Outriders will know, because that's their Calling."

"You think."

Dyan shrugged.

"We should probably also assume that Magisters will know," Jak said.

Dyan looked surprised. "Because … because of the spying device the Magisters carry?"

"That," Jak agreed, "and also because the Magisters may have known you were going to become one of them. Don't you think? Surely they were informed, so they could get a cot ready, and a position for you to take. Only then you didn't."

"So we stay away from the Creche." Dyan looked disappointed.

"Ironic and unfortunate, since it's the part of the System you know best."

Dyan only snorted.

"Show me where this Garage is," Jak suggested.

The center of the Buza System was busy. There were a few thoroughfares large enough for wagons; elsewhere, people rode horses or walked. Crossing one of the largest boulevards, Dyan pointed it out and called it "Capitol." She nodded to their left subtly, as they passed over the middle of the road.

"Look that way but don't make a big deal of it," she said.

"Of course." Jak rode with head high and shoulders back. "I'm Outrider Jass. I was born and raised here. Nothing is new or surprising to me about Buza System. What is there to make a big deal of?"

He looked left, faking a yawn. Atop a slight slope, with the foothills looming behind it, squatted a towering dome of white stone. It was the only dome he'd seen in the System, most of whose buildings seemed to be rectangular.

"The Council Hall," Dyan said behind him. "The Cogitant Council meets there."

Jak reined in his horse and yawned again. Two Guardsmen strolled past. South, where Capitol rose up toward the bluff and another gate and, far beyond, eventually, Ratsnay Station, he saw several Collectors' wagons rolling in his direction.

"We've got a good view here," he said. "Why don't you tell me a little about what I'm seeing?"

Dyan circled him and then stopped her horse parallel to his but facing the other direction, so she could look Jak in the face. "Okay," she said. "I'll tell you things, but I'm not going to look at them."

"Understood."

"This green space surrounding Capitol is the Garden."

"Lovely."

"Ahead of you and to your right you will see a cleared yard with a scaffold in it. The scaffold has five horizontal beams. If you look at it from the right angle, you'll notice the scaffold resembles the mark of the System."

"Whatever it's called."

"Do you see it?"

"I see it, barely."

"The square around it is Rose Plaza. The scaffolding is the Gallows Tree. Four times a year, all the Crechelings, along with other witnesses, gather in Rose Plaza to see five people hung on the Gallows Tree."

"Killed?"

"Killed."

"Always five? And only four times a year?"

Dyan nodded. A single tear trickled down each of her cheeks. Jak wanted to wipe the tears away, but didn't. Neither of them touched Dyan's tears, which gently descended to her jaw and then her neck and then disappeared under the Outrider's coat she wore.

Jak considered what he was hearing. Five was a doomed number, it seemed. Once a year, a Magister came from Buza

System and Selected five youth for the Cull. Always five, no matter what.

These killings were not about guilt. They were about ritual. They were about power. They were about communicating who was in charge.

"The four times a year must be the two solstices and the equinoxes," Jak said, using ancient words.

Dyan's startlement showed in her face. "Yes. The shortest day of the year, the longest, and the two days when day and night are of equal length."

"Life. Death. The universe. Secret names." Jak nodded. "Tell me about the other big buildings."

"The tall one over against the foothills is the Cradle. Babies are born there, and then delivered to the Nursery, which is out of sight in the foothills with the Creche. The lower buildings around it are the Shackups."

"For the Love-Matched. So where's the Camp?"

"Also out of sight. Off to your left, in the mountains. In a canyon up among the peaks called Bogo's Basin."

"Who was Bogo?"

Dyan shrugged. "An early Outrider? A builder? A legend? A monster? I've never heard. Who was Ratsnay?"

"Right. And the squat building, the big one, straight ahead of me?"

"It's the Prison. Zarah's there."

If she's alive, Jak thought, but he didn't say it.

"Beside the Prison is the Citadel. The Guardsmen live there."

"And what about the Garage?" Jak asked.

"Right here." Dyan turned her horse around to point it the same direction as Jak's. "Just ahead of us, on the edge of the Garden."

CHAPTER FOUR

Beyond the Garden stood five large buildings arrayed in a loose circle around green grass and a fountain. One of them, it turned out, was the Garage, home of the Mechanicals.

There were also a Gallery, a Croft, a Loom, and a Quarry—each of these, Dyan told Jak as they passed among the buildings, housed holders of one of the Callings of people who made things. Artists made the exterior decorations of things, which as far as Jak could tell meant they put the System's five-fingered emblem on many surfaces. Crafters made tools and vehicles. Seamstresses made clothing. Masons made buildings and roads. Each of these Callings had a slightly different uniform, and although Dyan carefully pointed them out as they passed, Jak's head spun with new information and he had a hard time telling them apart.

He didn't like the fact that these Callings added up to five. It made him think of the Gallows Tree and the Cull.

The stream of Mechanicals coming out of the Garage seemed to be picking up speed. Jak squinted at the sun overhead and guessed the midday meal must be ending.

"No guarantee Deek is actually here, though?" he asked.

"No guarantee," Dyan agreed. "He could be out working on something—like those Mechanicals we saw on the river, or even on some project outside the walls of the System itself."

"Like the Dam at the end of the Lull Sea," Jak said.

"Right. The System maintains and defends that."

"Defends it against what? Bears?"

"If anyone were ever to destroy the Dam," Dyan said, "whether by deliberate attack or as an act of vandalism, the Lull Sea would drain, destroying Nemap and Cowell as port towns, removing a primary source of irrigation from the agriculture of the Treasure Valley, and damaging fishing as a source of protein for the System and its inhabitants."

Her voice was monotone, and Jak raised an eyebrow in her direction. "You're quoting a Magister, aren't you?"

"I am." Dyan blushed and looked away. "I'm quoting a factvid."

Jak chuckled. "It still sounds true. Who makes the vids, anyway?"

"Hitchcocks. They live in the Cinema, there beneath the Council Hall. Beside it is the Library."

Jak nodded, taking it in. Magister Stanton had shown his pupils factvids and funvids both, all borrowed from the System and its Library. "And why is this called the Treasure Valley? Any idea?"

Dyan frowned. "I don't know. Maybe the System is the treasure?"

"Or maybe that's the name of the symbol. Huh. Ancient words, again. Come on, we can't just stand here in front of the Garage and make it *look* like we're waiting for someone."

Jak turned his horse to follow a pair of Seamstresses. They were both men, dressed in knee-length tunics with the System's emblem over their left breasts. Jak was careful not to accelerate onto their heels and didn't look at them, to avoid giving them the impression he wanted to talk to the Seamstresses themselves.

"Is it acceptable to water our horses in the fountain?" he asked as they approached the water feature.

Dyan hesitated. "I think so."

"You're not sure." Jak grunted. "Well, unless we see someone else doing it, let's hold off." The fountain itself was a silver-metallic rendition of the System's emblem. With five arms radiating outward rather than up, it looked just like the Gallows Tree.

The System didn't want to let anyone forget.

As Jak neared the fountain, with Dyan at his shoulder, a solitary man approached head-on. He was tall, with a nose like a hawk and tiny ears. Over his shaved skull he wore a silver circlet. His clothing was a simple white tunic and matching white trousers; the System's emblem on his chest was enormous and black. His feet were bare.

Jak wanted to ask Dyan what Calling the man had, but the newcomer was too close and would hear. Instead, he nodded at the barefoot man and shot him a lopsided grin.

The man stopped. Their gazes met, and Jak felt a curious tickling at the base of his spine.

The man's eyes were flat and cold. They almost didn't look like eyes at all. They looked like *paintings* of eyes.

Jak would have said they were *dead* eyes, except the man was walking.

"Rider," the man said.

Dyan's horse surged slightly ahead of Jak, and he sighed in relief. Watching her out of the corner of his eye, he tried to follow her lead.

"Cogitant," Dyan said. Those were the thinkers and planners of the System, Jak remembered. They lived and worked in the big dome over at the base of the foothills, the Council Hall. In a sense, they must be the System's leaders, and the thought made Jak want to whip a bola from its holster and try his first real-life throw.

He mastered the urge. They were here to try to get to Zarah, and to succeed they were going to have to enlist Deek's help.

"Cogitant," Jak mumbled, trying to sound natural.

The man said nothing. Jak wouldn't have sworn to it, but he thought the Cogitant was looking at Dyan rather than at him.

"I've a message for you to carry to the Prison," the Cogitant said.

Jak's ears pricked up. The Prison! Maybe they didn't need Deek. Maybe they could walk right into Zarah's cell with a legitimate purpose. He leaned forward in his saddle.

"Yes, Cogitant," he and Dyan said together.

"Report to the Keeper and tell her Cogitant Yurvek said *five is the number.*"

And then Jak knew he wouldn't be carrying a message to the Prison.

"Five is the number," Jak repeated. Dyan just nodded.

Cogitant Yurvek turned and continued his walk. Jak forced himself to ride in the direction of the Prison, or at least the direction in which the Prison lay, to the best of his memory. Dyan followed.

Dyan caught up to Jak as they passed a pair of Masons and moved into a tree-shadowed lane behind the Gallery.

"I'm not sure about this," she said to Jak.

"I, on the other hand, am completely sure about it."

"You are?"

"I am completely sure we're not going to the Prison with any such message."

Dyan stared at him. "You think it's a trap."

Jak looked about him at the white stone walls and the tall trees. "This whole thing is a trap," he said. "Can't you feel it? Death is everywhere, and it's announced in giant flaming letters. Death, death, death, get out of line and it's the gallows for you all."

"I ..." Uncertainty showed in Dyan's face.

"The System lies," Jak said fiercely. "It lied to you your whole life, and it lied to me. It lies for control. If that ... Cogitant had asked us to carry a message like 'please tell Jimi to come to the Camp,' I might have gone. But *five is the number*? It's some kind of code, and it's an instruction."

"You're afraid it means something like *kill me*."

Jak considered the question. "*Lock me up* is more likely," he decided. "Otherwise, I expect it would have been a message to go to the Citadel. That's where the Guardsmen live, isn't it? But it could be. It could be an instruction to the Guardsmen at the Prison to execute us. Wouldn't it be just like the System, to have an instruction it could give to its people to just have themselves locked up? Or murdered? Very convenient."

"I've never heard of any such thing," Dyan said slowly.

"But you wouldn't have, would you? You were a Crecheling, so you probably took a tour of the Prison, but you never learned the secrets of the Guardsmen."

"I did tour the Prison. That doesn't prove you're right."

Jak nodded. "But it's all consistent."

"You think Cogitant Yurvek recognized me?" Dyan asked.

"Probably. That's more likely than the possibility that he recognized *me*. Or he just realized there was something wrong with us. I don't know, something we're not doing right with the uniform ...? And rather than mess around, he ordered us to turn ourselves in." Jak looked behind himself, imagining a troop of Guardsmen with bows and vibro-blade swords.

"We need to leave," Dyan said.

"We need to find your friend Deek," Jak shot back. "Right now. And then get out of sight. Let's split up."

Dyan nodded. "Let's meet under the bridge in an hour."

Jak checked the sun. "The bridge? Where Capitol crosses the river? Will we be alone down there?"

"We won't be alone." Dyan laughed. "But the people down there will be ... lovers. People have picnics, go swimming in the river, and so on. Not Guardsmen. Not Guardsmen on duty, anyway."

"Or Outriders, looking for survivors of the Cull." Jak flashed his best grin. "Mind you, that doesn't mean it will be safe, since every single one of you is armed and dangerous." What he didn't say was: *Every single one of you earned his or her right to live here by murdering a Landsman like me.* "I'll see you in one hour."

He rested a hand on a bola as he rode. It made him feel safer, which was ridiculous, but he also hoped it made him look more dangerous. He wanted people to look away from him, and whether because of the hand on the bola or because of the Outrider's uniform and Jak's snarl, he got his wish.

He rode around behind the Gallery and the Quarry, although these five buildings looked similar enough that he couldn't really be sure. He crossed the small green plaza with the fountain in the center of the five buildings again.

He looked for Deek, a skinny boy whose face was burned into Jak's memory, and didn't see him.

He looked for Cogitants, too. Especially Cogitant Yurvek, but he saw no one in the white tunic and trousers, either.

Two Guardsmen stood by the fountain talking now. Jak made a point of riding close to them and waving, his breath held tightly in his chest.

They waved back, and Jak exhaled.

This was going to take forever.

He rode to the front door of the Garage. A silvery arch held up the massive pile of glittering white stone over the door and two Mechanicals walked out underneath it in their one-piece jumpsuits.

"You there." Jak used his sternest tones. "I'm looking for Mechanical Deek."

The taller of the two, a woman with orange hair and a bulbous nose, shrugged to her companion. The second Mechanical, dark and broad-shouldered, nodded. "He's new," she said. She pointed over her shoulder back into the building. "He's working with the Life Systems Maintenance crew."

"Ah," said Orange Hair. "A Creche-leaver."

"That's him." Jak dismounted. "Please tell him Outrider Jass needs to speak with him."

"Of course." Big Shoulders paused in turning to go back. "Can I tell him what it's about?"

Jak hesitated. He wanted Deek's help getting into the Prison, so at some point he would have to be honest with the Mechanical. "Tell him I have a message from Magister Dyan."

He really hoped that didn't give him and Dyan away.

Big Shoulders nodded, waved goodbye to Orange Hair, and went back into the Garage.

Jak waited. He kept the horse between himself and the building, with his face in the shadow of his wide hat brim. Even if Deek was willing to come talk with Dyan and not give her away, that didn't mean he'd be interested in talking to Jak. He might know Jak had killed his Crechemate Wayland. He might think Jak had corrupted Dyan.

Deek came out alone, dressed in a Mechanical's jumpsuit, with the gear and emblem on the chest. His clothing and his face were smudged black and his hair was a tousled mess.

"Outrider Jass?" he said.

Jak stepped around the front of his horse, openly holding a monofilament bola in his hand. "I'm not here to hurt you."

Deek blinked. "You're the boy. The one from Ratsnay Station."

"We've met," Jak admitted.

"You're the one who caused all the trouble."

Jak ground his teeth together. "That's not really how I see it," he said.

Deek's shoulders sagged. "I'm sorry."

"I'm sorry, too."

"Is this a trick?" Deek asked.

Jak was puzzled. He also felt itchy; the longer he stood in the doorway of the Garage, the more conspicuous he was. "What do you mean?"

"Dyan. Is she alive? Is she with you?"

Jak holstered the bola. "Dyan's alive. We need your help."

Deek looked all around before nodding. "Well," he said. "You'd better take me to Dyan, I guess."

So far, so good. Jak's hands trembled slightly, but he decided to extend his risk and show more trust. "Follow me," he said. Then he turned his back and walked toward the river.

Deek didn't run. He caught up with Jak with a few quick steps and matched his pace. "You're in disguise," the Mechanical said, "so I'm guessing you're an outlaw. You're both outlaws."

"I guess so," Jak agreed.

"I care a lot about Dyan," Deek said.

Jak nodded. Otherwise, the System-raised boy was telling him, he'd have yelled for the Guardsmen, and Jak would now be sliced into pieces at their hands. Or, in all likelihood, at his own hands as he tried to defend himself with the still essentially unfamiliar weapons of the System.

"She must have come back for Zarah," Deek said.

Jak looked at the other boy. "Does everyone know Zarah is arrested?" He tried to keep his voice calm, but suddenly he had the feeling ten thousand eyes were watching his every step.

"No," Deek said. "I know because my last Magister was supposed to participate in some of my early ... activities as a Mechanical. Only Zarah can't. She's been arrested and is in the Old Pen."

The Old Pen, not the Prison. The System had the strangest names for everything. "Why?" Jak asked. He was manipulating Deek a bit, not revealing what he himself understood, but he didn't feel bad about it. He needed every advantage he could get here to survive.

Deek shrugged. "I think it's because the Selection went wrong." He looked closely at Jak's face. "Really, I think it's because of you."

Jak just nodded.

On the near side of Capitol, Jak now noticed that the grass of the parks around the center of the System descended in easy slopes to the banks of the Buza River. He and Deek walked down to the water. He did his best to stay between Deek and the horse. If Cogitant Yurvek, or anyone else who might know Jak's face, happened along, he wanted to be tucked away out of sight.

Dyan had been right. Along the banks of the river there, Gardeners were at work, raking fallen leaves out of the reeds along the water's edge and trimming tall grass. Otherwise, people seemed to be here in a recreational mode—a few paddled small boats in the river; others ate on blankets spread along the banks. Beneath the bridge was a shaded walkway, and Jak looked there, expecting to see Dyan.

She wasn't under the bridge.

He checked the sun. It had been an hour, he judged.

"I guess this is where we're supposed to meet?" Deek asked.

"Yeah." Jak turned and walked back up the grass to look at Capitol, the Cogitant Council's dome, the squat Prison, and the rest of the System.

Deek came right at his shoulder. And when they emerged from the river depression, Jak saw Dyan.

She was a long bola's throw away, standing right in the middle of Capitol.

Surrounded by four Guardsmen with their swords out.

CHAPTER FIVE

eek immediately grabbed Jak's right arm, just as Jak put his hand on the bola holster. "Don't!" Deek whispered.

"You want her captured? Or dead?"

"Look around you," Deek suggested. He didn't let go of Jak's arm.

Jak trembled and wanted to throw the bola, but he did as Deek suggested.

Not everyone around was armed. But there were plenty of Outriders and Guardsmen armed to the teeth, and when Jak looked closely he spotted vibro-blade knives and swords hanging from the belts of many people of other Callings.

"You'll both die," Deek said. "There's no point."

"So we let them kill her?"

"They're not killing her. We watch."

Others were watching, too, from a respectful distance, so Jak didn't feel too conspicuous just standing in place and observing. Would Dyan give him away? Her eyes scanned the crowds around her and she must have seen Jak, but she didn't cry out or give any other indication.

From a tense pose, looking prepared to sprint, Dyan stood straight up and relaxed. The men surrounding her disarmed her carefully, taking the whip and the two bolas. They also pulled away the Outrider's coat, which made sense as a protective measure—who could know what an Outrider was hiding in those deep pockets?

And where was Dyan's horse?

Lastly, one of them knocked the hat off her head with his knuckles.

"My people!" Dyan called out. Her voice was loud, in the way you make a voice loud by speaking with your belly rather than your throat. It was a public speaker's voice, a teacher's voice. "I am innocent!"

What was she doing? The System never let anyone go.

Jak heard murmurs, but didn't make out what people were saying. He kept his eyes on Dyan. Days earlier, he had asked her to be his Goodwife. Now he feared he might see her sliced into so many chunks of meat before his eyes.

Deek let go of his arm.

Jak didn't take his hand off the bola.

"Come with us," one of the Guardsmen said. He grabbed Dyan roughly by the back of her neck and pushed her. The four warriors marched across the green, Dyan looking like a child in their midst. Two of them men held swords openly in their hands as they walked.

"You are also innocent!" Dyan cried again. "You must see that! You must believe it! You can still choose!"

One of the Guardsmen marching behind Dyan clubbed her across the back of her head with the hilt of his sword. She sobbed and fell silent.

"Not another word," the Guardsman growled.

Deek lurched forward, and this time Jak caught *him* by the shoulder.

"Wait," he said to the Mechanical.

"Don't you want to see where they're taking her?" Deek asked.

"Won't it be the Prison or the Old Pen? And won't you be able to find out afterward?"

"The way they're headed it must be the Old Pen, but—"

"Look, but don't stare," Jak told Deek. "Just on the other side of Capitol."

The Mechanical did a creditable job of pretending he wasn't looking, shaking his head and throwing up his arms in a gesture of disgust as he turned.

"What are you worried about?" he asked Jak.

"The Cogitant," Jak said. He wasn't sure he could explain what he was thinking to the other boy, but he was sure the Cogitant was observing, and Jak desperately wanted not to be noticed.

Deek didn't argue. "Fine," he said. "Look, I don't hold any grudge against you. I …" He looked down at his feet. "Anyway, if you just ride south on Capitol, in the uniform you're wearing no one's going to stop you. Capitol ends in a gate. In two days' ride, you'll be back in Ratsnay Station."

"I'm not leaving," Jak said. "Not yet. And not without her."

Deek looked up at him, a curious gleam in his eye. "Then what?"

Jak turned slowly, nonchalantly, and ambled back down the slope to the water. Deek followed. "First," he told the other boy, "we get to the Old Pen before the Guardsmen do. Just to be sure that's where they're taking Dyan."

"They've got a head start," Deek pointed.

"Yeah," Jak said. "And we have a horse."

Down in the river's depression, Jak looked around to be sure he couldn't see Yurvek or any other Cogitant. The Cogitant had almost certainly recognized Dyan. He had ordered Jak and Dyan to turn themselves in, but he had also alerted the Guardsmen to their presence.

The Guardsmen must know what *Jak* looked like, too.

Jak climbed awkwardly into the saddle and then helped Deek up behind him. He was relieved that Deek was not much more natural a rider than Jak, and they were both lean enough that the big Outrider's horse didn't protest at the extra burden.

Keeping his face down to hide his eyes as much as he could behind the brim of his hat, Jak kicked the horse into a slight canter.

He kept the animal on the bank of the river, which alternated between neatly trimmed lawn and pebbly beach. Gardeners raked at the stones in some patches or cut the greenery, but Jak had no trouble circling around them. He did find, though, that he was once again giving the horse too much free rein. His intended canter was coming close to a gallop.

"Whoa," Deek whispered, probably inadvertently. The Mechanical's muscles tensed.

Jak gathered in the animal's reins and slowed the horse to a trot.

"The Old Pen is this way, right?" he asked Deek.

"They're probably on horseback by now, too," Deek said. "Or on a wagon. So don't slow down too much." He pointed past Jak's shoulder at another upcoming bridge. "That's Broadway. Beyond it the river will turn south, and then you'll want to continue east instead. Pick any street."

Jak went ahead and let out the reins.

It made him nervous, banging along on the back of the stolen horse with Deek holding onto him for dear life. He also worried about the possibility Dyan wouldn't be brought to the Old Pen after all. She could be executed at any place. She could be held somewhere besides the Old Pen, including the Prison.

But no, Jak reminded himself. The Guardsmen had been coming this way. And it was a *System*, after all. It was lying and murderous, but it had order.

The Old Pen was a complex of squarish buildings behind a stone wall. The wall was not so high; Jak pulled the horse to a stop in its shade and estimated that from a standing start in the horse's saddle, he could probably grab the parapet and pull himself up.

But prisoners inside wouldn't have horses to jump from, of course. And Guardsmen walked the parapet, bows in hand.

Jak urged his horse on, finding a shaded corner between a tree and a plain white building from which he could see the Old Pen's gate. The gate was a metal double door set into a fortress built into and above the wall itself. Jak hitched the horse to a tree, and he and Deek both hunkered down to watch.

Three minutes later, the four Guardsmen appeared. They had indeed taken a wagon, and as the wagon approached the Old Pen's gate, the gate opened. Jak scooted forward, pressing himself against the edge of the wall to see.

The wagon disappeared into the darkness of the gate. Jak's last glimpse of Dyan was of her cringing, surrounded by four burly armed men.

"Holy Mother," Jak muttered.

He would *need* to be Redcap Rider. Now there were *two* Chained Princesses.

He turned and froze.

Deek stood three paces away, holding a bola in his hand. He had armed it by extending the counterweight, which now dangled in that disturbing fashion below the body of the bola, their connection invisible and only as thick as a single molecule, whatever that was.

Jak looked down at his own holster and found it empty.

He could grab for the bola on his left side as a bluff, but in actual fact the weapon would be worse than useless. Jak was right handed. He'd slice himself to pieces for sure with his left hand, and in the time it would take him to draw the bola, switch hands, and prepare to use it, Deek could have killed him several times over.

"I guess I'm the fool here," Jak said.

"I'm glad I have your attention," Deek said slowly, "because there's something I really want you to hear."

"I'm not going anywhere." Jak eased slowly forward onto his knees and held his hands up in surrender. Without being able to articulate exactly why, he felt that, if he was going to be killed by the System, he was glad it was at the hands of one of Dyan's Crechemates.

"I could kill you."

"I know it. All of you Systemoids get trained to use those things, even when your job is to sweep the floors."

"Or I could call out and the Guardsmen would be here in moments, and then you'd be tossed into the Old Pen. Maybe they'd kill you on the spot, maybe they'd hang you now. Maybe they'd hang you at midwinter."

Jak cracked his best defiant grin. "Am I being offered a choice?"

"No." Deek carefully returned the bola's counterweight to its disarmed position and dropped the bola harmlessly in the grass at his feet. "I'm showing you that you can trust me."

Jak exhaled a tight breath and collapsed back against the wall. "You could have just said it, Deek."

"People *say* many things," Deek said. "In the end, isn't it what you *do* that matters?"

Jak just nodded.

"You came here with Dyan." Deek nodded in the direction of the Old Pen. "You could have left her. I don't really know why you're helping her, but I want to help her, too."

"Even though she's an outlaw?"

Deek looked down at his feet. "Yes."

"I don't have a way in," Jak said. "Can you help me?"

"Maybe. Help you. Help her. Help *me*." Deek looked up. "But first, we have to hide you."

They remounted and rode away from the Old Pen along the foothills, behind buildings whose plain white facades gave away nothing about what happened inside. Jak thought they were what Dyan had identified as the Shackups, where Love-Matched Systemoids lived, but he couldn't think of a way to ask Deek that didn't sound awkward in his head.

Instead, he asked something else. "You have a Prison," he said, "and the Old Pen. That's an awful lot of capacity for locking people up."

Deek was quiet for a while. "I guess the System has lots of enemies," he eventually said. "I hadn't really thought about it."

At Deek's direction, Jak dropped the Mechanical off a few minutes' walk from the Garage, at a long, low building with the word HYDRO written over the door. "I'm learning to work with the water supply," Deek said. "I'm late."

"They going to hang you for it?" Jak meant this as a joke, but Deek's expression immediately fell and he wondered whether Deek had been asking himself the same question.

"Being late isn't good, but I think I can tell them I lost my way. I'm still new."

Then the Mechanical disappeared through the doors.

Again following Deek's directions, Jak rode to the Buza River and dropped out of sight. As the sun was descending now in the west, there were fewer people recreating along the river, which made it even better as a way to stay out of sight.

Jak did meet three Outriders coming the other direction. His heart beat faster, and he deliberately loosened his grip on the reins a bit to speed up.

But they only waved, and he waved back, and then they passed each other.

Deek's directions had been very clear. At the third weir breaking the flow of the river, Jak found a catwalk crossing the water. It was too narrow for the horse, and Jak was reluctant to give the animal up, so he rode across the river itself instead. On the far side was a small open-air amphitheater built into the slope of the bluff overlooking the river. Jak tethered his horse in a grove of tall, scabby-barked cottonwood trees and walked to the top of the amphitheater to sit at the highest bench.

From here, he couldn't be surprised. He held a bola in his hand, careful not to arm it accidentally, and waited. Across the river, in and around white stone buildings whose purpose he didn't know, he watched streams of people pulse to and fro.

Vaguely, ominously, the streams of people felt to him like the bola in his hands. He knew they were dangerous. He didn't know how they worked or why, though he was sure the System had a logic to it. If he wasn't careful, he was going to get himself sliced in half.

Like Eirig.

Somehow, Jak closed his eyes and dozed a little.

In the afternoon, people in brown trousers and tunics—Gardeners—swept the floor of the amphitheater, trimmed branches off surrounding trees, and raked a thick bank of leaves into a black bag that they hauled away with them. Jak ignored them, and they ignored him back.

At dusk, Deek appeared again. The Mechanical jogged up from the river with a bundle under one arm. "Quickly!" he called. He loosed the horse's tether without waiting for confirmation and mounted as Jak was still descending the amphitheater's steps.

They rode west along the river. The leaves were turning orange and falling in large drifts, so that even though Gardeners had plucked the leaves from these paths during the day, the horse's hooves still kicked up jets of orange and gold.

"Where is this secret place where you're going to hide me?" Jak asked.

As he asked it, Deek reined in the horse and climbed down. They were in a stand of cottonwoods, screened off from the outside world by a further veil of young aspen trees. Deek waved the bundle he was carrying at Jak. "These are for you. Hop off."

Jak climbed down and took the bundle. "These are clothes. They're *your* clothes." Deek had brought a Mechanical's uniform. Wrapped inside the uniform was a belt of tools Jak mostly didn't recognize.

"Right. Pretty sure we're about the same size. Your head's bigger, but there's no hat to wear. You get changed and I'll explain."

Jak didn't love taking all his clothes off. It made him feel unprotected and exposed. He dropped the Outrider's outfit into a puddle on the ground.

"I think I can get us inside the Old Pen," Deek said.

"How?"

"Let me finish, blast you. I work in Hydro, that's the water systems. Just Maintenance, because I'm new and I have to learn how the basic systems work before I can start doing anything really interesting. I think I can get us both into the Old Pen on a maintenance shift, but not for a couple of days. So you're going to hide out in the Bothies."

Despite his short nap, or maybe because of it, Jak felt irritable and tired. "What is that, where you keep tools?"

Deek laughed. "Sort of. Bothies are the buildings where the Gardeners live. Mostly at the west end of the System."

"The long, low buildings around the west gate."

"Yeah. Gardeners are used to having Mechanicals stay with them when we're working on an extended task. For instance, when one of the Bothies has a Hydro Maintenance problem that takes a day or two to resolve. Easier to sleep out there than to ride back and forth to the Garage, you see? Especially if you end up working late."

"Fine. But I can't fix a Hydro Maintenance problem."

"Fortunately for you, there isn't any real problem. You're going to walk up to one of the Bothies and tell them you'll be working on an issue with one of the weirs. By day, you hang out at the river, pretend you're doing things with the water systems.

Stay away from any real Mechanicals. By night, you sleep on a pallet in the Bothies."

"No one's going to question me?"

Deek shook his head. "This happens all the time. The Gardeners will assume you're a real Mechanical because they host real Mechanicals like this, and they have no one in particular to report it to. And no one else will miss you."

Jak thought about the Cogitant with the dead eyes. "The System ... may already be looking for me."

"So stay away from Outriders, too. There are rations in the belt. Just keep your head down, and if any of the Gardeners get too close, just act ..." Deek trailed off.

"Just act like I'm too good to mix with them?"

"That'd do it."

Jak reached into the puddle of Outrider's gear. He took out the ration bars he had left, along with the two bolas, and tucked it all into the Mechanical's belt, which he buckled around his hips.

"Okay," he said. "Take me to your Gardeners."

CHAPTER SIX

Deek wrapped the remaining Outrider gear in a single bundle with the coat on the outside, weighted it down with a big rock, and pushed the whole thing into the river. Then they left the horse in the trees and walked.

The weir was taller than Jak, creating a deep pond on its upstream side. In its middle was a metal gate. Crossing the weir by the metal lattice walkway along its top, water rushing over its height just beneath their feet, Deek stopped at the water gate. He tapped the wheel-like horizontal handle capping a long screw that descended into its depths.

"This will raise and lower the gate. Don't do it too much, or you may attract attention to yourself from somebody downstream."

"I'll just pretend to play around with this for a day or two until you come back for me with a plan to get into the Old Pen." Jak trusted Deek, or at least he trusted him to help Jak help Dyan, but he didn't like the idea of doing nothing.

"I have to arrange for us to get inside the Old Pen," Deek said. "This is just a way to hide you."

"How do you know a real Maintenance team won't come to work on this in the meantime and catch me?"

Deek grinned, his teeth white in the darkness. "Because I just finished the Maintenance work here myself. It's perfect. The only reason it can possibly malfunction in the next two days is if you do something to break it. And I'm pretty sure you can avoid breaking it."

"I like your confidence." Jak looked at the north bank of the river. He saw the long, low Bothies where the Gardeners lived. Beyond them lay the road he and Dyan had traveled from the west gate into the System. "Anything else you want to tell me about the Gardeners?"

Deek shrugged. "Be polite, but they should basically be willing to do anything you ask. Each Bothy has a Headman, and the Headman is responsible for everyone in the Bothy. You should probably just pick one, knock on a door, and ask to talk to the Headman."

"Got it."

Deek walked away. "I'll be back tomorrow," he said before he passed out of earshot. "Or the next day at the latest."

The Mechanical disappeared into the trees.

"Summer Son, help me," Jak muttered.

He trudged across the weir alone, gripping his heavy tool belt with both hands to reassure himself that, alone as he might be, he wasn't unarmed. He shot a look heavenward, but the powered lights—one globe above each door in the Bothies, and additional lights atop metal poles he hadn't previously noticed along the main street—hid the stars behind a veil of white light. "Holy Mother, don't leave me now."

Between the Buza River and the Bothies was a short strip of grass. Jak stopped at its edge and looked at the grass. Something about it bothered him, and it took him a few moments to realize what.

No evidence of children.

Nothing resembling a toy, or a child's shoe, or a place to play.

Some part of him, he realized, had been relieved to try to hide himself amongst the System's Gardeners. The way Deek talked about them, Jak had thought of them as Landsmen, like him. People who did real things to the earth, to trees and other plants. Farmers.

This lack of evidence of children was a good reminder that the Gardeners were just a different kind of Systemoid.

Jak crossed the grass and knocked at the nearest door.

The woman who opened the door was old enough to be his mother, with curly brown hair just beginning to be flecked with white. Her eyes sparkled, and though it might be from the cold, her cheeks had red cherries in them over deep dimples, which together made her face look merry. She wore a long brown tunic.

Beyond her, though Jak didn't mean to spy, he saw two other women and a small room with bunks along all the walls.

"Mechanical?" the woman said.

"Jass," Jak said. "Mechanical Jass. I'm looking for your Headman."

"You're in luck." The woman smiled. "I'm Headman Anji. Whitwark Bothy."

"Good." Jak nodded. So the Bothies had names. "I'll be working on your weir tomorrow." Would the Headman think of it as *her* weir, or might it be the *System's* weir? Too late. Then he almost asked permission to stay, but he caught himself in time. "Where can I sleep?"

"As it happens, you're in luck," Headman Anji said. She stepped out onto the white stone walkway running in front of the Bothies. Then she sighed. "The Overseer took two men yesterday, leaving me two empty cots. Otherwise, you'd have been on the floor somewhere."

"I'm not particular." Jak grinned as he caught Headman Anji's eye. "A floor would have been fine. As long as you didn't put me in the quarters of some energetic young Love-Match."

Anji squinted at Jak and frowned. "You're a recent Creche-leaver."

"I'm not as young as I look," Jak said. He regretted his defensive words immediately.

"They don't teach you much about us over on the other side of the Camel's Back." Anji stopped and folded her arms over her chest. "We don't have Love-Matches, Mechanical. And all male Gardeners are chemically sterilized. That doesn't mean they don't get frisky, but … they know the consequences. They'll leave you alone if you aren't interested."

Jak wasn't sure how it would be done chemically, but he had spent enough time around sheep and cattle to know what sterilization was. Curious that it was the males alone who were sterilized, though of course you only needed to sterilize either the males or the females to stop reproduction.

Not that he knew why the System didn't want the Gardeners to reproduce, but he wasn't all that surprised. After all, the System interfered with his own people, the Landsmen, by removing its brightest children from their people when they reached adulthood.

The brightest children, like himself and his sister Aleena.

Did the System interfere with the Shoshan or the Basku? What might that interference look like?

He almost apologized for his mistake, but caught himself.

"So I guess that won't be a problem." He gestured at the path, though with his other hand he squeezed one of the bolas in his tool belt to reassure himself. "Lead the way, Headman."

Headman Anji nodded and continued.

In the darkness, they almost bumped into another Gardener. He was a narrow-faced man, whose eyes in the light looked sour and yellow. A wide scar ran through both his eyebrows. The Gardener grinned at the Headman.

"Tulit," the Headman said. "It's after curfew."

Tulit nodded at Jak. "We have a guest."

"Jass," Jak said. He didn't offer his hand, taking his cue from Anji, who seemed annoyed at Tulit's presence.

"Will I be so honored as to have Mechanical Jass stay with me tonight?" Tulit grinned widely. "I do love conversations with new friends."

Anji kept walking. "You will be so honored as to have work to do and food to eat tomorrow," she snorted over her shoulder. "Now get inside!"

Jak followed.

The Headman stopped again several doors down to knock. "Headman!" she called.

A younger man, Jak's age, maybe, opened the door. His blond hair hung in wet tangles around his ears—one of which was smaller than the other, and shriveled—and he had a long drying cloth wrapped around his waist.

"Headman." He nodded.

Headman Anji jerked a thumb in Jak's direction. "You got a Mechanical." She turned and walked back down the path toward her own room. "He's young, respect his boundaries."

"How long?" the blond man called after her.

She threw her hands over her head. "Long as he's here."

Jak reminded himself not to treat these men as peers, but he didn't have to be rude. "Whichever bed is empty is fine."

"Good." The blond man threw the door open and stepped aside. "Because you're not really my type."

With the door open, Jak saw four bunks, a high and low bunk on the walls to the right and left. Against the back wall were two closets, and between them a shut curtain. Steam coming out from behind the curtain and the sound of running water suggested that it was some kind of bathing space. One of the closet doors was open, revealing shelves stacked with very little: several sets of identical brown clothing, a few small hand tools, some kind of wrapped rations, a partly whittled chunk of wood. The walls of the room were white, but not bare; one featured a painted picture of the Jawtooths, and another a sketch of fish, probably drawn in charcoal. The space was illuminated by a pair of glowing glass tubes affixed to the ceiling.

And on the inside surface of the door, Jak saw as the door shut, was the System's emblem, painted in black.

These were the Bothies. These were people the System hated enough to sterilize and who only existed to do menial labor, but they still lived in rooms nicer than any Jak had ever known.

Both upper bunks were bare; the lower bunks had clothing strewn on them. Jak gestured noncommittally. "Do you care where I sleep?"

The blond man laughed. "That bunk," he pointed, "was Rimbo's. Yesterday the Overseer killed him because he'd stolen dessert rations and was trading them with some Landsy girl outside the wall. That one was Hoff's. The Overseer killed him for napping during his shift."

Jak kept his expression neutral and nodded slowly.

He took off his tool belt and slung it onto the first bunk. "Rimbo's it is. Sounds like better luck to me. But really, I thought you Gardeners were all sterilized."

"No *babies*," the blond man chuckled. "That doesn't mean no *fun*."

The sound of running water stopped and the curtain opened. The man behind it was older and heavier, but he still had thick, dark hair to match a thick beard. Beneath his mustache, Jak spotted a hint of a cleft palate. "No babies means *more* fun. No babies means no responsibility."

"This is Klem," the blond man said, introducing the older man. "I'm Barstow."

"System feeds me, houses me, and surrounds me with occasionally willing women," Klem grunted. His eyes flickered briefly to Barstow. "Or men." Barstow smiled faintly, but otherwise didn't acknowledge Klem's reference. "All I have to do is push around a rake or a pair of shears? Sounds like a bargain to me."

"I'm Jass," Jak said, remembering his assumed name just in time. "Mechanical Jass."

"We know Mechanicals when we see them," Klem said, pointing at Jak's uniform. "Mechanicals and Overseers is all we ever see down here in the Bothies. Other than people riding by on horseback."

"Right." Jak realized, standing in the presence of these just-cleaned men, how much he stank. He carried several days' worth of sweat under his borrowed Mechanical uniform. He pointed at Barstow's drying cloth. "You have another one of those?"

"Use Rimbo's. It's on the bunk."

Jak stripped down, piling his uniform on top of his tool belt. He didn't like leaving the monofilament bolas out here in the room while he washed, but unless the Gardeners got training the Landsmen didn't, he didn't think Klem or Barstow could threaten him with the weapons.

Besides, so far Deek's advice seemed to be right. These people were used to Systemoid visitors—*Mechanical* visitors, anyway—and were deferential.

But what was the Overseer?

The bathing space was a stone-walled chamber with just room enough to stand. By pulling on levers in the wall, Jak made hot water pour from a spout in the ceiling. He scraped the dirt and oils off his body with a crescent-shaped fin he found on a narrow shelf in the washing chamber and watched it swirl in streaks down a drain in the floor.

When he was clean, he dressed again in the Mechanical jumpsuit, laid his tools carefully by his side and stretched out to sleep.

Despite his exhaustion, sleep didn't come.

His body and heart both aching, he lay awake a long time, remembering Dyan's face as the gates of the Old Pen shut behind her.

Later still, he drifted off of sleep to the soft sound of male voices whispering and laughing softly in the darkness.

$$*\qquad*\qquad*$$

No one offered him food in the morning, and Jak didn't stick around the Bothies long enough to see where and how the Gardeners ate. He was already pushing his luck pretty hard, so before the sun was up he buckled his belt, stepped into his boots, and marched over to the weir.

Some of the tools on his belt were self-explanatory. A hammer and a knife, for starters. He didn't know their names, but he could see that some of the other devices were clearly suited for poking or prodding, and others made sense as levers to turn tight bolts. One was a light stick. Some weren't so obvious in what they did, and Jak was afraid they might be dangerous in unexpected ways, like a monofilament or vibro-blade cutter.

He proceeded carefully.

As the sun rose, the Gardeners of his Bothy took large tools, and sometimes small carts, out of one of the Bothy's rooms and trundled off to work, upstream, downstream, north toward the foothills, and even south. Jak scooted to one side to let those who wished to pass him on the walkway over the weir.

Then Jak positioned himself by the water gate in the weir's center. More to entertain himself than for any other reason, he turned the wheel to lower the gate a hand's breadth, watching the water rush over in a thick torrent. A couple of thick-bodied fish went with it, and then he raised the gate again and watched the pool upstream.

With the water lowered, he could now see the river was full of fish. Maybe that's what the weirs were for—they created deeper than natural pools for the fish to swim in. Or maybe the System tapped those pools for its other water needs, like drinking water and bathing? He hadn't seen any food crops or livestock within the System's walls, so Jak assumed the System ate entirely off what it took from the Landsmen, and maybe others, outside the System.

Deek could probably tell him. Young as he was, he was a Mechanical, and in Hydro Maintenance. *Hydro* meant *water.*

The Old Pen had to have water. The prisoners drank, and probably they washed, too. And there would be latrines, which might be flushed by flowing water.

Lying on his belly with a metal rod in his hand, Jak reached down and pretended to tinker. In reality, he thought about Dyan in the Old Pen. Would her cell look at all like the room in the Bothies where Jak had spent the night? Would she be in a room with three other prisoners? Would they have a washing chamber? Where would their food come from?

Or was it just a filthy pit? Had Dyan slept on cold stone?

"Mother!" Jak cursed. He banged a tool against the stone in frustration and doubt, and only succeeded in knocking it out of his own hands. He lunged for it but missed, and then watched uselessly as the tool sank past a trio of fleeing fish and disappeared into the unseen depths of the weir's pond.

He looked up to be certain no one was watching, and saw something on the highway that caught his eye.

Two riders.

Outriders, by their costumes. It was the long dark coats that had caught Jak's gaze at first, but he kept looking because he noticed one of the Outriders was dusky and the other fair and the combination rang a dark bell within him.

He flattened himself on the weir, pressing his face against the base of the gate's control wheel to try to stay out of sight and watched.

The riders were Shad and Cheela.

They had come to Ratsnay Station with Dyan, Deek, and the dead Healer-designate Wayland to carry out the Cull. With Magister Haika, they had further pursued Dyan and Jak into the Wahai, and after rescuing Jak, Dyan had spared their lives and left them behind, on foot in the mountains on the other side of the Lull Sea.

Now they rode into the System on the same road Jak and Dyan had used. They looked tired but determined. Cheela in particular had a set to her jaw that was positively murderous. They rode smaller horses than the big mounts Outriders were known for—Shoshan ponies, or some other Landsman or Basku breed.

Jak had believed the Outriders a few days behind.

Clearly, he had been mistaken.

"Mother blast me," Jak muttered.

CHAPTER SEVEN

Jak stayed hidden and the two young Outriders passed.
Should he race after them? If they were looking for
Dyan, surely they'd go straight to the Prison or the Old
Pen. If they didn't find her themselves immediately, *someone* would
tell them their old Crechemate, the Magister-designate-turned-
renegade-and-Landsy-lover, had been captured.

But so what? Jak forced himself to lie still and watch the
horses receding up the highway toward the heart of the System.
Dyan was already captured, so what did it matter if Shad and
Cheela found out? Dyan would be punished, or maybe there
would be a trial, but Jak didn't see how it was worse for her for
the Outriders' presence.

Unless they were so angry at having been outwitted that they
walked right into her cell in the Old Pen and murdered her.

Possible, but it didn't seem likely.

On the other hand, it occurred to Jak, their return to the System
might make things worse for *him*. They knew his face from Ratsnay
Station and Marsick. They knew he had been with Dyan out in the
Wahai. Wouldn't they assume he might be here, too?

But if Dyan was captured, wasn't it because the Cogitant had
recognized her? And the Cogitant had seen Jak, too.

Or maybe someone else had recognized Dyan, and the
Cogitant's strange words had been a genuine message and not a

trap, but now Shad and Cheela's presence put Jak in real danger for the first time.

Jak shook himself.

He'd never be certain, so he just had to make a decision. The Outriders were gone from his sight so he stood and stretched, looking westward along the river, toward all the things he couldn't see: the wall, the gate, the Lull Sea, Cowell.

Sayatil? Portolan?

The Summer Son, once night had fallen.

The Summer Son had killed the Rattler, despite the fact that it sprouted extra heads as he chopped them off. He had killed it by knowing its secret name, which let him seal off the heads as he severed them. He'd cleaned out the filthy Palace of King Simple, when it was full of the corpses of his dead servants, by running the Snaik River through it. He'd killed the Lion Queen of the Wahai, worn her skin, and planted her teeth—which had sprouted into the Jawtooth Mountains.

The Summer Son wouldn't have run away, and he wouldn't care whether the Systemoids found him or not. *The Summer Son gets the job done,* Jak's mother had told him many times.

Jak could get the job done. He could be the Summer Son.

He could be Redcap Rider, rescuing chained princesses.

He turned away from the west and ideas of flight, to notice that a troop of Gardeners had worked its way downstream on the north bank of the river and was getting quite close to him.

Randomly selecting a tool from his belt, Jak stalked across the catwalk in the other direction, getting away from the Gardeners. When he reached the far end of the weir, he sat down and pretended to fiddle with bolts holding the catwalk in place.

There was no point in getting involved with Gardeners, beyond the need to have somewhere to sleep other than on the open ground.

Several of the Gardeners, including Klem, the older man whose room in the Bothy Jak had shared, swung long-handled scythes to cut the tall grass along the river's edge. Others raked the cut grass into piles. Others gathered piles of grass into carts. Other groups still worked on the red carpet of fallen leaves, raking it and gathering it into other carts.

Full carts were pushed out of Jak's sight. To be composted somewhere?

Headman Anji pushed a rake, but also called a constant stream of direction to the people around her. It didn't sound angry. Anji was sometimes encouraging, sometimes cajoling, and sometimes bullying, but her words were never angry or cruel. She had the knack of sounding patient even as she was bellowing.

Jak realized he had been watching for several minutes without even pretending to work on the bridge; he changed tool and shifted his position, turning his face away from the Gardeners and tapping on the catwalk under his feet.

He hadn't seen Barstow, the young, blond man. At that moment, a man in a red cloak strolled out from behind the nearest Bothy. He was tall, narrow in the waist, and broad in the hip, with curling hair down to his shoulders.

Really, the cloaked man was what the Summer Son should look like. Or Redcap Rider; the monster slayer was not said to wear a cape, but surely he must cut a similarly heroic figure to this man.

The man in the red cloak held a trailing leash in his right hand. A moment after he appeared, the creature at the end of the leash staggered into view—

The creature at the end of the leash was Barstow.

Barstow stared at his feet and muttered. Just at the edge of visibility he seemed to resist, digging in his heels.

Red Cape twitched the leash and Barstow screamed.

It was a scream without words, and Barstow staggered forward again.

Jak looked at the Gardeners—they all seemed to be intensifying their efforts to be busy, hewing and gathering grass even faster than before.

"Headman Anji!" Red Cape called. "Whitwark Bothy!"

Jak couldn't look away, but he didn't want to be caught staring. He slipped down the dirt riverbank, hiding his body behind the weir and looking under the catwalk. He gripped the bars of the catwalk and pretended to be testing it, but with little energy.

The Gardeners all turned to face Red Cape.

"Yes?" Anji laid her rake down and folded her hands in front of her.

"Is this Gardener Barstow of Whitwark?" Red Cape looked absolutely calm. Barstow was trembling.

"He is," Anji agreed. She looked calm, too, but there was a slight cracking in her voice when she spoke.

"This Gardener is guilty. He has been making indecent propositions to an Urbane."

"Blasted idiot," Klem spat out. Other Gardeners muttered, but Red Cape ignored them.

"I ask for your clemency, Overseer," Anji said. "Barstow is young. Making mistakes and receiving mercy is one of the ways young people learn."

So *this* was the Overseer.

"This Gardener has been guilty before," the Overseer said.

"Of shirking, once," Anji said. "Not of indecent propositions."

The Overseer said nothing. He pulled his cape off one shoulder, exposing a range of tools on his belt Jak didn't recognize, and a few he did, including a sword and a whip. The Overseer took the belt from his whip and threw it to Headman Anji—

"Mother!" Jak flinched.

But the whip wasn't a monofilament whip. Jak could see its length, and when Anji made no effort to catch the whip, it fell to the ground at her feet.

"Please, Overseer," she said. "I ask for mercy for this man."

"Pick up the whip," the Overseer snarled.

"Whip me instead." Anji's voice caught in her throat as she spoke, but she looked resolute.

"Not an option, Headman." The Overseer spoke slowly and drew his sword. "No one takes the punishment for another. On the other hand, if you refuse to whip this Gardener, that will be a dereliction of your duties as Headman, and I will be forced to remove you from your position."

The Overseer's sword began to whine softly. The blade appeared blurred, like a smudged image on glass.

Anji picked up the whip. She shook out the long strand of it and turned to face Barstow squarely.

Barstow whimpered.

"The switch, Headman."

Anji said nothing. She touched the handle of the whip with her free hand, though, and Jak smelled a faint burning odor in the breeze.

The other Gardeners stood back. Anji cursed, but only through clenched teeth and directed at their own feet.

"Twenty for indecent propositions," the Overseer said.

Anji nodded and drew her arm over her shoulder.

"Ten more for your delay in carrying out sentence."

Anji turned her head sharply. "Overseer! If there is a punishment for my delay, *I* must bear it!"

The Overseer smiled at her. He looked just as strong and handsome as before, just as much like Jak thought the Summer Son would look, but the smile on his face made Jak's stomach twist. He found himself spitting bile into the river.

"I'm glad to find we share a common idea of justice." The Overseer smiled pleasantly. "Now would you like him to have yet another ten strokes?"

Snap!

Anji cracked the whip. As the lash struck Barstow, he raised an arm to protect himself, but then shrieked. His body jerked and twisted as each blow fell on him, and the burning smell in Jak's nostrils changed slightly.

It stank of scorched flesh.

He looked away, but he couldn't block the sounds from his ears.

"Count!" the Overseer shouted.

"Five!" someone shouted back. Maybe Klem?

Snap!

"No!" the Overseer roared. "Start with *one*!"

"One!" The voice was Anji's. It wasn't a sob, not quite, but it was close. *Snap!*

Jak found himself counting out loud, his arms wrapped around the struts of the weir. He reached ten when he heard Barstow begging for mercy. He couldn't bring himself to look at what was happening.

"Please!" Anji cried. "Eleven!"

But she snapped the whip again, and the Overseer offered no mercy.

Fifteen. Eighteen. Twenty.

Why were these people taking this?

"He's dying!" Anji was weeping now.

"You will administer all thirty," the Overseer said. "Or we will start over and administer thirty lashes to someone else."

"Twenty-one." *Snap!*

Then Jak heard a roar.

He popped his head up over the top of the weir just in time to see Klem charge.

Klem didn't have the Overseer's heroic build or his height. He was older and slower, but he was thick in the thigh and in the arm, and he was swinging a long-handled scythe, howling at the top of his lungs.

"Leave him be!" the older man shouted.

"No!" Anji shouted. She snapped the whip again, this time at Klem. She struck him on the shoulder and a red welt appeared. The air already stank of burned flesh, and Klem didn't slow down.

In the Overseer's place, Jak would have dodged, or run.

The Overseer stepped into Klem's charge and raised his whining, blurry blade up to parry the attack.

Except that when the sword and the scythe handle met, the scythe handle split neatly in two. The Overseer's weapon, a vibro-blade, cut the grass-trimming tool as easily as it would have cut through water.

The head of the scythe hurtled through the air and bounced harmlessly of the wall of Whitwark Bothy.

Then the Overseer stepped aside. Off balance, Klem stumbled and fell to the ground. He lay facedown on the grass and sobbed, but his sobs didn't last. Stepping forward, the Overseer ran his sword through Klem's neck, and the Gardener's head popped neatly from his shoulders and fell over sideways in the grass.

Eyes staring at Jak.

Throughout the short encounter, the Overseer had never released his grip on Barstow's leash. Now he turned to face the Gardeners of Whitwark Bothy again.

"What was this Gardener's name?" he asked.

"Klem." Anji's voice was so soft Jak could barely hear it over the rippling of the Buza River.

"Sentence has been carried out on Gardener Klem for insurrection," the Overseer said. He wasn't breathing hard. His voice sounded cheerful.

Silence.

"Now we must finish with Gardener Barstow of Whitwark Bothy."

Anji nodded. She turned to face Barstow again, who was just a lump of trembling flesh, emitting soft whimpering noises. She raised her whip.

"One." The Overseer smiled.

Anji didn't argue.

Snap!

Jak turned his back to the scene of death and pressed his shoulder blades against the cold metal of the weir. He heard the count of thirty. He heard the Overseer warn all the Gardeners that it was very important for them to keep all the System's rules, because without rules there was no order, and without order the System didn't function. When he had gone, Jak heard the Gardeners go slowly back to work.

Later, while the others were eating, Jak crouched in the shadow of the weir and heard Headman Anji, standing on the catwalk above him, weeping.

*   *   *

Jak ate alone, at noon and in the evening. He would have wanted to in any case, to keep his identity a secret, but now he had no will to look any of the Gardeners of Whitwark Bothy in the eye. But lying on his back across the river from where the Gardeners sat at long trestle tables (produced from doors in the Bothy that must open into storage sheds rather than sleeping quarters) and ate, Jak heard the enormity of the Gardeners' silence. It matched a deep silence inside his own heart.

Jak stood a long time that night in the hot water of the bathing chamber, but felt no cleaner for it. Then he dressed again in the Mechanical uniform Deek had given him and sat on Klem's bunk, staring across the room at Barstow's empty sleeping space.

Without warning, the door opened and Headman Anji entered. She stood a moment in the doorway looking at him.

"I'm sorry," she said. "I thought you had gone."

"You were looking for a place to be alone," Jak guessed numbly. It was what he wanted, too.

Anji turned to leave.

"Please sit," Jak said. He pointed at the opposite bunk. "This is your Bothy."

She sat slowly. "It's the System's Bothy. As I've been reminded today."

Jak had nothing to say. He wanted to comfort her. *You tried!* he wanted to scream. In his mind, he saw over and over Klem's death, cut with memories of Eirig, coming to rescue Jak from the Cull on a high bluff over the Snaik River. *The System came for your people and you tried to save them! It's not your fault the System is too powerful for you!*

But he said nothing. He just stared at the weathered, sad face of Headman Anji until exhaustion finally dragged him off to sleep. Something about the way she held herself, or the set of her jaw, reminded him of his own mother.

What would the Summer Son do for the Gardeners of Whitwark Bothy? There wasn't even a monster to kill here, not unless you imagined the System itself was a monster. But that made no sense—the System was a people. It was everybody. It was even, Jak realized, the people of Ratsnay Station, who in their peripheral and subjugated way took part in the vast mechanism of rules and deeds that had today crushed Barstow and Klem.

There was no monster to slay, and the number of princesses to rescue was practically infinite. Jak would need to be an army of Redcap Riders.

He wondered, as he finally sank into unconsciousness, whether he was crying.

CHAPTER EIGHT

Jak awoke late in the morning, to the sound of galloping horses.

Staggering to the Bothy door, he opened it a crack, just in time to see the back of a band of Outriders, galloping away down the highway, westwards. At least eight of them, which was the most Outriders Jak had ever seen together in one place.

Turning, he found he was not alone.

Headman Anji sat on Barstow's bunk. Her eyes were red but wide open and she watched Jak. Her hands were folded together in her lap.

"Good morning," Jak said.

"You're not a Mechanical."

Jak froze.

This woman had kindness in her. She had tried to save Klem, even offered to take his punishment herself. So she had courage as well as compassion. But in the end, she had cooperated with the Overseer. Her hand had held the whip that killed Klem.

Jak bit his lip.

"There's nothing wrong with that weir. And also, I don't think you were even born in the System. No product of the Creches feels as much pain as you did over the suffering of another human being."

Jak realized his belt, with the bolas inside, was across the room on the bunk. If he killed Anji, he'd have to run again. Since

D.J. Butler

Klem and Barstow were both dead, maybe the other Gardeners of Whitwark Bothy wouldn't be able to identify him. Maybe he wouldn't have to run very far.

He drifted slowly across the room toward his belt. "Don't the Gardeners need to be out working?"

"The Gardeners *are* out working. As Headman of this Bothy, I'm checking on our guest. Who are you?"

Jak picked up his belt and wrapped it around his waist. He tried to make the action look as casual as he could, but his heart sank as he did it.

The belt was too light.

He looked again at Headman Anji. She opened her folded hands to reveal two monofilament bolas.

If he were going to leap across the room, seize the bolas from the Headman, and kill her with them, now was the time.

Jak considered committing murder. Instead, he sat down.

In part, he didn't think he could kill Anji before she could make a noise to alert the Gardeners. He might not be able to kill her at all—for all he knew, she was skilled with the bolas herself, or had some other weapon he couldn't see.

But his restraint was more than that. Anji was like Jak. She wasn't a Systemoid, not really. And in fact, the System had taken from her people she'd cared about. And she had tried to resist. She had offered to sacrifice herself to the System in someone else's place.

He couldn't kill her. He *was* her.

"I'm nobody," Jak said.

"You don't look Basku or Shoshan. Are you a Landsman?" Anji shook her head. "Never mind, it doesn't really matter. What I really want to know is this: what are you doing here? If you don't have to be in the System, why are you here?"

Jak remembered the things Klem had said in the same room, two days earlier. He could tell her he was here for food and shelter, but it felt like a lie she wouldn't believe. Jak wouldn't believe the lie, if someone else told it to him. Food and shelter could be had elsewhere; that was the least of the things the System offered.

"Do you know the story of Redcap Rider?"

Anji shook her head.

Jak sighed. "I'm trying to rescue someone."

"A prisoner of the System?"

Jak nodded. "The odds are pretty bad, and I might even be doomed to fail. But I have to try."

Headman Anji was silent for a long time.

"I try to rescue people," she said. "People who are prisoners of the System, in a way. Prisoners like me. I try it every day. Most days and most times, I succeed. Yesterday you saw me fail."

"Yesterday I saw you *try*," Jak said. "You risked yourself to try to save Barstow."

"But now what you have to wonder is whether my desire to save the people in Whitwark Bothy will cause me to look the other way, or lead me to report you to the Overseer."

"That's about right."

"You'd feel much more comfortable if you had these bolas in your hands, wouldn't you? I notice you walked to pick them up." Headman Anji's face gave away no trace of any emotion.

"Of course," Jak said. "Don't you feel more comfortable for the fact that you're holding them now?"

Anji laughed. She set both bolas on Barstow's bunk, stood, and walked to the door.

"Wait," Jak said. "Are you not going to tell me your decision?"

"Would it matter if I did?" she asked. "You couldn't take my words at face value anyway. You'd have to make a judgment call based on the other information you have. About me. About the System. About yourself."

"Yeah." Jak couldn't think of anything else to say.

"Yeah." Headman Anji turned to leave.

"Wait—"

Anji turned back, and Jak dropped to his knees on the floor. The Headman furrowed her brows, so before she could say anything in objection, Jak spat out his words.

"I don't know how I'm going to do this," he said, his tongue tripping over itself. "I don't know how I'm going to rescue … my friend. But I won't leave you here, either. I will come back for you."

"Don't promise what you don't mean." Anji blinked, and her eyes were bright with tears.

"By the Holy Mother," Jak said. "By my sister Aleena. By my best friend Eirig. And by everything else I hold dear. I won't leave you here."

Anji looked into Jak's eyes for a long time without saying anything. Finally, she nodded and left. Jak looked at the bolas on the other bunk a long time before he stood and picked them up.

*   *   *

Jak was pretending to work on the weir again when Deek returned.

With relief, Jak put his tools back into his belt beside his bolas and stood to greet the Mechanical.

"We've got a ticket," Deek said. He held a squarish piece of thick paper in his hand, no bigger than a thumb's length across. He seemed excited.

"What's a ticket?" Jak asked.

Deek showed him. The tiny sheet was covered with numbers, and made no sense to Jak. "Help me out here. This is going to get Dyan out of the Old Pen?"

"Nope. It will get us *in.*"

Out of sheer reflex, Jak rested his hands on his belt above where the bolas hung.

"And we just walk out with her."

"More or less," Deek said. He shook, as if he were cold.

"Thanks for helping us, Deek," Jak said to the Mechanical.

"For Dyan. And ..." Deek looked down at his feet. "For Dyan."

Jak passed Headman Anji on his way out of Whitwark Bothy. He nodded slightly to her, and her nod back to him was nearly imperceptible.

Deek had two horses. As they rode, he explained his plan. Jak didn't follow all the details but he gathered the ticket was a way of assigning tasks to Mechanicals. Someone, not Deek and not Jak, had received the assignment to enter the Old Pen and deal with a routine Hydro Maintenance issue. Deek had the ticket, so he and Jak would walk into the Old Pen.

Jak failed to follow quite how Deek had obtained the ticket. "Did you trade something for it?" he asked the other boy.

"Yes," Deek said. "I traded something. But really it was something I had already given away."

When Jak pressed, Deek would say no more.

The Mechanicals had a closet in the Old Pen, Deek further explained. This closet contained tools, including a cart. Deek described the cart, and it sounded more like a box with wheels on it. He was sure Dyan would fit inside, and they could wheel her right out of the Old Pen.

"The numbers on the ticket ... one thing they show is who has the ticket, right? I mean, the other Mechanicals you traded with?"

"True," Deek admitted. "But the Guardsmen at the Old Pen won't read the number."

"They won't?"

"I'm pretty sure they can't read the number."

"How sure is pretty sure?"

"Trust me," Deek said. "You are about to see the power of a uniform."

Jak pondered the other man's words. Would the Mechanical uniform Jak was wearing be enough to hide him from the gaze of Cogitant Yurvek?

"The Cogitants," Jak said as they rode past the Garage. "They're the ... leaders?" This was as much as he knew, from his classes with Magister Stanton in Ratsnay Station, and from what Dyan had said.

He hoped Deek would give him additional information. Instead, the Mechanical seemed reluctant even to confirm what Jak already knew. He said nothing in answer to Jak's question.

"I mean the Cogitant Council," Jak continued. "They rule the System."

Deek turned to look Jak in the eye. "Why do you care?"

Jak shrugged. "I'm just trying to understand the System. What's going on around me."

"My advice? Don't. Don't try to understand it. Just get Dyan out and get the blazes out of the System. And don't ever come back." Deek's voice was unexpectedly fierce.

"Okay," Jak said. "Sounds good to me."

"And stop trying to learn things. Take my word for it, some things, you'd be better off if you never knew them."

"I know," Jak said. "Remember me? I'm the guy whose sister was kidnapped, and later killed. I was happiest when I believed she was just living a good life in the System, Love-Matched to some fat Collector. Holy Mother, I wish I was still ignorant."

Deek looked like he was about to say something, but then he didn't. Instead, he shook his head and looked away. Finally: "Yeah. Yeah, that's right. Just take Dyan and get the blazes out of here."

Outside the Old Pen, they tied their horses next to others on a hitching post. Deek showed his tickets to the Guardsmen in front of the main gate. Their leader, a thickset man with bouncing jowls, made a show of closely reading it. As instructed in advance by Deek, Jak hooked his thumbs in his belt and looked up at the gate in front of him. He felt naked, he felt highly visible, as if he were *showing off* his face rather than trying to hide it.

And that was the point. The uniform was hiding him, and turning his face away could only attract attention.

"Okay," the Guardsman said. "Clink five."

"Yeah." Deek shrugged. "You know how Hydro is, though. Pipes all over, all of it closely connected, so I'll probably have to check all the Clinks."

"Nice Calling." One of the other Guardsmen, a tall man with two missing fingers on his left hand, snickered. "Fool around half the day, call it one ticket."

"Not half so nice as being a Guardsman," Deek shot back. "Sit around all day every day, tell people you have a Calling."

The muscles in Jak's back tightened with each word, but then Missing Fingers sneered at Deek and they both laughed.

"Take your time," the thickset Guardsman said, joining in the laughter. "Just get it done today, will you? The prisoners in five aren't getting water, which means we have to actually take it to them in buckets."

"What, your Lot Letter didn't mention you'd be carrying water around for prisoners?"

"Like yours didn't mention the possibility of having a whole squad of Guardsmen angry with you, I'm guessing."

"Yeah, yeah," Deek agreed. "I'm on it."

Then the gate opened, and he and Jak walked in.

The gate opened into a passage, with a door and a window set into the left wall. Deek waved his ticket through the window at a Guardsman sitting behind the glass, and then the gate at the far end of the passage opened, and the Hydro Maintenance detail entered the Old Pen's yard.

Small buildings stood in rows inside the enclosure. They were two stories tall and close to square, but otherwise reminded Jak of nothing so much as the Bothies. Jak saw two plain metal doors on the ground floor of each building, and no windows.

"Those buildings," Jak whispered to Deek. "Those are called 'Clinks'?"

Deek nodded.

A box-like wagon with four large wheels stood between two of the Clinks, with four heavy horses hitched to the front of it. The wagon was painted white, with the System's tree on its side painted in red.

"Sick Wagon," Deek said, nodding at the vehicle. "Takes prisoners to the Cradle."

Jak frowned. "What, if they're going to give birth?"

Deek just shook his head.

"We should split up," Jak suggested. "We'll go faster."

Deek looked at him with an expression Jak couldn't read. It was a childlike expression, and a fearful one. Whatever Deek was feeling, though, all he said was: "That's a good idea."

"What do I say if anyone tries to talk to me?"

"'Hydro Maintenance. Any problems with the water?'"

"And what do I do if they say there are problems?"

"You'll come back later. Remember, you don't actually care whether they have any water or not. You just want to look into each of the cells and find Dyan."

"And when no one fixes the real problem they have ... I mean, I'll be gone, but won't you have to be accountable? Later?"

"I'll be accountable," Deek agreed. "You don't need to worry about it."

"If I find Dyan, I'll finish checking the water in the cells of the ... Clink she's in first. For appearance's sake."

"Right. Then come find me."

Jak entered the Clink in the northeast corner of the enclosure. A Guardsman let him in at his knock and then strolled up and down the two halls, one on the ground floor and one on the upper story, while Jak asked each prisoner about the water. The answers he got were mixed, and he stopped noticing what the answers even were after the third cell. He focused his attention on the people in each cell.

The cells, it turns out, were smaller than the rooms in Whitwark Bothy. The cells were windowless, with a small latrine and a drinking pipe in one corner, and the wall facing the interior of the building entirely consisting of floor-to-ceiling iron bars. Each cell had a cot bolted to the wall and held a single occupant. Each was lit by a single light tube bolted to the ceilings, like the tubes in the Bothy's sleeping rooms. Some of the prisoners looked like Systemoids, but Jak would have pegged others for Shoshan or Basku or Landsmen. They all wore plain white tunics and trousers, without the mark of the System on them.

In the second floor hallway waited a cart. It was long and wheeled, padded on top, and underneath there was a single large shelf. A man with ragged brown hair lay on the cart and was strapped to it; a long white sheet covered his body, with only his head and restrained hands and feet showing.

The man turned to look at Jak. "Please," he said. "Just kill me now. Don't stretch this out."

Jak ignored him and finished checking the floor. Behind him, he heard whimpering.

No Dyan.

When he had seen all the prisoners, he went to the next Clink, passing the Sick Wagon on the way. Again, a Guardsman let him in. Jak heard muffled voices from the upper floor but ignored them, concentrating on his task of checking the occupant of each cell.

"You got water?" Ignore the answer. A tanned, lean man with white hair.

"You got water?" Ignore the answer. A woman, surprisingly young, and pale.

"You got water?" Ignore the answer. A fat man with a thick, curly beard.

Jak climbed the steps. He realized the voices had stopped as he put his foot on the bottom step. At the top step he paused. A man stood next to one of the cells, his back to Jak, his features hidden by an Outrider's coat and hat.

Jak put his hand on one of his bolas.

"Oh, no," said a woman's voice behind him, and at the same moment something touched his shoulder.

A monofilament whip. Jak nearly jumped, but the whip's counterweight was not extended. If it had been, Jak would now be in two pieces.

The voice belonged to Cheela.

The man turned to face Jak: he was Shad, and he grinned from ear to ear. It wasn't a malicious grin, but it was definitely a grin that said *I beat you*.

"Why look, Dyan." Shad the Outrider stepped in close to undo the buckle of Jak's belt, which fell to the floor. "You have a visitor."

CHAPTER NINE

ak looked into the cell and saw Dyan rise from the bunk. She wore the white tunic and trousers worn by other prisoners.

Other prisoners and, oddly, the Cogitant. Though the Cogitant had the System's tree on his chest in black as well.

"Jak!" Dyan looked as if she wanted to say more.

Jak's back was to the wall, but was there some way to play this meeting for his advantage, or for Dyan's? Could he pretend at this point that he had coerced Dyan into doing everything she had done and clear her name?

Not likely. Among other things, Dyan had rescued Jak from Cheela and Shad, leaving them stranded without horses in the Wahai. The Outriders probably knew she'd killed Magister Haika, too.

And what Jak knew was that Cheela—long-legged, good-looking Cheela whose hair was long, curly, and bronzed by the sun—had killed his best friend, Eirig. Jak hadn't seen the killing; he'd been riding to try to prevent it and had arrived too late.

But Dyan had told him the bola had been Cheela's.

"I guess you thought the Landsy would run away, huh?" Jak cracked a grin.

"No." She grinned back. "Not this Landsy." She didn't look like she had been tortured, but her hair was a tangled mess and her eyes showed fatigue.

"*I* was sure you would run, though." This from Cheela. Jak turned around to face her. She held the whip back now, ready to snap it forward. "I was convinced when you left the Wahai you'd head right back to the rotten little Landsy hole you were spawned in. What's it called? Rat Station?" She sneered.

"Ratsnay." Jak controlled his voice. "Are you relieved? I made your job easier."

"I'm disappointed."

Jak wished he had a bola and was aiming it at the two Outriders, rather than the other way around. He had nothing. Shad was behind him and would stop him trying to run; to his right were Dyan's bars; to his left was a sharp drop onto cement, but he had to go over a waist-high railing before the drop, and Cheela would have him sliced in two before he even put his hand on the rail.

All he had left was reasoning. It was not a strong card.

"Look," he said. "I don't want to hurt you. I don't want to be an … outlaw. I don't want to damage your System, and I won't tell anybody in Ratsnay Station anything. There's no one there I care about anymore anyway." That was a lie. There was his mother. Of course, Rosyn was old enough she would never be taken in the Cull, and in fact too old to have another child who could be Culled. Maybe at this point, the System would be basically a good thing for his mother. "Let us go. We'll just disappear. We'll go to, I don't know, Satulak."

"Satulak's just ruins," Shad said quickly. "And there's a lot of wilderness between here and there."

"Sayatil, then. I don't care. We'll go anywhere. We'll go where you tell us is acceptable. Just let us go."

"Cowardly little Landsy." Cheela sneered even wider. "Look at him, pleading for his life."

"He isn't pleading for *his* life." Shad sounded thoughtful. "He's pleading for *Dyan's*."

"You aren't seriously thinking about letting that little vixen *go*?" Cheela's voice rose nearly an octave as she spoke, her final word twisting into a blood-curdling yelp.

"No." Shad looked at Dyan and shook his head. "I wish I could. If we were out in the Wahai or the Jawtooths, maybe there'd be room for … discretion. But we're not, and there isn't."

"Have you forgotten she's one of the Midwinter Five?"

Jak guessed what the words meant: Dyan was not only condemned to die, she was to be hanged publicly.

"Along with Magister Zarah?" he asked.

"Not your concern, Landsy!" Cheela shook her whip.

"Yes," Shad said gravely. "Dyan and Zarah have both … made serious enough errors to come before the Cogitant Council for judgment. Both will be hanged at midwinter."

"You, on the other hand," Cheela said, "are just a nobody Landsy vermin. We had the good fortune of catching you trying to rescue this prisoner here, and we're going to kill you on the spot."

"Capture or kill," Shad said, but he was stepping back as he said it, getting out of the range of Cheela's monofilament whip.

Cheela raised her arm.

"Stop or I'll kill you."

The voice came from behind Cheela, and it was Deek's. The little Mechanical stood behind his Outrider former Crechemate with his own monofilament whip raised and ready to attack.

"The blazes?" Shad mumbled, but he and Cheela froze.

Jak wasted no time. He slipped behind Shad and disarmed the Outrider, taking his belt and holsters and wrapping them around Jak's own waist. Without waiting, he extended the handle of the whip through the bars to Dyan, holding onto the counterweight.

Dyan understood. She extended the filament, stepped back one pace, and moved right to slice through the bars of her cell.

"Landsy-lover," Cheela spat.

"Don't do this, Deek," Shad said. "If you help Dyan escape, or you hurt either one of us, you know what will happen."

"You'll die." Cheela sounded happy.

"I died already." Deek's arm trembled and his face was red.

Jak and Dyan lowered the whip and sliced back through the same bars going the opposite direction. *CLANG!* The bars fell to the floor in a heap, leaving a neat hole easily big enough to step through.

Dyan climbed out. Carefully, Jak handed her the whip. He kept the two bolas for himself, just in case.

"What are you talking about?" Shad pressed the Mechanical.

"All I ever wanted was to make things," Deek said. Tears streamed down his cheeks. "The most interesting things, the exciting technology. The day I got my Lot Letter and learned I was going to be a Mechanical was the best day of my life. And then Zarah took me out there to the Snaik ... and I ... I ..."

"You did your duty," Shad said. "You chose life."

"You chose *death!*" Jak hissed. The arguing Systemoids didn't hear him.

"You chose the System," Cheela continued.

"No!" Deek's voice was strangled. "I didn't choose; I just did what I was told. I guess that's a choice, but it's a nightmare choice. I haven't slept since. I see ... her hands. The hands I chopped off. I see her face. All the time."

"Put the whip down."

This was a new voice again, and it belonged to the Clink's Guardsman. He'd come up behind Deek, up the stairs, and as he spoke he activated his vibro-blade, filling the air with its high-pitched whine.

Jak didn't wait. He threw one of his bolas. He didn't have time to spin it twice over his head like Dyan had made him practice, but he got off his shot quick and straight—

And right through the Guardsman's chest.

At the same moment, Cheela snapped her arm forward—

But Deek was faster. With a quick snap of his elbow, and as the severed halves of the Guardsman collapsed in a red fountain behind him, Cheela's arm, neatly sliced off mid-forearm, also tumbled to the floor.

The Guardsman's torso, bouncing forward, still held the humming vibro-blade in its right hand. As Deek yanked his hand back over his head to retract the whip, the 'blade passed through his thigh. Off balance, Deek crumbled back into the railing, and pulled the filament of his whip back through his own neck. His blood sprayed onto the wall, the floor, and the railing asDeek fell apart into three pieces. His severed head banged off the railing and fell to the floor below with a sickening *splat*.

Jak thought the last expression on the Mechanical's face as it disconnected from his body was one of peace.

Cheela fell to her knees in the sudden pool of blood and screamed. All over the prison building, faces pressed themselves against bars to see what has happening.

"Holy Mother!" Jak's breath was thin and squashed in his chest. His hands shook, but he grabbed his other bola and aimed it.

Shad raised his hands over his head. "Stop!" the Outrider said. "Capture or kill."

"Your rule, not mine," Jak said. "In fact, it isn't even your rule. It's just the thing you say to your friend here to remind her about the option you never choose."

"He's right," Dyan said. Jak turned to her and realized with surprise she meant *Shad is right.* "We don't have to kill them."

Cheela clutched the stump of her arm and stared at Jak. She had stopped howling and her jaw hung open. She looked astonished.

And afraid?

"We do if we want to escape," Jak said, ignoring the injured Outrider. "Because I don't trust any Systemoid to tell the truth or keep a promise."

A look of hurt flashed over Dyan's face.

"I'm sorry—"

"No, you're right. I just hope you don't include me in the category of *Systemoid.*"

Cheela collapsed forward onto the floor.

"I have to help her," Shad said. "Kill me if you want."

Jak raised his bola, prepared to strike the Outrider down, but the bigger man only walked along the hall to the far wall and took down a medikit held there in a bracket. Faces stared at him from the cells he passed, and he ignored them.

"We can lock them up," Dyan said. She pointed at the Guardsman. "He may have a key."

Jak nodded. "Keep an eye on these two."

He put away the bolas and knelt beside Shad in the blood. While Shad did the same things for Cheela's arm that Jak had done for Eirig's only a few days earlier—ointments to cauterize the flesh and force skin regrowth, antibiotics, a pain killer—Jak slid around in the gore searching for keys.

When he stood he had no key, and blood all over his hands. Cheela had passed out, either from shock or from something Shad had given her.

"No luck," Jak said. He pointed at the sleeping Outrider. "But this gives me an idea."

Shad nodded and handed him a vial of tablets. There were no instructions printed on the outside. "Will this do it?" Jak asked Dyan.

"One will just numb pain," she said. "Too many will kill him. Maybe three?"

"Right." Jak shook four tablets into his palm and handed them to the Outrider. "Down they go," he said, repeating an incantation Magister Stanton had said to him many times as a child, when dosing him for fevers or pain.

Shad wiped the blood off the tablets as best he could on the lapels of his coat and then swallowed them. He opened his mouth so Jak could see they had really gone down his throat. "It will take a few minutes to take effect," he said.

"Good," Jak said. "That gives you time to drag your friends into Dyan's cell and lie down." He gestured as he spoke at both Cheela and the two corpses. "And give Dyan your coat and hat."

"Deek was my friend, too," Dyan said.

Jak sighed, but he nodded. He dragged Deek inside the cell himself, leg first and then body and then Jak stumbled down the stairs to pick up Deek's head. He tried not to think about what he was carrying, tried to think of himself as Redcap Rider carrying the head of the Snake Witch and when he returned to the cell he arranged Deek's body in something resembling its normal order.

It was too little, but he owed something to the Mechanical who had died to help him rescue Dyan.

Cheela snored in the bunk against one wall of the cell. Shad stood against the back wall, his eyes fluttering as he resisted sleep. Dyan still wore her white prisoner's garb, but over it she now carried Shad's Outrider hat and coat.

Dyan looked at the pools of blood. "We'll never clean this up."

Jak shoved the severed bars of the cell back under Cheela's bunk. "No, we won't," he said. "Anybody who looks in this building is going to see something terrible has happened, and I guess that will be public knowledge quite soon. So you and I need to get out of here."

"Do you have a plan?"

Jak laughed, a hollow sound. "No." He pointed at Deek. "*He* had the plan."

Dyan laughed too, but it came out as a sob. "We can try just walking out. If we dress in Shad's and Cheela's clothes, maybe the Guardsmen won't recognize us."

Jak snorted. "Sadly, I think they would. Even if Cheela's coat weren't missing a sleeve." He felt as if he were stealing a joke from his dead friend Eirig. "But I'm willing to try." He reached out to take Dyan's hand.

"Wait."

Jak cocked his head to one side. "For …?"

Dyan half turned, pointing at the far end of the walkway, to the cells into which Jak hadn't yet looked. "Zarah," she said.

Shad collapsed.

Jak pointed a thumb at the Outrider and whispered. "How sure are you he's asleep?"

"I'm surprised he stayed awake as long as he did. The dosage you gave him might be lethal."

Jak nodded. "If he dies, it's my fault. You tried to save him. And I will sing him a lovely song."

"Zarah," Dyan said again. She turned and walked to the far end of the walkway.

Jak followed her, and stopped at the cell where she stopped.

Inside, sitting on her bunk with her hands clasped on her knees, sat Zarah. Jak could never forget the woman's face—this same person had condemned him to death under cover of a public ceremony. Guided by this woman's ritual, Jak's mother had celebrated Jak's murder … as she and Jak had years earlier celebrated the murder of Jak's sister Aleena.

And this woman was Dyan's mother.

"You're not in the Prison after all," he said. "What are the odds?"

She looked more tired now, haggard, beaten. Without the black cloak of her authority she seemed tiny. Her iron gray hair hung around her face without order, and as she looked up at Jak her eyes seemed bottomless.

"You don't forgive me," she said.

"Not yet."

"I don't forgive myself, either. I have done terrible things, worse than you know. And I have suffered some of the same things you suffered."

"Your sufferings don't really help me."

"Will my death console you at all?"

Dyan made a sound. Jak turned to her and saw that she was weeping. The tears were quiet and dignified, but there were a lot of them and they flowed down her face in a sheet.

"Mother blast that," Jak said. He took the whip from Dyan's unresisting hand and passed the handle between the bars, retaining his grip on the counterweight. "You let Dyan live. I can't do any less for you."

Urbane

CHAPTER TEN

I
t took a few moments of explanation, but once Zarah realized what Jak had in mind, slicing through the iron bars was as easy as snapping twigs. Then, despite what he'd said about the sleeve, Jak took Cheela's coat and hat and helped the former Magister into them. While he was at it, he stripped the Outriders of their boots and Dyan and Zarah each stepped into a pair. Dyan in particular looked ridiculous in Shad's boots, like a child shuffling in its parent's footwear.

"Better than nothing," he mumbled.

He was surprised to hear Zarah humming. He was even more surprised to realize he knew the tune.

"Ironically, that was one of Eirig's favorites." He couldn't help himself, and although he heard the bitterness in his own voice, he couldn't stop it. "Even though he didn't know what half of it meant."

"A *soldier* is like a Guardsman." Zarah had the same tone in her voice that Magister Stanton had when explaining where bears went in the winter. Jak tried not to stare as he helped the older woman step around the puddles of gore Jak had left on the walkway. "A *pistol* is an ancient weapon. But isn't it obvious what the song means? It's about forbidden love, and the consequences."

85

Zarah seemed to be saying *this song is about Dyan*, and Jak snapped his head up with a retort on the tip of his tongue to the effect that Dyan wasn't anybody else's Goodwife—

But the retort died in his mouth. Zarah wasn't looking at him. Her eyes were glassed over as if she were thinking about a distant time and place, and someone else entirely.

Besides, the consequences of the song's forbidden love seemed to be that most of the people involved died, and that, at least, rang too true a bell for Jak to dismiss her comment entirely.

"Anyway," he said, "I'm just impressed you still have a voice."

They stood on the ground floor of the building now, and Jak gestured up at the faces above them and in front of them, all pressed against the bars, staring. The silence of the prisoners was eerie. "If I were locked in here, I'd be screaming and banging things on the bars. These poor ..." he had intended to say *people*, but somehow that didn't seem right, "folks are quiet as shadows."

Zarah looked at the other prisoners and furrowed her brow. "A voice can consent or protest," she said softly. "When the power to do both those things has been taken away, what point is there to speech?"

"Well," Jak said, "for starters, there's cussing."

"Tell me this is not insane," Dyan said.

He looked at the two women in their Outrider garb. If they kept their coats closed and if nobody recognized their faces, this just might work. "This is definitely insane. On the other hand, I've been walking around dressed as a Mechanical for two days and nobody has realized I didn't belong."

"Nobody?"

What about Headman Anji? "Almost nobody. Nobody who wanted to capture or kill me." He grinned. "So this is close enough to sane that it just might work."

"I have something I want to tell you," Zarah said softly. She said it to Dyan, but something in her voice made Jak curious to hear whatever it was she wanted to share, too.

"I may know what it is," Dyan said.

"Go ahead and talk." Jak opened the door to the Old Pen's yard. "Just keep your coats shut and, Zarah, keep your hand in your pocket. With a little luck, it just might hide the fact that you're missing half your sleeve."

The light of day was harsh after the softer lighting inside the Clink. This was a good thing. The women both tilted their chins down, so the brims of their hats would keep the sun from their eyes, and that gesture had the effect of concealing their faces. At least partially.

Jak shielded his eyes with his hand, which accomplished the same.

At least the Systemoid fabric the Mechanical's jumpsuit and the Outriders' coats were made of seemed to have shed the blood without acquiring a stain. That made sense—if you worked with grease and dirt and sweat all day, a fabric that didn't take a stain would be useful. Interestingly, the white prisoners' outfits the women wore did not have the same resistance, and under their stolen coats Dyan and Zarah were both spattered with dark, clotting red.

"You know I'm your mother," Zarah said. "You must know, or you would not have come."

"You let me go and saved my life," Dyan said. "I had to do the same for you, whether you were my mother or not."

"I let you go and saved your life knowing it would mean my own death," Zarah said. The Outrider boots they wore crunched loudly on the gravel of the Old Pen's yard. "I accepted it. I was willing to do it because you're my child. Those connections matter, regardless of what the System tells us."

"The System breaks those connections *because* they matter," Dyan said. "The fact that the System goes to so much effort to break them tells us it understands perfectly well how powerful those connections are."

Jak walked ahead of the two women and he was grateful for it. His eyes were tearing up slightly, and he was happy to keep that information to himself. "I hate to be the goose honking among the sparrows," he said, "but please remember you are Outriders leaving the Old Pen after having beat up a prisoner. If you two hug or even hold hands, it's going to look wrong."

"Outriders can be Love-Matched," Dyan said. There were tears in her voice.

"As we all know," Jak agreed. "But they don't get to live in the Shackups, apparently. And I still don't think they get all mushy in public."

"Those connections do matter," Zarah pressed on. The teaching edge had faded from her voice, which was softer now. "That's why I want you to know something else. Something … I have long kept secret."

"I'm listening," Dyan said.

"Don't stop walking, even if what I say shocks you."

They had reached the gate. A Guardsman looked down from the wall above and Jak waved at him.

"Hydro fixed?" the Guardsman called down.

Jak grimaced, uncomfortable talking with the Guardsman, the soldier of the System. On the other hand, as long as the man was chatting with Jak about the Hydro problem he thought Jak was trying to repair, he wasn't looking at Zarah and Dyan.

"Not yet," Jak recovered and called back. "I need to get a part from the Garage." He really hoped that made sense, but the Guardsman, at least, didn't object. Stepping back away from the edge of the parapet, he must have signaled someone, because the inner gate swung slowly open.

Willing his legs to be firm and step confidently, Jak walked into the darkness. The women followed.

The short passage through the wall was empty, without even a watcher behind the window to wave them through. Zarah resumed her revelation. "You've seen your father."

Despite Zarah's warning, Dyan stopped walking. She nearly stumbled, and then stepped quickly to catch up. "I'm sorry."

Zarah said nothing.

Jak said nothing, either. His head tingled.

"When did I meet my father?"

"I didn't say *met*. I said *seen*."

"No one is supposed to know their father."

"Or their mother," Zarah reminded Dyan.

Ahead of them, the outer gate opened. Beyond, rumbling down towards the Buza River and the main center of the System, Jak saw the Sick Wagon.

"Is he a Magister?"

Zarah hesitated. "You saw him only on the day he died."

"Died?"

"At the Hanging."

They stepped through the gates and were out of the Old Pen. Jak waved at the leader of the Guardsmen on duty as he and the escaped prisoners ambled towards the hitched horses.

"Part, huh?" the Guardsman grunted.

"Yeah." Jak jerked a thumb back in the direction of the Old Pen's yard. "My friend's getting the joints greased and ready." He was talking gibberish; he hoped it was *convincing* gibberish.

The Guardsman snorted.

Jak climbed awkwardly into his saddle. The two women were already mounted and Zarah was singing:

> *Sally, she married a soldier*
> *A captain named William Lee*

"My father was not a man of the System," Dyan said. "Forbidden love."

"Forbidden love," Zarah agreed. "Consequences."

They rode away. "They're going to find out you escaped," Jak said. "They're going to find it out soon, and then there will be Outriders after us."

"What are you saying, Jak, son of Rosyn?" Zarah asked. Her use of the same formulation she had used to identify him in the Cull made Jak flinch. "We must ride like the wind?" She laughed, but only a little.

Jak laughed, too. "Like the Outriders in Magister Stanton's funvids. No, I'm not saying that. Riding like the wind is exactly what we'd be expected to do. So instead I think we need to hide right here."

"In the System?" Zarah looked at Jak with a curious light in her eyes.

"Yeah. Right now we need to go deeper in, and not run. And we need to find a place to hide for a while."

Hiding would also give him time to think about how to deal with Whitwark Bothy and his promise to Headman Anji.

"You say that as if you have someplace in mind."

Jak shrugged. "Maybe. It's hard to know who to trust around here, but maybe. But first we need to get there without being stopped." He nodded his head toward a thicket at the edge of the river. "This is going to sound odd, but I think the thing we need to do immediately is switch clothes."

"It doesn't sound odd at all, Jak." Zarah turned her horse down towards the river with no further prompting. Jak and Dyan followed. "People will be alerted to two female prisoners who escaped dressed as Outriders. Therefore, we should present a male and a female outrider."

"Right. And for the same reason, we need to split up and meet somewhere else."

In the thicket, Zarah dismounted and shrugged out of her coat. "I'll be the Mechanical," she suggested.

Jak climbed down and started to strip.

"I was supposed to Cull your father," Zarah said. Dressed in bloodied prisoner's whites, her words rang honest and powerful. The white fabric and the blood seemed like witnesses to the truth of her words, somehow. Jak really wished he wasn't in the act of taking off all his clothing.

"But you didn't."

"I couldn't. I found I loved him, and I let him escape."

"He was whistling the same song," Dyan said. "On the Gallows."

"I was sent to track him, you see. I followed him out beyond the Wahai, west, a long way. The Buza flows into a bigger river that flows west, and I caught up to him on the banks of that river, many days' ride from here."

"Sayatil?" Jak asked.

Zarah shook her head. "I don't know whether Sayatil exists. Or Portolan. But I reached a river beyond the lands of the Shoshan, in deserts inhabited by people calling themselves the Ka-Yoss and the Wallalla. I caught up to him, and again I could not kill him. Instead, I lived the winter with him. He taught me the song."

"Only the single winter?" Dyan asked.

"That's all. And in the winter I killed a man. A different man, a scavenger. No one of importance."

"But innocent," Jak said. He stood in his underwear, shivering.

"Innocent," Zarah agreed. "But my choices were all terrible."

"I understand what that's like," Jak said.

"I could kill my lover. Or I could let myself be killed. Or I could be an outlaw. Or I could kill this innocent man. I chose the last. At the time, it seemed like the least worst of all the options."

"And now?" Jak pressed.

"I have carried a heavy burden since," Zarah said slowly. "I do not know whether any of the other burdens would have been lighter."

"You brought the dead man back to the System and convinced everyone it was the boy you were supposed to Cull," Dyan said.

"I believed at the time I had convinced them." Zarah stepped into the Mechanical's uniform and Jak suited up as an Outrider, albeit an Outrider wearing only underwear and boots under his coat. "But earlier this year, your father was arrested. The Cogitants knew who he was immediately, and I expected to be arrested too, because I had let him live and I had lied about the Cull. But I wasn't."

"I don't quite follow." Jak clambered back onto his horse.

"I think I do," Dyan said. "You're saying the System knew all along you hadn't Culled the boy you were supposed to Cull. But it didn't care, because you had killed *someone*."

"I think with respect to *him*, the System cared that he had survived the Cull. It had continued to hunt him for ... well, for your entire life. Survivors of the Cull cannot be permitted, because they know too much. And they can tell. But with respect to *me*, the System was satisfied. It had forced me to kill. It had placed guilt upon me. It was enough. If anything, my lies only laid *more* guilt upon me."

"This is sick." Jak wiped his mouth, feeling as if he had just vomited. "This is not how things are supposed to be."

"If you mean *this is not how nature would order us*, I think you are right," Zarah agreed. "The System is very unnatural indeed. But who determines what is *supposed* to be?"

"Order is necessary for human beings to survive. The world is harsh, and the System preserves." Dyan looked startled at her own words. "I mean, that's what I was always taught."

"Order is necessary," Zarah agreed.

"Yeah," Jak said. "But there are other kinds of order. There are kinds of order that don't require killing people. Outside the System, for instance. There's Ratsnay Station and Marsick and Nemap. They're ordered. And I'm willing to go out on a limb that the urge to vomit I felt when I first learned about the Cull is a reliable indicator that things are not *supposed* to be like this."

"Your willingness speaks well of you, Jak," Zarah said. "But others might feel differently. Others certainly *do* feel differently. Whose feelings ought to govern us? The feelings of the greater number? The feelings of the Cogitant Council? The feelings of a young Landsman from Ratsnay Station?"

"Drop the Magister nonsense," Jak said. "I'm not your Crecheling. I am what I am. I feel what I feel. I can only fight for the world as I think it ought to be."

Zarah nodded.

"Marsick and Nemap are part of the System, too, though," Dyan pointed out. "They feed the System with their crops."

"And with their young." Jak's words were lead in his mouth.

"Yes," Zarah said. "Jak, I am sorry."

"Everybody's sorry, aren't they? Only sorry isn't enough." Jak pointed along the river to where he could just see the top of the Sick Wagon. "That goes to the Cradle, doesn't it?"

"It should."

"So Dyan and I will follow the Sick Wagon. If we ride right behind it, people will see us and think we're guarding the wagon, or following a prisoner in the wagon, and won't even think of us as two lone Outriders. You meet us at the Cradle."

Zarah nodded. "Among the Wrongborn."

Jak turned his horse and rode after the Sick Wagon.

He had an uncomfortable feeling in his chest, and he was beginning to suspect the feeling was compassion.

CHAPTER ELEVEN

Jak and Dyan rode only slightly faster than the Sick Wagon. Jak wanted to catch up and appear to be part of the Wagon's entourage, but he didn't want to draw attention to himself. In the Wagon's wake, they were again on one of the System's black, slightly springy roads, and other riders passed them, coming and going in all directions.

"The Wrongborn." Dyan's speech was slow and thoughtful.

"Funny," Jak said. "I've felt pretty wrong-born myself, pretty much since the day I ..." He realized he didn't have a way to end his sentence without possibly hurting Dyan. "Since I met Magister Zarah."

"I think she wants to meet us there because the Wrongborn get less attention in the Cradle. They're born with weaknesses, sicknesses. They're more likely to die."

"You *think*?"

Dyan shrugged. "I haven't seen the Wrongborn, only been told about them. I think I would have learned more after the ... Selection."

The Cull! Jak wanted to scream. Instead, he laughed; if he and Dyan were going to be sensitive about the words they used, they couldn't be in each other's presence.

"You mean you think that part of the Cradle will have fewer watching eyes? No Guardsmen?"

"Yes. But I haven't seen it."

Jak chuckled. "Why did I ever imagine the people living in the System knew everything?"

"I was raised in the Creche." Dyan pointed at a ridge at the beginning of the Jawtooths. "I know a lot more about what goes on in the Creches. Over that hill, the Camel's Back."

"What's a camel?" Jak asked.

"Knowledge is power," Dyan said. "I have no idea what a camel is. It's some kind of animal. I see now one reason I wanted to be a Magister is that Magisters *did* seem to know everything, and I wanted that. In my heart, Jak, I'd like nothing better than for a young Crecheling to ask me what a camel is, so I can explain it to her. But of course, if knowledge is power, then controlling access to knowledge is one way to control people."

"It's all your System cares about, isn't it? Control."

"It isn't *my* System." Dyan looked away. "Not anymore."

Jak regretted his use of the word *your*. "Doesn't it seem backward, though, that the children born sick in the System get less attention than the healthy ones? The System can split stone in half at the touch. Is it not *able* to heal sick kids? That can't be possible—when your ... Crechemate Cheela broke her ankle, she was just fine a few days later. And I have experience with how great the System's medikits are, so it must have the ability to help kids who are born ... with challenges. Does it not *want* to help them?"

"It seems ... regrettable. Strange. But might it not be necessary to let some of the weaker members of the System go untreated? The System's future does not depend on the survival of a sickly child, but it does depend on the health and activity of its strong adults. Maybe the System is able to split stone in two at the touch, and fix Cheela's ankle, precisely because it does not spend its resources healing its weakest children."

Jak couldn't deny there was a logic to it. "Still, it feels like the System is treating people like cattle."

Dyan turned to look him in the eyes. "It is. So maybe it lets the sick die to improve the breed."

"That's sick." Jak could barely breathe. "That *idea* is sick."

"I'm not saying it isn't."

"Shouldn't human brains be worth something?" Jak asked. "Isn't it worth something to the System to help its weak become strong, so they can contribute? Is there any reason a person born, say, with bad legs, couldn't be just as powerful as a Cogitant as the man we saw the other day? Cogitant Yurvek?"

"I don't disagree, Jak." Dyan shrugged. "I'm just trying to tell you what I know."

"And what you *don't.*"

"Yes," Dyan agreed. "Which is by far the biggest part."

A squad of four Outriders galloped towards them from the center of the System. In his gut, Jak wanted to jump down from the horse and dash to the Buza River, but instead he slightly tightened his grip on the reins and smiled. Mimicking Dyan, he nodded and waved to the riders, making room for them as they rushed past.

Afterwards, trying to keep his movements as casual as he could, he looked back over his shoulder. "I think they're headed to the southeastern gate."

Dyan didn't look back, but she nodded. "Let's hope they don't find Zarah."

"Your mother," Jak said. He immediately wished he hadn't, because his words pushed Dyan into a deep pool of silence. Had Zarah given her too much to think about, with her confession? Was Dyan thinking about her father and his death?

They continued following the Sick Wagon, turning right, toward the Jawtooths, the Camp, and the Creche on the other side of the Camel's Back, before they reached the Garage and the Gardens.

They approached the Cradle. From this angle, Jak could see it consisted of two identical buildings, constructed of the same white stone that made up every other building he'd seen in the System. The buildings shared a circular stone plaza, but otherwise didn't seem to be connected. Around the plaza were the Shackups, which were cubes. Each cube contained four two-story living spaces, with a different "front" entrance on each side of the cube.

Dyan directed their path toward the easternmost of the two, finally breaking communion with the Sick Wagon, which turned left and west toward the other half of the Cradle.

"We Crechelings were told, when we visited, that some of the Wrongborn were contagious, and others were fragile, and therefore we couldn't go in to see them," she said. "I didn't know any better than to accept that, at the time."

They tied their horses to a hitching post. At the door, a young woman in a gray robe with the System's tree on her chest, opened them by pulling on one side of the double glass door and stepping inward to make way.

"Healer?" Jak whispered after they'd passed.

Dyan nodded.

But inside the Wrongborn Cradle they saw few Healers. The ones they did see were mostly young, and they were all harried, pacing quickly from place to place, taking information in the form of brusquely shouted numbers, and giving orders back in the same tone.

The others who were taking direction from the Healers wore the brown tunic and trousers of Gardeners.

"Gardeners." Dyan voiced the thought at the same moment that Jak arrived at it.

"That pretty clearly tells us what the System thinks of the Wrongborn," Jak said.

"They're dirt." Dyan's voice cracked. "Plants to be tended."

A circular desk and six immense pillars dominated the center of the floor. On the desk sat sheaves of paper. Behind the desk was a room in the very center of the floor that seemed to be a storeroom of some kind—at Healers' directions, Gardeners went into it and came out holding supplies Jak knew as components of a medikit.

So the System wasn't completely indifferent to the fate of the Wrongborn.

Around the outside of the floor, like wedges sliced out of a pie, were large spaces crammed full of tiny beds. The spaces were separated from each other and from the center by floor-to-ceiling walls of glass and lit dimly by softly-glowing bulbs hanging from the ceiling in strings. The beds stood in tight rows, parted and made navigable by clear aisles passing among them like the spokes of a wheel.

Of course they had arrived before Zarah, but it wouldn't do to stand around looking conspicuous until she caught up. Jak took Dyan by the elbow and guided her to the nearest cluster of beds.

"You're thinking this is where the Gardeners come from," Jak said softly. He made a show of bending over one of the beds and inspecting the baby inside. The child had a purple blotch on its cheek, and Jak thought of Barstow and Klem—a shriveled ear and a cleft palate. And Tulit, too, who had a big scar running through both eyebrows.

What were the odds?

"That's exactly what I think."

Jak felt heavy. "You know they sterilize the Gardeners."

Dyan stared at him.

He looked around at the tiny cots. "The males. They may have sterilized all these babies already." Jak nodded. "So, I guess where they come from is they're the weak ones, the ones who are born with bad hearts and missing fingers and so on. The System doesn't put them into the Creche at all, or it doesn't put them in with people like you."

"I assumed it did." Dyan shook her head. "I assumed some of my Crechemates had probably been Wrongborn, and when they were healthy enough, they had been put in the Creche."

"Because ... what else would you do with them, right? Because that's the reasonable things to do with a baby that survives birth, even if it's got a little mark on it, or an extra finger or something."

"I guess you can make them Gardeners. Have them cut grass and carry dirt for their healthier neighbors."

"Not neighbors," Jak said. "Family members. Because two babies could have exactly the same parents, Love-Matched, and the healthy one would go into the Creche and become a Magister or a Mechanical or a Seamstress."

"And the sickly one would shovel manure." Tears slid down Dyan's cheeks. "Family members," she agreed. "Even twins."

Could their guesses possibly be true? It seemed too monstrous. On the other hand, the conclusions also seemed unavoidable. "You ever see a Crecheling with a missing eye? Or a stunted hand? Or a birthmark?"

Dyan shook her head again.

"Mother blast these people."

"Who?"

"I don't mean to curse these poor wretches." Jak waved discreetly at the babies surrounding them. He also lowered his voice, conscious that there were Healers and Gardeners in the Cradle who might hear him. The room had an antiseptic smell that at that moment struck him as anti-human. "Summer Son help them, they've already been cursed enough. I mean—"

"You mean the System." Dyan smiled sadly. "I agree. Mother blast the whole System. The Cogitant Council, the Magisters ... all of it."

"You realize this is the mirror image of what the System does to the Landsmen?"

Dyan's eyes sharpened. "The brightest Landsmen are killed."

"Rendering the remaining stock more stupid." Jak ground his teeth. "You're right. Like cattle, they breed us."

"But in the System the healthiest live and have children—"

"Only you don't *have* children, do you?" Jak asked. "You just *generate* them. The System *has* them. The System's *people* just *breed*."

"Like cattle."

"And the weak are sterilized. So this herd becomes healthier and smarter and faster, and is controlled by guilt. Guilt and ritual. Everyone is pushed to the ultimate line, committing murder, because the System knows that if it can make you kill, there's nothing it *can't* make you do."

"And the Landsmen herd gets Culled."

Dyan's words hit Jak like the bedrock at the bottom of a long fall. "And the Gardeners do the heavy lifting, and are kept dumb and mostly happy. Mostly."

"I would not have believed any of this if you had just told it to me a month ago," Dyan whispered. "I can only believe it because of what I've seen."

Jak tried not to think of all the things he'd seen. "We'll get Zarah and we'll get out of here," he said. "We can slip through the gate one by one, or hide in a Collector's wagon, or climb the Jawtooths. We won't wait." He remembered his promise to Headman Anji as he spoke, but he told himself he could come back for the Gardeners of Whitwark Bothy. He didn't know how, but he could come back.

"You were right before," Dyan said. "We need to hide for a day or two. Don't panic. The Wrongborn were doomed to become Gardeners before we ever knew about their fate. Knowledge doesn't make our needs any more urgent."

"Okay." Jak took a deep breath. "Keep quiet until they forget about us, or assume we've run off to join the Ka-Yoss or whoever, and then get out of here. We can go find the river Zarah … your mother was talking about. Rivers have to go somewhere; they have to go to the sea."

"Sayatil?"

"I don't know anything about Sayatil," Jak said. "But people live on water. So I bet if we get to the river and follow it, we'll find people all along it. And when we get to the sea, I bet we'll find people there, too."

"You will." This was Zarah's voice, and suddenly she was with them. Jak realized too late that he and Dyan had been huddled so intently over the mewling Wrongborn infant, talking softer and softer, that anyone could have approached them without being noticed.

Luckily it had only been Zarah.

"What do you mean *you* will?" Dyan asked. "You're coming with us."

Zarah's face looked weary. She slowly shook her head. "Thank you, daughter. You have given me a gift."

"Your freedom isn't a gift if you won't take it," Jak said.

"Not that," Zarah said. "You're right, I won't take it. I *can't* take it. I don't know *how*."

"It's easy." Jak's head spun. Had he really come this far for nothing? "We walk out and go away from here in a straight line."

"It's that easy for you, Jak. You haven't lived with this weight all your life. You haven't been bent by the System."

"I've carried my share of weight," Jak muttered. "I've carried plenty."

"I think you'd find that once you were out of the System you would unbend." Dyan's voice trembled.

"I don't want to find that. I don't deserve that. The weights I have borne have been less than I merit. I cannot leave here. What was outside … for me, it was a fantasy. A dream I dreamed when I was a young woman. But the dream was never real, and I cannot go back."

"So … you're going to go surrender yourself to the Guardsmen?"

Zarah ignored Jak. "Thank you," she said again to Dyan.

"For what?" Dyan asked.

"For choosing not to cooperate. For choosing not to kill. You made the choices I could not. You made the choices I wish I had made." Zarah looked at Jak. "Perhaps you'll live the dream I could only briefly see."

"I've killed," Dyan said. "I live with it."

"It's not the same," Zarah said. "And I cannot live with it any longer."

Jak was looking at Zarah as she said her last words. As she said *longer*, a thin red line appeared across her forehead.

"Mother?" Dyan said.

Zarah's lips worked, her mouth opening and shutting without any sound. Then her eyes rolled up to stare into her own cranium, becoming all white. Beads of blood welled up along the red line.

"Mother!"

Zarah toppled forward. She banged against the crib and then fell down with her arms around it, as if she were trying to hold the Wrongborn infant and its bed in her arms.

When her knees hit the floor, the top of her skull fell off.

Jak saw spongy white and gray matter inside the Magister's skull. The top of Zarah's head fell into the baby's bed and hit the baby, who screamed.

Dyan screamed, too, but Jak barely heard it. He felt as if he were standing on the bottom of a river, moving slowly and hearing all sound muffled and far away.

Someone had killed Magister Zarah with one of the System's monofilament weapons. Jak turned to see who.

Cogitant Yurvek stood behind Zarah and to one side. Meeting Jak's gaze, he bowed slightly.

Zarah's corpse toppled to the floor.

CHAPTER TWELVE

Jak grabbed for the bolas in his holsters, but the Cogitant raised his arm over his shoulder, and Jak saw the hawk-nosed, small-eared man with the shaved skull held a whip.

"*Stop.*" It wasn't a shout, but the Cogitant's voice was as emphatic as it was calm. To match his voice, Yurvek's eyes showed no emotion whatsoever.

The voice didn't bother him, but Jak knew very well what the whip could do. He froze.

The baby wailed. Jak was very aware of Magister Zarah lying dead at his feet, the top of her skull neatly removed. Out of the corner of his eye, he saw Dyan moving. Kneeling to see to her dead mother, Jak thought, but he didn't dare look.

But then he heard soft shushing sounds. Turning his head slightly, he saw Dyan push the top of her mother's skull aside and pick up the blotch-faced baby in both arms. Whispering reassuring sounds, she pressed the baby to her shoulder. Her voice trembled slightly.

She was to have been a Magister. She had *wanted* to be a Magister.

The held baby began quieting.

Around him, though, Jak heard the soft whimpering sounds as other Wrongborn babies, disturbed by the noise, began to complain. He realized there were no Gardeners in the room with them.

In fact, as he looked through the glass walls he realized there were no Gardeners on the floor at all. And the Healers were gone as well. He was alone with Dyan, Cogitant Yurvek, and the imperfect infants.

"So," Jak said. "You followed a defenseless woman here and murdered her. Does that make you feel in control?"

Yurvek smiled, but didn't lower his arm. "It isn't murder when the System chooses who dies. And Magister Zarah wasn't defenseless."

"The System chose to kill my sister, and my best friend, and me. You can probably guess how I feel about the System's choices about life and death."

"Will it help you if we tell you Magister Zarah *herself* chose to die?"

"Liar," Jak said, but Dyan gasped and he feared the Cogitant might be telling the truth.

"You heard her. She was tired, and she wanted to be finished. She found us and turned herself in to us, asking only two things in return."

"I don't think I want to hear this," Jak said.

Dyan stepped forward. "Go on."

"She asked not to know the moment of her own death."

"Maybe she imagined you'd let her actually finish the conversation, though." Jak's fingers itched. He really wanted to throw a bola.

"Perhaps. But we kept the terms of the bargain."

"Who's *we*?" Jak asked. "You're alone here."

Cogitant Yurvek said nothing.

"What's the second thing she asked?" Dyan wanted to know.

"She requested that we let you go. Which we will do." Yurvek lowered his arm and dropped the whip.

Jak snatched a bola from its holster and held it high and ready to throw. The babies' crying was growing louder. "I don't get it," he said. "I could kill you."

"We fully expect it."

"In fact, I either have to kill you so you won't sound an alarm, or I have to take you with us. And I have to tell you, I've taken hostages before. On balance, they're much more trouble than they're worth."

Yurvek laughed dryly. His eyes still looked dead. "We understand your reference, Jak, son of Rosyn. You are witty. As an alternative to killing me, perhaps you would consider joining us?"

Jak hesitated, though a voice in the back of his head yelled at him to strike the big-nosed man down. "Really? Just like that?"

Yurvek shook his head. "Nothing is ever *just like that*, Jak. You should know better by now. There would be reconditioning. You would need to be fitted."

"To be what?" Jak asked. "A Mechanical? A Guardsman? A Gardener?"

Dyan took a step back, almost disappearing from Jak's sight. "He's offering you something else, Jak."

"Cogitant," Yurvek said.

"Cogitant." Jak snorted. "So I could dress like a prisoner and meet under the big dome to decide who lives and dies. Why me?"

Yurvek's smile was cold. "You are strong-willed. A strong will helps a candidate survive the reconditioning. Also, we like you. After all these long dusty years, irrationality still has something to do with our choices. Just how we're made, in the end, blame the Creators."

"Improving the breed, eh?"

"Maybe that as well."

Something was wrong with Yurvek's words, but Jak wasn't quite sure what. The Cogitant's reference to *Creators* sounded spiritual, but Jak had never heard Dyan mention anything that sounded like worship or a reference to divinity.

"Dyan went to school her whole life just to become an apprentice Magister. How long would I have to study to become a Cogitant?" Maybe he was willing to live with the death and the lies, as long as he could stop living in fear.

His arm, holding the bola, was very, very tired.

"There would be no study involved," the Cogitant said. "To be a Cogitant is not to have a Calling like any other Systemoid, Jak."

The word *Systemoid* sounded friendly, almost conspiratorial on the Cogitant's lips. It sounded self-mocking, which was not the attitude Jak had come to expect from the System.

"Are you saying there are no skills involved? Nothing to learn? I find that hard to believe." Jak waved his arm around, trying to capture not just the Wrongborn Cradle but the System beyond it. "This is a complex place. Don't you rule it? You and the rest of the Cogitant Council? Don't you have to understand how it works?"

"You misunderstand my nature. You fail to see me for what I am, Jak."

A murderer! Jak wanted to scream. But he didn't. "Explain."

"You will see shortly."

"You expect me to take you up on your offer to become a Cogitant, but you have no intention of explaining what you're talking about. You don't want to tell me about your *nature*, or what you *are*. Seriously?"

"We expect you to reject our offer," Yurvek said. "This time. But you are already thinking about it. And you are about to see something that will cause you to think about it even more. And the second time the offer is made, we believe you will accept it."

"You're insane. You plan to make me this offer twice?"

"Not *I*, Jak. Not *this* Cogitant, necessarily. Who knows how long *this* Cogitant may survive? But there will be revelation, and then fear and reflection, and then we will make the offer again. And then, yes, we believe you will accept."

These were, hands down, the strangest words Jak had ever heard.

"Why did you send the Healers out?" he asked. "And the Gardeners?"

"You are about to see something they are not fit to see, Jak."

"I don't like this at all." Jak tightened his grip on the bola. He heard Dyan hushing other babies.

"I am unarmed. After you and I are done, Jak, you will leave. There is a door over there," the Cogitant pointed, "that connects to the other half of the Cradle. It is unguarded. You will simply walk through it. There are two horses, saddled and equipped, waiting for you on the outside."

"That doesn't seem like a very Systemoid thing to do."

"I am not a Systemoid such as you have known, Jak. I am a Cogitant."

"So you're fancier."

"No. I am a different kind of thing altogether."

"Don't you want to control me, though?" Jak nodded at Zarah's corpse at his feet. "Like you controlled Zarah, with guilt and fear? Like you controlled Dyan, with ritual and a death sentence?"

"No, Jak." The Cogitant smiled. "Not like them."

"You'll follow me. Or sound an alarm."

"You won't believe me when I tell you I haven't already sounded an alarm, but I have not. So instead, Jak, you will take your chances and kill me. This is the right thing to do. And you will find that when you pass through the Cradle and beyond, no one will molest you."

"Outriders are looking for me."

"But as you have already calculated, they have ridden out the south gate of the System. You will take another path, and will ride free."

"There's a catch. There's a trick here. Why are you doing this? Are you going to spy on me, like you spied on Zarah?"

"We only ask you two things, Jak."

"Go ahead and ask," Jak said. "And then I'm going to have to kill you."

"Jak," Dyan said softly.

"No," Jak said, "he's right. I don't really have a choice. The thing I don't understand is that he's forcing me to kill him, and I don't know why. But I'll do it, because I want to live and I want you to live. We failed to save Zarah, but I'm not leaving you behind, not if I have to dam up the Buza and flood this whole stable."

If the smug, strange-talking Cogitant caught Jak's Summer Son reference, his face didn't show it.

"Maybe we did save Zarah," Dyan suggested.

"Maybe in a way," Jak agreed. "But not in the way I had in mind." He faced the Cogitant again. "All right, then, Yurvek. What do you want?"

"First, tell us a secret, Jak. Tell me something we do not know, and cannot know. And then I will ask you a second favor."

Jak stared at the Cogitant. It felt wrong. It felt as if the Cogitant wanted to cast a spell over Jak, and knowing a secret of Jak's would give the Cogitant control.

But that was madness. That was the kind of nonsense you'd hear from root-digging crones down on the Snaik, and not from this man.

He shrugged. "Fine. I'll tell you this. I spied on Zarah, too. We spied on Magister Zarah and her Crechelings as they came down to Ratsnay Station. We sneaked up to their camp at night and listened to them talk. And then we did it again the night after the Selection. That's how Eirig and I knew what was coming. We knew about the Cull."

"A sneak and a spy." Cogitant Yurvek cocked his head to one side. "And you told the others?"

"I told the others who were going to be Culled. We debated what to do." Jak wasn't sure why he felt he could report these things to the Cogitant, except that he *had* decided to kill the man, so what Yurvek knew didn't matter anymore. "We didn't tell anyone else at the Station."

"Because the knowledge might put them in danger."

"Yes. And because we couldn't be sure they weren't in on it. For all we knew, they were well aware we were being sacrificed." He choked back a sudden sob at the memory that he had once suspected his mother of conniving at his sister's murder.

"Jak," Dyan murmured.

Cogitant Yurvek nodded. "Will it put your mind at ease if I assure you that, other than Magister Stanton, the people of Ratsnay Station have no awareness of the true nature of the Cull?"

"I don't want my mind put at ease," Jak said. "I want to kill you and get the blazes out of this Mother-cursed place."

Yurvek nodded again. "In that case, I must ask you the second favor."

Jak raised his bola higher, feeling his arm and shoulder muscles knotting. "Now's the time."

"Kill me as I killed Zarah." The Cogitant pointed at the dead Magister.

"Believe me, I'm going to kill you."

"Cut my head open."

"What?" Jak lowered his arm. It was a show of weakness, but the Cogitant had dropped his whip in any case.

"Slice off the top of my head," Yurvek said. He drew his index finger across the front of his face at eye level. "Right there. Open my head."

"I get that you might just want out," Jak said. "But I don't understand why you would want to be beheaded in particular."

"We want it. Isn't that enough? And know this one last thing: I remember." His eyes were still cold and flat, but a single tear trickled down Cogitant Yurvek's cheek.

"Jak," Dyan said. "Don't do it."

"You're sick." Jak raised the bola. "But I don't care."

"Please!" Dyan grabbed Jak's elbow. It was a dangerous move, because Jak nearly lost his control over his weapon, but she restrained him. "Kill him if you must. But don't kill him because he asks. Don't kill because the System tells you to, don't you see? It's no different from what they ordered me to do."

"It's a *little* different," Jak said. "It's different because Cogitant Yurvek is a murderer and scum and deserves what I'm going to do to him."

Jak was distracted, but as he said the words *do to him*, he saw the Cogitant step forward in his peripheral vision and bend to pick up his whip again. Jak pulled his arm free—

The Cogitant slightly extended the counterweight at the end of the whip—

Jak raised his arm—

"I remember," the Cogitant said, and he pulled the invisible monofilament line forward through his own eyes.

Jak froze.

The Cogitant dropped the whip and his hands fell to his sides. Blood beaded at Yurvek's temples and on the bridge of his nose. His eyes, though … there was something wrong with them.

A crack of *light* shone through Yurvek's eyes.

"The blazes?" Jak said.

He reached forward and pulled Yurvek's shoulder. Yurvek fell forward and, as Jak had expected, the top of his skull fell off and bounced across the floor.

But that was where the resemblance with Magister Zarah's death ended. Because Jak could still see the spongy gray and white pulp that had filled Zarah's head, and that now pooled around her face on the floor.

The inside of Yurvek's head was different.

Yurvek had gray and white brain matter, but much less than Zarah. Maybe a third of his skull was full of brain.

The rest seemed to be full of some kind of device. There were wires in Yurvek's head, and metal prongs, and a black square like a chunk of the glass-like volcanic rock you could sometimes find along the Snaik.

And the inside of Yurvek's eyes, split neatly open, glowed with an artificial blue light.

Jak threw up.

"Come on, Jak," Dyan said. Somehow, she was not vomiting, but Jak convulsed half a dozen times until his stomach hurt and there was no ration bar inside him left to come up.

Finally, Dyan turned and led the way towards the other half of the Cradle.

Jak followed.

It was only when they had passed through the Cradle where healthy Systemoid babies were housed and were exiting on the far side that Jak realized Dyan was still carrying the Wrongborn baby.

CHAPTER THIRTEEN

I 'll name the baby Zarah," Dyan said.

They were the first words she had spoken since they'd left the Cradle. Yurvek had been telling the truth at least this far: outside the Cradle waited two Outriders' horses, fresh, saddled, and with full saddlebags. Without hesitation, Jak had helped Dyan by holding the baby while she climbed into her saddle and then handing it up to her.

He had had an impulse to set the baby down instead and leave it there but had immediately felt guilty for the impulse. Besides, Dyan would have simply dismounted to get the child.

Then he'd crawled into his saddle and they'd ridden west.

Dyan had said nothing, and so Jak said nothing, either. They'd passed the Garden and Capitol and the Cogitants' dome. Jak had seen the Camel's Back off to his right and had shot a glance at the Camp, half expecting to hear the galloping of horses and see a gang of Outriders in pursuit.

But the System seemed to go about its business without paying attention to the two fleeing outlaws.

Somehow, outlaws had seemed different in Magister Stanton's funvids. More ... wicked. Despicable. And a little romantic, maybe.

But Jak just felt no different, only battered and exhausted and confused. He tried not to think about Cogitant Yurvek and the surprising contents of his skull.

When they had ridden past Whitwark Bothy, Jak looked for Headman Anji. He'd found her after a little scanning; she directed the cutting down of a large dead cottonwood tree on the far side of the river from the Bothies. Not far from where Jak had crouched beneath the weir in hiding as Anji had tried to defend two of her Gardeners. Tried and failed.

If Anji noticed the two people in Outriders' coats riding past her Bothy, she gave no sign of it. Jak plunged the arm with the sliced sleeve deeper into the coat pocket.

He'd made her an oath, and now he was leaving the System without her.

His mouth tasted like ashes.

At the gate, no one had asked any questions and Jak had volunteered nothing. What did they think about the fact that one of the Outriders passing through their midst held a baby in one arm?

Maybe they just didn't notice.

Once beyond the gravel band encircling the System's walls, Jak had breathed easier. He'd breathed even easier when they'd ridden another hour and turned to cross the river at a pair of fords and a long island.

A hide and board building on the center of the island, right on the track connecting the two fords, seemed to be a trading post. Two Shoshan had nodded at Jak and he'd raised a hand in greeting back. Having crossed the second ford, they had ridden to the top of the bluff overlooking the Buza River, and Jak finally had stopped them.

"I will name the baby Zarah."

"That is an excellent name." Jak felt tired, burned up, consumed. "I think all three of us could use a change of clothing. I, for one, have nothing under this torn coat except a breechcloth, so I'm really hoping one of these saddlebags has extra clothing. And while you're changing its swaddling, you might double check to be sure that little creature is in fact a female."

"She's not a *creature*." Dyan's voice was surprisingly fierce. "She's a *child*. She's my daughter."

Jak fell off his horse more than he dismounted. "Okay," he said. "She's your daughter." He rummaged in the saddlebags and was relieved to find a pair of trousers and a shirt, as well as a coat that wasn't missing a sleeve. The garments all seemed even to be in his size.

"I was wrong in what I said earlier."

Jak heaved the sleeveless coat into a thicket and pulled the shirt over his head. "About what?"

"The future of the System … no, that's not right." Dyan looked down at the baby she held. "The future of a people. Maybe not the System, because the System doesn't see it this way. The System is a different … there's something wrong with it. There's something not human about it."

Jak remembered Cogitant Yurvek's brain and shivered despite the afternoon sun's warmth. He pulled the trousers up and stepped into better-fitting boots.

"But I think the future of a people *does* depend on its sickest, weakest children."

"Little Zarah's got a blot on her face," Jak said. "It doesn't make her weak or sick. And it certainly doesn't mean she can't be smart, or inventive, or funny, or a great leader. Or beautiful."

"True," Dyan agreed. "It's not what I meant."

"Let me take her." Jak reached up to take the baby. "You have to get out of those prisoners' whites."

He held the baby while Dyan dressed. Jak turned and looked away over the desert. He didn't know whether she expected him to give her privacy, but they weren't Goodman and Goodwife yet—hadn't yet held hands at a shrine of the Holy Mother in the presence of the community to exchange promises of loyalty and protection—and perhaps they never would be. There was a little more space between them than there had been before.

She had, after all, said that Zarah was *her* child. Not *their* child.

Jak looked down at the baby. Her face was wrinkled and the skin around one eye was a blotchy purple. The blotch was vaguely star-shaped. He sang to her, a little:

Sally, she married a soldier
A captain named William Lee
I guess in his fashion he loved her
But Sally always loved me

Zarah emitted a sharp sound that was half-angry cat and half-terrified frog.

"I think the baby's hungry," he said. "Or possibly she just hates music. I'm not an expert."

"Maybe we can mash up a ration bar with some water," Dyan said. "It isn't perfect, but it will have to do."

Jak opened his saddlebags half-expecting to discover that Cogitant Yurvek had provided for the baby as well, with some kind of baby Outrider rations. When he found the usual stash of slender brown ration bars and water he laughed at his own foolishness.

What had he imagined, really? Sealed packets of milk? Canisters of puréed fruit?

Of course the Cogitant hadn't expected them to take the Wrongborn baby with them.

Dyan took the baby back. Out of the medikit's mirror and the heavy butt end of a vial of painkillers Jak fashioned a crude mortar and pestle, and in short order he'd reduced the ration bar to a muddy paste.

"It doesn't smell any better wet," he observed. "Actually, it smells a lot worse. I'm starting to wonder why I was ever willing to eat these things."

Dyan smiled, took the mirror, and put a little of the food in Zarah's mouth on the tip of her finger. The baby quieted down and began to suckle. "You were willing because you were hungry."

"I'll make a sling," Jak offered. "You don't want to carry the baby in your arms the whole way."

"The whole way to where?" Dyan asked.

Jak hesitated. "You said Magister Haika told you Zarah had been observed."

"Yes," Dyan said. "All along, apparently. The Magister's medallion she wore was also a recording and transmitting device. The System spied on her through it, I think her entire adult life. I think maybe all Magisters are watched that way."

"It's not surprising, really. The more I see of the System, the more it seems to be just a collection of mechanisms for dominating everyone involved." Jak gestured at the horses and their gear. "In fact, maybe everyone from the System is observed. Maybe Outriders are. Wouldn't you want to keep an eye on your agents out among the Landsies? Maybe Cogitant Yurvek gave us this stuff precisely so he could plant spying devices on us."

"If Cogitant Yurvek wanted us dead, why didn't he just call in the Guardsmen?"

"That's a good question. There are lots of good questions. Why was Cogitant Yurvek willing to die? In fact, did he *want* to die? It sort of seemed like he did. And what on earth did he mean by *I remember*? And ... well ... you saw what was inside his head. But the existence of *more* questions just makes me feel *less* comfortable."

Jak carefully split a microfiber blanket to make a piece of cloth the right size for a sling. Across the saddle of his horse, he began to fold and knot it.

"I have no ideas," Dyan said. "I feel ... I feel as if I'm in the grip of enormous powers, or being carried along on a fast current. I can't see where it's taking me, and I think I might not like the place when I arrive."

"The current's always there." Jak hung the sling around Dyan's neck and shoulder and tucked Baby Zarah into it. "The Summer Son tells us we have to swim. He tells us there's an opposite bank and we can reach it, even if we don't see it."

"I'm out of ideas of where to swim to." There were tears in Dyan's eyes. "I don't think I can see the shore."

"I've got an idea about that," Jak said. "From something Zarah, Magister Zarah, said. Pistols are a weapon, she said."

Dyan looked at him wordlessly.

"So I don't know about you, but I feel like I'll take all the weapons I can get. Especially if they're weapons that might be mysterious. You know, ancient. Pre-Cataclysmic. Beyond the control of the System."

"Pistols," Dyan said slowly.

"So, I think you have an idea of where I want to go. But I want to go by an indirect route. And as soon as we can, I want to get rid of everything we're carrying and replace it with wool and leather. Material I can trust. Things I know the System isn't using to listen to our conversations."

"You want to get rid of *everything*?" Dyan asked. "Medikits, even?"

"That's a scary thought," Jak admitted. "But if you were going to place a listening device in something because you wanted us to carry it around, wouldn't a medikit be exactly the kind of object you'd use? Innocent, harmless, useful?"

"Ration bars?"

Jak considered the question, and then shrugged. "I just don't know. Do *you* know? I mean, it's hard to imagine the ration bar itself has a recording tool in it, but what about the wrapper? The System makes whips one follicle thick, why not listening devices?"

Dyan laughed. She seemed to be laughing at him, but Jak didn't mind—it was good to see her laugh, and the baby responded with a charming gurgle before taking another blob of soggy ration bar into its mouth.

"What is it?" he asked. "Did I say something stupid?"

"No."

"Yes, I did. Admit it."

"Well ... a little."

"I'll take that. I can live with *a little stupid*. Now give me the sling, and once I'm on my horse, I want you to hand me up the baby. It's my turn to carry her for a while." Jak took the sling, shrugged into it, and climbed up onto his mount.

Wearing the sling sort of made him feel like a Goodman.

Dyan handed up the baby. "Her name is Zarah."

*　　*　　*

Without speaking any place names or directions out loud, Jak and Dyan rode to Marsick. They stopped to feed and change Baby Zarah as often as the child seemed to need it, filling her belly with ration bar mush and wrapping her in fresh sheets of microfiber cloth. They avoided trails, riding in a straight line across the long rise above the Buza River, and then back down towards the Lull Sea and the Snaik.

They crossed and circled ruins of various kinds. The Treasure Valley had many more ruins than the hills around Ratsnay Station. This must once have been a great city, but Jak had a hard time imagining what it would have looked like. It seemed to have been criss-crossed by pebbly black roads not very different from the paved paths of the System, and its buildings, as he'd observed before, seemed almost built to be temporary by design.

Or maybe it wasn't that they were temporary, it was that they were cheap. Building made of paper and dust wrapped around skeletons of wood.

So if the city that had once filled the Treasure Valley had been vast, maybe it had also been poor.

On the other hand, Jak and Dyan also rode over the crumbled remnants of ancient cement canals. Now they lay full of sand and grown thick with yellow grass, but once the canals must have carried large amounts of water across the bluff. Jak tried to imagine what that had looked like—the canals must have carried water to the people who lived in the high ground here in the center of the valley, and some of the fields they passed seemed to be cut by irrigation ditches. The city had had farms inside it.

Jak let that thought lie inside him and grow as he rode.

The city that had once filled the Treasure Valley had had farms within its walls. Inside it, fed by artificial conduits.

It had treated its farmers just as it treated its other residents. They lived and farmed within the city, with neighbors and the privileges of city life. In his mind's eye, the ruins around Jak rose into restored homes, and they were beautiful, no matter how cheap the materials out of which they were constructed. Water flowed freely among them, and fed tall groves of exotic trees he had no name for. The slabbed footpaths he crossed became ringed and bordered with bright flowers.

What had happened? How had such a paradise been lost?

As the sun sank behind the Wahai to his right, they crossed a vast highway lying shattered in the sand, and beneath a second arm of the same highway that rose several stories high into the air, still standing on cement pylons thicker than ten people bunched together.

Jak found himself crying silently.

*   *   *

They camped huddled on the banks of the Snaik, within sight of Marsick.

"I'll go into town tomorrow," he told Dyan. "We want to get in and out quickly, without attracting the attention of anybody. But especially without attracting the attention of the Sheriff."

Jak tried not to, but he spent the night awake, staring across the cold river at the canyon mouth where his sister and her brutal Goodman, or rather captor, Narl had once herded sheep.

Someone else would have taken over the land by now. And if not, Jak told himself, he didn't really want to see the log building where his sister had been cut down in cold blood by the System she had once escaped.

Dawn, and Dyan's hand on his shoulder, surprised him at the same moment, finding him still awake and staring at the hills.

*   *   *

Jak had seen Orvyl Rich's store before, on his previous and ill-fated visit to Marsick. As Rich opened his door that morning, sweeping dust out toward the street with a broom of bundled straw, Jak entered directly behind the merchant. He had trading on his mind.

He had all the Scrip he had pulled together from the various coats and saddlebags he and Dyan had, and all the additional accessories he judged it was safe to sell. He doubted real Outriders would sell their coats, for instance, so he seemed stuck with those. But medikits and ration bars and blankets?

Why not?

Orvyl Rich didn't bat an eye. He took a broad range of supplies from the young man who introduced himself as Outrider Jass. He even took the Outrider's horses, which was the biggest gamble Jak was making, and a purse full of Scrip.

In return, Jak walked away with wool serapes, cotton shirts and trousers, leather boots, several bedrolls, a thick stack of furs, a tent, large quantities of dried beef and parched grain, two long knives, and two different horses, which were distinctly smaller, though Dyan assured him, when he rejoined her at the edge of town, that they would do. Whenever possible, Jak chose items whose appearance was completely forgettable—simple, plain, and brown.

Across the Snaik from Aleena's former cottage, Jak dug a hole and tossed in the few items they hadn't sold. They threw petrofuel over their Outriders' coats and hats and lit them all on fire, tossing in the petrofuel bottle after.

"And the weapons?" Dyan asked.

"I wish I could keep them." Jak dropped his bolas and whip onto the fire, and Dyan did the same.

He had imagined that switching his gear would leave him feeling lighter, relieved of a burden. Instead, Jak felt a pressure on his chest.

"My turn for the baby again," he said. "Let's get on the road. It's a long way to Farkill."

CHAPTER FOURTEEN

T he boots are the thing," Jak said. "You don't realize how bad your shoes are until you've been able to wear the System's boots for a couple of weeks. I feel like my feet have been pounded thoroughly flat between two rocks and are now ready to be spiced and hung up to dry in the air."

"Disgusting." Dyan made a face, but it was a faint one. She seemed older since they'd picked up Baby Zarah—for that matter, she seemed to have aged a hundred years since Jak had met her on the evening before the Selection—so it was good to see she could still respond to a little humor, even if she wasn't falling out of her saddle with laughter. "Besides, you're forgetting medikits."

"I haven't had the need to use a medikit once since we sold ours." Jak shrugged. "In fact, as I recall, we sold ours on purpose, in part so the System's Outriders couldn't follow us, injure us, and cause us to need medikits." He chuckled at his own wit, small as it was.

"Funny. But wait 'til you're bit by a rattler, or fall and break a leg, or drink bad water and throw up until your stomach bleeds. You'll forget all about your shoes and be begging for a little painkiller and antiseptic."

"True," Jak agreed. "So don't fall. But Rattler can't bite me; I'm the Summer Son."

And there were still stables to clean. Jak remembered the look on Headman Anji's face as she warned him not to make promises he wouldn't keep and felt a twinge inside his chest.

They stood at the top of a high cliff on the south bank of the Snaik River. Behind them rose drifts of sand dunes, and a watering hole where they had spent the night, huddling within their tightly sealed tent against the extremely bold and thumbnail-sized flying insects that made the marsh at the edge of the water their home.

Ratsnay Station was out of sight, across the river and away north and east, closer to the mountains. The dunes were not within the Station's cultivated land, but occasionally as a boy Jak had herded sheep in the area, or hunted, or just wandered. The dunes had no grass, but there was forage down around the water itself, and the dunes were confined to a small area—a short walk from the water, and the usual tall desert grasses resumed.

Jak was not quite home, but almost.

Directly across the Snaik lay the ruins of Farkill.

Farkill was much larger in area than Ratsnay Station, even including all the Station's planted land. From where they stood, Jak saw walls, domes, whole buildings, and large flat areas of paved earth. In stark contrast to the soft crumbling ruins of the Treasure Valley, these buildings all looked hardened. They were made of stone and cement. Built to survive impact.

"There's the trail." Jak pointed at a steep defile running up through cement rubble and eventually disappearing into the tangle of tumbled stone. "I think the crack there eroded recently. Well, since Farkill stopped being used, anyway."

"Is the whole thing walled in? Like a fortress?"

"It was," Jak said. "The wall's fallen down in many places. This is a good road because I know how to get up it. And also because it's on the far side from Ratsnay Station, so there's less chance we'll run into anybody we might recognize."

"It looks steep."

"I know for a fact you've climbed steeper. Let me take the baby."

"Zarah."

"I remember her name." Jak took the sling and settled it around himself, and then tucked Baby Zarah into it. She sucked contentedly at her own fingers and looked at him. She looked a bit like an animal, with that mark around her eye. Or a person wearing a mask. "I just like calling her the baby."

He didn't say that *the baby* sounded very close in his ears to *our baby*.

"I just want you to remember she's a person."

"A baby is a person," Jak said. He didn't say *I'm the one who was going to be Culled, remember? I'm the one who was treated as less than a person.* Whatever Dyan was going through inside, she had taken to making these declarations. As if she were clarifying principles, or thinking out loud. Maybe it was her Magister training, taking hold. She wanted to *teach* Jak. It kind of made her sound like a priestess. "When I start calling her *the puppy*, you can be worried."

Dyan laughed.

"Come on," Jak said. "Watch your step and don't rush."

The left their horses picketed in the shade of a thicket of thornbush trees. As a little extra precaution, Jak had packed most of their gear and walked it along a long stretch of slickrock where he would leave no tracks, to hide it away from the horses in the hollow of a large rock. He'd piled more stones on top of the gear to keep animals away from the food.

The Snaik's canyon was deep here, but there was a long defile that was wide enough to hold shelves of sand, grass, and actual trees, and that wound slowly down into the canyon. Maybe once there had been a stream flowing into the river through this crack, but now it was a steady, easy path that brought them, after half an hour of careful stepping, down to the water.

Jak looked downstream. A few miles north and west of here, on a high bluff on the other side of the river, he had been slated to be Culled. He had fought back, survived, killed the Healer-designate Wayland, and kidnapped Dyan. Beyond, the same river flowed past Marsick, where his sister Aleena had tried to protect him from her own husband and from the System, and had only succeeded in dying in his place. Eventually, the river flowed into the Lull Sea, on the shores of which Jak had got two Outriders drunk and then beheaded them in their sleep.

He pulled his mind away from those savage memories and looked forward.

Above him towered a bulwark of red stone. Across its height crept a cement wall. The fact that its construction resembled the fallen highways of Treasure Valley and not the sparkling white stone construction of the System filled him with sudden hope.

Farkill. Jak had spent the night there once, just within the wall, afraid of the malign spirits Pistols and Guns. But Magister Zarah had told him a *pistol* was an ancient weapon, and now he was here hoping to find a pistol, whatever exactly it was. He wanted weapons to protect himself, and Dyan, and their Wrongborn baby, from the System.

Even if he *did* find a pistol, of course, there was no guarantee he'd be able to figure out how to use it. And as the System's whips and bolas demonstrated, sometimes it was safer not to have a weapon at all than to have one you couldn't wield.

"Was it a city?" Dyan asked.

Jak splashed into the river. The water was cold and brown, and although the current was slow, it was strong. He stepped forward carefully, feeling for footing solidified by pebbles embedded in the clay and not letting his foot sink into deep mud.

"I don't know," he admitted. "I can you tell it's haunted by Pistols and Guns, or anyway so I was always told. The stories say Pistols and Guns are servants of a king who used to live here. So I guess maybe this was his city."

"Or his palace."

"Could be. The buildings are pretty grand."

Dyan said nothing, so Jak finally turned around and looked to make sure all was well with her. She stood in the middle of the river, staring up at the massive rock face above them.

Jak waited quietly, but Zarah let out a sharp yelp as cold water sloshed against her leg. Dyan's eyes snapped into focus and she looked at Jak sharply.

Jak looked sharply back, and Dyan relaxed.

"Maybe," she said. "I think cities used to be much larger than they are now."

"Yeah," Jak agreed, thinking of their recent ride south out of the System. "The Treasure Valley … I guess it used to be all one city."

"It seems like it. So maybe Farkill was a city, too. What was the king's name?"

Jak turned and resumed forward progress, yanking his left foot from thick clay that sucked at it. "Yuess Airfo, I think. I suppose he lived a long time ago. Before the Cataclysm Magister Stanton was always on about. And when he died, Pistols and Guns stayed behind."

"Or they all died, but pistols and guns came back as ghosts?"

Jak laughed. "Anyway, yeah, Magister Zarah said pistols were some kind of weapon. Which makes sense, doesn't it? *Pulling his pistol, he pushed her* could be a weapon. Maybe a pushing weapon? Although a pushing weapon just sounds like a club, and that's not very impressive. Maybe something that can push really hard? Or push from far away? Or both?"

"What did you use to think *pulling his pistol* meant?"

Jak clambered out on the far bank and stood, letting water stream from his trousers and shoes. "Something magical, I guess. Maybe accidentally attracting the attention of Pistols. Maybe something nonsensical, like *tra la la*."

"It still could be something nonsensical."

"Yeah." Jak gave Dyan his hand and helped her climb out onto the pebble-studded sandbar on which he stood. "But probably not, right?"

"Probably not."

"And anyway, we're a day's ride further away from the System. So if we look around here and find nothing, the worst case is we just keep riding. See if we can make it to Satulak, or find somewhere too far away for the Outriders to care about and just run sheep."

"It's not such a bad worst-case." Dyan smiled at Jak, but something in the twist at the corner of her mouth told Jak she didn't think the two of them would ever be shepherds.

"Come on," Jak said. "Young Zarah would love it. Little woolly lambs to play with. Lambs are cute."

"Sheep are stinky animals that have to be sheared or their own feces sticks to them."

"Well, yeah," Jak admitted. "But young Zarah would love that, too."

"Yuck."

"And *lambs* are cute. Admit it. And delicious."

Dyan raised a hand in surrender. "Fine, I haven't said no."

"You haven't said yes, either."

"True." Dyan walked past Jak and into the defile on the other side.

This was a steeper and narrower crack. Jak had forgotten how much of a scramble it had really been, the first time he had climbed up it. He could manage, with water and some dried beef over one shoulder and Baby Zarah over the other, because his hands were free and he could lean in to the rock to keep his balance. He wasn't looking forward to the off-balance scramble the descent would no doubt be.

Halfway up the defile, Dyan stopped in a swirled bowl of stone sluiced out of the rock by rainwater and waited for Jak. "How will we identify a pistol if we find it?" she asked as his head poked over the lip of the bowl.

Jak crawled up on two knees and one hand, his other hand steadying Zarah against his chest. She was crying, but it was a soft sort of weeping, an expression of concern rather than terror.

"How should I have any idea?" Jak countered once he'd caught his breath. He offered Dyan water, and when she refused he gave Zarah a sip and then put the water away without tasting it himself. "How will we know when the System has stopped looking for us?"

"How should I have any idea?" Dyan's voice was flat.

"That's just life, isn't it? Uncertainty."

"I'd offer to take the baby, but I don't think I could do it."

"It's my rugged Landsy physique that lets me scramble up the rock and carry Zarah, too. Don't worry, I've got her. It's nice carrying her, she smells better than I do." Jak didn't point out that Dyan had referred to Zarah as *the baby*. "Even when she's soiled herself, frankly."

"Don't take this the wrong way, but *rugged* is not the word I would have chosen." Dyan sighed, climbed to her feet, and marched up the defile.

"How could I possibly take *that* wrong?" Jak called after her ascending back. He turned his face to the open air above the river and sucked in deep breaths, cleaning out his lungs before he, too, stood and resumed the climb.

A length of Farkill's wall passed overhead. It was three times thicker than Jak was tall, at least, and its underside was a combination of the native rock and, where the stone had been scraped away, bare white cement with rusted iron bars jutting down.

Jak remembered this part; it had seemed more ominous before, the bars reminding Jak of red fangs, and the canyon feeling like a gigantic throat, when he had been on the trail of mysterious ghosts he was afraid might kill him in the night. That was probably ironic and backward; now there were definitely mysterious powers on his trail that might kill him, and if anything, the famous pistols might turn out to be something useful. Or could be nothing at all, a complete myth.

So why did he feel so good?

He wasn't calm; Jak's heart beat fast from the exertion of the climb and also from the thrilling, horrifying knowledge of the danger he was constantly in. But he was alive.

Zarah cried a little and then got a fist into her mouth.

"Good girl," Jak told her.

Shortly afterward the crack became gentler in its slope, and then opened into a sandy funnel in what had once been some kind of open yard. Dyan stood there, on an immense cracked flagstone, to take Baby Zarah.

"Thanks," Jak said. Then he waved at the ruins around them. "This is it."

The open yard was a sea of shifting sand. In some places the sand swept into high drifts, as against the outside walls, where it mostly buried something emerging from the sand in large metal tubes pointing skyward and out. Like chimneys, Jak thought, though they emitted no smoke. There were wagons, too, though they lacked anything resembling traces to hook them to draft animals, and their wheels were a soft black substance collapsing to the ground in bell-shaped skirts, so Jak didn't see how they could actually move. There were other things less obvious in their use and meaning, too, things with scales and wheels and bands. Surrounding the yard were buildings, all two or three stories tall and made of the same cement as Farkill's outer walls.

And there were corpses.

Two skeletal feet protruded from one dune. A complete skeleton wearing a faded, splotchy jumpsuit that had once been colored a mixture of green and brown lay slumped forward on the driver's seat of one of the wagons. A pile of skulls stood exposed on one flagstone.

"You forgot to tell me about the skulls," Dyan said.

"Yeah. Sorry." It was a pointless gesture, but Jak moved to stand between Dyan and the pile of severed, wind-scoured heads.

"So which way do we go? Any suggestions?"

"I never found pistols and guns, remember?" Jak pointed at an angle formed by two walls of a building roofless but otherwise intact. "I didn't even go inside the buildings. I sat right there and waited for dawn."

"And counted yourself lucky you didn't meet evil spirits."

Jak grinned. "But swore up and down to every kid younger than me that I had. Of course."

Dyan pointed directly away from the defile up which they'd climbed. "This way, more or less, must lie the center."

Jak started walking.

They passed among buildings, at first, but when a staved-in door presented itself, Jak stepped inside. Within, the structure was a dusty labyrinth of shattered glass, scorched cement, and more skeletons.

"A war has been fought here," Dyan observed. "I wonder who was fighting."

"I guess Pistols and Guns didn't save Yuess Airfo. Can you read any of the writing on the walls?"

Jak could read, of course. He had been one of the best readers of Ratsnay Station, better than most of the adults. But though some of the letters painted in square characters on many of the walls looked familiar, he could make out none of the words.

Dyan shook her head. "I think our writing has changed since the Cataclysm. Shapes of letters, spelling, sounds. It would take someone much more learned than me to read this."

"Who would that be?" Jak asked.

Dyan shrugged slowly. "A Cogitant? Maybe a Magister specializing in the pre-Cataclysm world? Someone who had spent much more time in the Library than I have."

A voice behind them spoke.

CHAPTER FIFTEEN

A t first, Jak didn't understand the words.

The voice was harsh and abrupt, and Jak spun around and pulled the long knife he'd bought from Orvyl Rich from the sheath at his belt. The sudden movement surprised Baby Zarah, who cried out sharply and then fell quiet again.

The thing from which the voice emanated looked a bit like a living creature. It had an identifiable head, although the head was a wedge-shaped block of black glass, with red dots on opposing sides of the wedge, like a bird's eyes. The head rose on a flexible stalk that wove left and right as the thing continued to speak, like a chicken getting a closer look at something and deciding whether to peck it. The base of the stalk was attached to what Jak perceived as the body—a broad, low polyhedron with segmented steel belts running around two sides. The sounds came from a trio of holes punched into a plate surrounding the base of the stalk.

The thing spoke again. Or might that be mere noise, rather than speech? A near imitation of speech, like some birds can make? But then Jak heard the word *identify*.

It was spoken in a strange accent, harder to understand than a Shoshan or a Basku. The thing said *ai-DENT-i-fai*, instead of *i-dinn-I-fee* like Jak did, but once he unriddled the word, he began to be able to make out others.

"You are trespassing in a secure zone. Identify yourselves or prepare for destruction." *That* he understood.

"Whoa!" Jak shouted. He raised his knife defensively and grabbed Dyan's hand. "We're not trespassing! We're just ..." He had been about to say *looking for Pistols and Guns*, but of course if those were really weapons, that might reinforce this thing's intention to destroy them.

"We are peaceful." Dyan must have understood the thing, too. "Do you serve King Yuess Airfo?"

The thing made a dry clicking sound; it could have been a chuckle. "Are you people of Ratsnay Station?"

"*I* am," Jak admitted.

"You have come quite far in," the thing said. "Usually your people cower by the edge of the mesa."

"I didn't think of myself as *cowering*."

"Fearing evil spirits like any primitive, you huddle and wait for the salvation of dawn. Then you return to your camp whooping and hollering with the thrill of having survived. This is behavior barely elevated above the antics of squirrels. If not *cowering*, what word *would* you use?"

Dyan looked at Jak with laughter in her eyes.

"Okay," he admitted. He didn't lower his knife. "That's basically right. I was cowering."

"I have always wondered about your people and their rituals," the thing continued. "What do you receive after this trial? Does surviving the night in the Airfo Space make you an adult? Do you return to your tribe with the right to marry or own land?"

Airfo Space. So that much at least of the old stories was true. *Space* seemed like a bland word to Jak, but maybe it meant something different in the days of King Yuess. It was strange having a conversation with this mechanical creature, but feeling strange was preferable to being destroyed, by a long ways.

"Mostly you get bragging rights," Jak said. "You get to tell everybody you slept with Pistols and Guns and survived. It's kind of ... it's not something everybody can do. It shows you're brave."

"Slept with pistols and guns." More dry clicking. "It has been a long time since I heard those words spoken aloud."

"Do you remember me?" Jak wanted to know. "From when I spent the night in the Space?"

"I remember everything, and I don't remember you."

Jak knit his brow. "Are you saying I didn't spend the night here?"

"I'm saying you spent the night unnoticed. Security systems are not what they once were."

"Who *are* you?" Dyan asked. She peered closely at the nearer of the two red lights Jak thought of as the thing's eyes. "Or *what*? How *old* are you?"

The thing turned its wedge face in her direction. "Interesting. You betray a consciousness of history and maybe some knowledge of it. Those are not the questions of a tribeswoman of Ratsnay Station."

"You make us sound like we run around naked and eat bugs," Jak objected. The baby fussed, so he stroked and shushed her. He finally lowered his knife, but kept it in front of him with the tip pointed down, ready to defend himself with it if necessary. "We build buildings, we herd cattle. We have families. We can read."

"I am not of Ratsnay Station. I come from Buza System."

The thing bent its neck, looking Dyan up and down. "Has the System ceased?"

"He means your clothes," Jak said, trying to be helpful. "You're dressed like you come from Marsick."

Dyan nodded. "I was raised in the System. I've abandoned it."

"Interesting." The belts on both sides of the thing's base turned simultaneously, dragging it several steps away from Dyan. It cocked its neck into a goose-like crook and stared at her. Jak found himself irrationally wishing the red eyes would blink. "Are you a criminal? A *renegade*?"

"Yes, in the System's eyes."

"Renegade, one who reneges," the thing said. "One who fails to keep a vow. Except that a true promise isn't obtained by compulsion. Choosing not to keep a compelled promise does not really make one a renegade."

Jak's ears perked up. "*Renegade's* the word they use, though."

"Were you made by the System?" Dyan asked.

Dry clicking. "This object you see in front of you is not *me*. It is just an avatar, if you will."

"What's an *avatar*?" Jak found he was clutching the baby tighter than she probably wanted, and forced himself to relax his grip.

"What you see is only a remote unit. It is a pair of eyes and a voice able to patrol the perimeter and keep watch. I built the avatar in my foundry. I built all my avatars in the foundry."

"You mean you and your foundry are somewhere else. Somewhere here in the Airfo Space?" Dyan knitted her brows.

Dry clicking. "Yes. Call it Mountain Home. I am elsewhere in Mountain Home, and the avatar allows me to see remotely. And communicate, of course, although I rarely have occasion to do so. Mostly"—*click click click*—"I only use my voice to frighten away children from Ratsnay Station."

"But you built the avatar with a voice. Who did you *expect* to talk to?"

The avatar said nothing for a moment. "I was not made by the System," it finally said. "The System and I had the same creators, an agency of the Yuess Government. The System is my sister, if you wish to think of us in those terms."

That didn't make any sense. The System was a place, or it was a group of people, the Systemoids. How could this contraption, which was apparently just a roaming manifestation of an entity existing somewhere else, be sister to a city full of people? "Isn't this King Yuess's palace?" Jak asked.

More clicking. "It's one of them. The Yuess had many large facilities once. This is but one Airfo Space, and not even a particularly large one."

King Yuess, then? Not King Yuess Airfo? Jak's head spun.

"So you're very old. Pre-Cataclysm," Dyan pressed on.

"*Cataclysm* is a peculiar word for it. I infer that this is the word chosen by your System to describe the events of its own prehistory."

"What do you mean *its* prehistory? Aren't we talking about the history of the world? I don't understand."

"Of course you do not." Jak realized the avatar's accent was getting better. It was learning, adjusting to and adopting the accents of Dyan and Jak. "You have been told that some disaster wrecked human civilization, and that those who remained created for themselves a System to enable them to survive the rigors of the new and broken world, haven't you? That the System protects humanity?"

"Is that not true?"

The avatar was silent for a long time.

"Come with me," it eventually said. Then the avatar turned and proceeded down a shadowed hallway.

"Come on, Jak." Dyan stepped forward.

"Wait." Jak touched her wrist and she stopped. Baby Zarah whimpered. "What do you hope to get from this?"

"Knowledge."

Of course. "To what end? Who cares about this ancient history? The Cataclysm happened. Whatever it was, what does it matter now? What we need is pistols and guns and the power to push Outriders from far away." The Summer Son wasn't especially a hero who *knew* things; he was a hero who accomplished great feats.

"Maybe the avatar can show us pistols and guns."

"Maybe we could at least ask it whether it can before we follow it blindly deeper into the Space."

They both turned to look at the avatar. It had paused, a stone's throw down the hallway, in a pool of light shining in through a hole in the ceiling. It said nothing and its eyes didn't blink.

"I don't think so," Dyan said. "I feel asking would be … inappropriate."

"Rude, you mean?" Jak pointed. Zarah whined louder. "Rude to our metal friend there?"

"That metal friend there, or the person looking through its eyes, is having a perfectly intelligible conversation. I have no reason to think it's any less smart than we are."

"It's not a *person*," Jak hissed. "It already told us it was *made*. So whatever it is, it might just be really good at faking it's a person. And you're about to fall for it." Jak shook his head, stiffening as his determined eyes met hers. "I'm taking the baby and getting out of here. I came for weapons to defend us with, and if there are no weapons I'm leaving and I'm riding south as fast as I can."

"I mean I think if we ask it for weapons, we'll be *disqualified*."

It was Jak's turn to struggle for words. "What?" he managed to spit out.

Dyan shrugged.

"Do you hear what you're telling me? You *feel* this thing is a *person*, and you're willing to walk into the darkness with it as a result. And you haven't even asked what *it* wants from *you*."

"Look, this person … or thing, fine, this *thing* built itself an avatar, and one thing he equipped it with was a *voice*. No arms, you see, no hands, no visible weapons, but a human voice and the power of speech."

"So?"

"So what for? Who did it think it would talk to? Did it plan just to send its avatar around to whisper frightening things to kids like you, hiding out and hoping not to see pistols and guns?"

"Hey." But Jak couldn't deny she was making sense.

"I think the avatar exists to meet people and ask them questions. And whatever we said convinced it to bring us deeper into the Airfo Space."

"Or possibly convinced it to lead us into a trap."

"Possibly." Dyan looked down at Baby Zarah. "I'm willing to take the risk. At least for me. I have nothing for this avatar to steal. But you're right: you should take Baby Zarah and get out of here. We can plan a meeting place, meet there tomorrow. In the dunes, for instance."

Jak sighed. "Okay. I'm willing to take the risk, too."

"What about Zarah?"

"I guess we're taking the risk for her. It's not fair, but I don't see any other way. Not without me leaving you, which I will not do."

Dyan shook her head. "Come on, then."

They followed the avatar. Their journey across the Space took half an hour of walking, and then the avatar led them into another building. It was windowless, and rubble blocked the apparent doors, but the avatar led them into a nearby canal cut into the cement, and from there into the gaping open mouth of a drain, perpendicular to the building.

During that time, the avatar kept slightly ahead of Jak and Dyan and out of the reach of comfortable conversation. When pressed with questions about where he was leading them, he said nothing.

As the moment when the darkness of the drain would have swallowed the avatar, its eyes blazed into light. A dim reddish flood illuminated the ground in front of it and, as it swung its head back and forth, to each side.

Dyan trotted to catch up, Jak stumbling in her wake.

The tunnel took a ninety-degree turn after a hundred steps, and then ended in a sheet of steel. As the avatar churned forward, the metal slab rose soundlessly, admitting the three of them into a broad passage.

"Do not touch the tubes you see pointing at you." They were the first words the avatar had spoken on their journey.

Jak held Zarah tighter to him. The walls and ceiling of the passage bristled with tubes and they all seemed to be pointing at him. "What are they?" He faltered and fell a step or two behind Dyan.

Click click click. "They are guns, man of Ratsnay. You have found the great demon of your childhood."

"Jak is my name. And will they push me?" *Pulling his pistol, he pushed her.* Or was it only pistols that pushed, and not guns?

More dry clicking. "They will shred your flesh, puncture your internal organs, reduce your brainpan to useless pulp, and spill your blood."

Jak looked at the nearest gun. "From how far away?"

"Don't touch."

Beyond the gun-filled hall there were further passages and doors. The avatar took them into a room that was bare but for a bulky, padded chair in the center, and a helmet hanging from the ceiling above it.

"Jak." The avatar's face bobbed in Jak's direction. "Stand in the corner."

"Keep my mouth shut and keep the baby quiet, right?" The helmet looked ominous. Jak wished he'd kept one of the bolas. Probably they didn't contain listening or tracking devices after all, and if this swollen chair turned out to be some sort of weapons platform, or if the guns came after him here, he had nothing but a knife with which to defend himself and the baby. "Only I'm not always so good at following orders."

The avatar nodded. "Make all the noise you like; once the process begins, the woman will be unable to hear you."

"Dyan," Jak said.

The avatar inclined its head in a nod. "But do not interfere. Touch nothing. Some of my defense systems—my *guns*—are automated. If I am distracted because I am conversing with this woman Dyan, I may not be able to protect you."

"You could turn off your defense systems."

"That would not be prudent."

"I'm not the only threat you're defending against, huh?" Jak chuckled uneasily.

"You are not a threat at all, Jak of Ratsnay Station."

Without being told to, Dyan had seated herself in the chair. It was raised two steps, and it looked like what Jak imagined a throne would look like. King Yuess's throne, and that made the helmet above it Yuess's crown.

The helmet descended. It rode on the end of curved and flexible rods, and as it came down Dyan raised her hands and pulled the helmet down onto her head. It covered her eyes and ears, and then she settled back.

"Good luck," Jak whispered, feeling shoved aside, a little.

The avatar turned to Jak. "What I want," it said, "is to tell someone. This is not why I was created, but it is why I persist. Others must know. If I could, I would tell all humans what I am about to tell your Dyan."

Light blazed all around the throne. Jak couldn't see where the light came from, other than it seemed also to be ascending out of the floor. The light split and branched as it rose, resembling a tree of pure radiation with Dyan at its center. It was a shimmering golden light, like fire or lightning, and Dyan disappeared behind it.

CHAPTER SIXTEEN

J ak thought he could see other people walking around behind the curtain of light with Dyan and the avatar, but that couldn't be true.

"Hush, hush, you're okay," he murmured to Baby Zarah when the brightness of the light made her cry. Reluctantly, he turned and blocked the light from her face with his own body, finally resheathing his knife. She continued to whimper, and his hushes migrated into an aimless melody, until somehow he was singing the same old song he still didn't understand.

Sally, she married a soldier

He strained his neck to watch over his shoulder as long as he could. Dyan's lips moved as if she were speaking, but he heard no words. The air in the small chamber slowly grew warmer and Jak wiped sweat from his forehead several times with his sleeve. He tried not to sweat on the baby, but Zarah was herself a ball of heat making his body sweat where she was pressed against him.

And then the light was gone.

Once Jak's eyes had adjusted, he realized there was still a single source of light. The light was reflected, and came from somewhere outside the room, but it was enough to see by.

"Dyan?" he asked.

Nothing.

Then breathing, but it quavered.

He looked for the glowing red eye-lights of the avatar and couldn't find them.

"Dyan!"

"I'm here, Jak." Her voice was small. "I'm awake."

Jak stepped forward and almost tripped over something waist-height in the darkness. He groped with his fingers, eventually deciding it was the avatar, now still, cold, and lightless.

He moved past it and found Dyan. He could see her dimly; the helmet had come off her head, presumably retreating up into the darkness near the ceiling. Taking Dyan's hand, Jak helped her step down from the throne.

Jak chose not to ask her what she had seen, heard, and said. Not yet.

They struggled together toward the source of light. The halls through which they moved were dark, and in Jak's imagination he saw rows of guns, pointing at him and ready to … shed his blood and pierce his brainpan and all the other horrible things the avatar had said they could do.

He didn't know what such an end would look like; his mind conjured images from the deaths he'd seen by monofilament whip and bola, of severed heads and limbs and great arterial sprays of blood.

But the guns left him alone.

The sole light came from a blue bulb set in the ceiling, near what Jak remembered as the exit. Jak pulled Dyan's hand to lead her past and out into the drainage tunnels, but she pulled away.

"Wait."

The wall here was divided into tall vertical panels. Two thirds of the way up the panel was a black dial with numbers printed on it.

"What are you doing?" Jak asked.

Dyan didn't answer. Instead, she leaned forward to look closely at the black dial. Taking it in her fingers, she turned it one way, then the other, then back again.

"I'm a little confused," Jak said.

The panel swung open, revealing itself to be a door.

"This is not for me," Dyan said. "It's for you. And for us. And for others who will come after."

"What is?"

Dyan reached into the door and pulled out a long bag with a strap. "This bag contains guns."

"Whoa." Jak took two steps back. "Is it safe?"

"I'll carry the guns." Dyan's smile was thin in the blue light. "I'll show you how to use them later."

Jak looked past Dyan into the dark depths beneath Farkill. He thought he saw movement, and maybe he even heard scuffling sounds, but he couldn't be sure. He pointed back the other direction, toward the exit.

"You can just see a sliver of light there," he pointed out. "You go first, and walk to the sliver. Zarah and I will bring up the rear."

Dyan led the way and Jak followed.

Jak drew his knife again. In his imagination, twisted metallic creatures—avatars—threatened Jak at every step. In fact, nothing happened. His steps were huge in the darkness, he occasionally tripped over rubble in his path, but he kept his balance and kept Baby Zarah reasonably quiet, and then they emerged in the bright sunlight in the courtyard of King Yuess's Airfo Space, or as the King's avatar had instructed them to call it, Mountain Home.

"What happened?" Jak asked. "I mean, what did you see?"

"It's getting dark soon." Dyan looked to the west, where the sun was now only an hour's journey above the horizon. "I'd rather not spend the night here."

Jak grinned. "Pistols and Guns."

*   *   *

The sun had set and the last traces of daylight were slipping from the sky as they crossed the Snaik again. By the time they had climbed the canyon on the other side and made their way back to the lake nestled among the dunes, full night had fallen and the stars were out.

"I'd like to risk a fire tonight," Dyan said.

Jak gathered wood. There was plenty of it. It drifted down the creeks, seasonal and non, feeding the small lake, and then piled up in the reeds and rocks on the outlet side.

He mentally added petrofuel to the list of things he missed from the System. This absence was particularly egregious, since he had a hard time imagining even the most clever of the System's Mechanicals could somehow hide a recording or tracking device inside a liquid.

Still, he had decided to be safe. Too late to rethink the decision.

So Jak struck the back of Orvyl Rich's knife against a piece of flint to catch sparks in a pile of wood shavings and dried yellow grass. The tongue of flame springing into birth from that matrix licked hungrily at the pyramid of twisted driftwood about it until Jak had a good fire going.

He had left the baby with Dyan on the assumption that she'd feed Zarah. But as Jak finished building and lighting the fire, he realized Dyan had sat perfectly immobile the entire time, and Zarah was fussing.

"Okay," he ground the words between his teeth, "I'll feed the baby."

Half a mashed avocado and some slices of melon later, Jak settled back against a drift of sand with Zarah asleep, lying on her belly on Jak's chest, and looked at Dyan. She finally moved, turning to look in his direction. Her eyes reflected the fire between them, which was beginning to burn down to a peaceful and powerful bed of embers.

"Whatever you want to tell me," Jak said, "I'm ready to hear it."

He expected her to explain to him what the guns were, maybe even open the bag she'd brought out from Farkill—Mountain Home—with them and show him how to use it. But the long bag lay ignored at her side as she started to speak.

"I have seen the Cataclysm," she said. "And the world before. Neither of them is what I imagined."

"Seen?" Jak asked.

"Recorded. Like factvids."

Jak nodded.

"I have stood unseen in the council of the women and men who decided, unknowing, to put an end to the world they had always lived in and replace it with a new world. They believed it would be a better one."

She then fell silent for a long time, her face still. Had she fallen asleep? No, her eyes still reflected the light of the fire.

"Was it?" he asked. "Was it better?"

It was as if he were playing his part in a ritual, asking the question he had been prompted to ask. There was no possible way that this world, the world in which he continued to live, the world guilty of murdering his sister Aleena and his best friend Eirig and thousands of others in order to exert control, could be better than ... than any other world Jak could imagine, really.

This world was a slaughterhouse.

"They were leaders. Thinkers. Builders. People who understood how the physical world worked. But maybe they didn't understand other human beings. Or they didn't understand them as well as they thought."

Jak nodded.

"Before the Cataclysm, this place—the Treasure Valley, the Wahai, and everything for many days' travel in all direction—were part of a single land."

"That's what I was always taught. I think you even told me that."

"It was ruled badly," Dyan said. "For a while, though, the misrule was not so terrible. The men who had designed the mechanisms of its rule had believed rulers would mostly rule badly, and they created a government they hoped would control the worst excesses and allow only the most important things to be done."

Jak sat up, nearly dislodging the baby. This was new. "You mean ... they thought rulers were evil?"

"They thought *people* were evil. Or at least, they thought people were *imperfect*. Including themselves. They believed that people, if they could, would make foolish, selfish, spiteful decisions. They thought that most people would never do anything but seek power, and popularity, and wealth, and satisfy their lusts. And the people, including their rulers, certainly lived up to the designers' expectations. Maybe they even exceeded them. The government of this land grew cruel and greedy, aggressive and proud."

Jak spat, thinking of the brutal face of Narl, his sister's Goodman.

"And so a later generation of leaders decided that the best solution was to replace the government's human and imperfect leaders with leaders who would be perfect. A leader who would not seek its own lusts and wealth, because it could not want such things in the first place."

Jak's mind, grinding through the story as Dyan told it, hit a wall. "Do you mean … not a human?" He looked up and saw, partly obscured by the firelight, the stars of the Summer Son's chest, disappearing below the western horizon. "Something more than human?"

"What they created was not the Buza System as we know it."

"I don't understand," Jak interrupted her. "The Buza System *as we know it* is a place. It is a collection of buildings, and a way of life, and a tribe of people, and a list of rules and mechanisms for controlling all the people that live around the System. It's the Magisters raising Crechelings and turning them into Urbanes, and it's the Wrongborn being sterilized and forced to work as Gardeners, and it's the people of Ratsnay Station giving their produce to the Collectors and their children to the Cull. It's the Cogitant Council at the top, dictating everything for everyone."

Dyan closed her eyes.

"So what in blazes are you talking about, Dyan?"

When she spoke, Dyan's voice was streaked through with unshed tears. "That is the System as I have known it also, Jak. As I have *lived* it. But behind all those things lies the true Buza System. The System is a mind, but it is a mind that is not human and never has been."

Jak remembered the sight of Cogitant Yurvek's skull sliced open to reveal contents that looked like a device, as well as his odd last words: *I remember.*

"Go on," he said.

"When the Buza System was created, it was but one of a group of minds. These minds were very powerful, and they resided inside machinery. Some of them were located in cities, and others were in fortresses, and others were hidden in the wilderness. They were connected, they spoke to each other, and they ruled."

"I feel like I'm saying *I don't understand* a lot," Jak said. "But that's because I *don't.* Are you saying there were machines that actually could think? People built objects, and the objects actually had minds of their own?" The idea seemed wrong to him, corrupt. And maybe impossible.

Dyan pondered for a moment. "I don't know," she said. "Maybe they actually did think. *Do* think. Maybe they just follow very complex instructions in such a way that they *seem* to think to us. I'm not sure their makers even knew. Practically speaking, I'm not sure it makes any difference to us."

Jak had a hard time wrapping his mind around the words Dyan was saying. He sucked in cold night air, spiced with a hint of campfire smoke, and beckoned for her to continue.

"For a time, the result was peace and prosperity. But then a division arose among the minds."

"The Systems," Jak said.

Dyan nodded. "Of which Buza System was only one, the mind contained in a machine in the ancient city of Buza."

"They disagreed over which of them should rule?"

Dyan shook her head. "That's a human way of thinking. They were happy to continue their rule or maybe, depending on how you think of it, continue to execute their instructions. But they differed in how to understand their instructions. They were instructed, *programmed*, to consider the wellbeing of the human race, and some of the Systems announced to the others their belief that the best way to improve total human wellbeing was to reduce the number of humans."

Jak sucked air through his teeth.

"Once the discussion had started, other Systems suggested that human existence was on balance a misery, and the most human wellbeing could be achieved by killing *all* the humans."

Jak chuckled painfully.

"There was war."

Jak looked up at the sky. The Summer Son had almost completely disappeared, but the Rattler straddled the northern void. As it always did.

"War in heaven," he said.

"If you will. But also here on the earth. Most of the fighting was done by machines. Flying machines, machines that caused massive explosions from a distance, earthquake machines, beams of … condensed light able to ignite immense fires from many days' travel away."

"And the humans? Did none of them resist?"

"They resisted. They sided with those minds of the System that understood their instructions not to include the murder of human beings. They fought with weapons such as you and I have never seen."

"Pistols and guns," Jak said.

"And flying armed servitors. And devices that …" Dyan groped for words, "that eliminated power. And with great fires and pollutions. And other things I can't describe very well."

"I see."

"The earth swam in the blood of its people, Jak."

Jak winced at a pain in his seat, shifting on the sandbank as if he were sitting on a tack. "And?"

"The humans lost," Dyan said.

"Nonsense," Jak said. "Humans still exist."

"The Buza System permits humans to exist. Maybe it needs human beings for something, or maybe it has lost the means to really wipe us out. But make no mistake: we are its slaves."

"Other Systems?" Jak croaked. Zarah slept on, and he envied her. "Are there places where humans live in freedom?"

"I don't know."

Jak stared into the fire. "Maybe tomorrow," he said, "you can show me how the guns work."

CHAPTER SEVENTEEN

In the morning, Zarah woke Jak with a loud yelp. Sitting up, he rubbed thick sleep from his eyes and looked around for Dyan. Shouldn't this be her turn to deal with the baby? But she was nowhere in sight.

Which was fine.

He changed the baby, unwrapping the cloth from around her legs and wiping away the filth. Folding the swaddling cloth with the dirty parts facing in, he set it aside and wrapped the girl in a clean cloth.

She yawned, burped, and then looked at him, snapping her fingers open and shut.

"You're like a raccoon, aren't you?" Jak laughed. "With that mask of yours over one eye, you're a little outlaw in the making. Well, your mask and your outlaw nature are both fine with me."

"Maaaaaaak," Baby Zarah croaked.

"Yeah," Jak agreed, "Maaaaaaak is right, whatever that is. Anyway, since you're not demanding food right now, and I don't see where Dyan is, you and I can go finish cleaning up this mess you've given me."

He picked up the re-swaddled baby without putting her in her sling and carried her from the dune-encircled hollow where they had camped, down to the water.

Might *Maaaaaak* be the Wrongborn baby's way of trying to say *Jak?*

That was silly ... wasn't it?

Jak considered the possibility. It seemed unlikely the baby was trying to say his name. On the other hand, babies sometimes showed surprisingly advanced development, even at young ages. His own mother had told Jak repeatedly that he had stood and walked at the age of six months.

He decided to choose to believe the baby was saying his name.

As he knelt and leaned over the water to wash out the soiled cloth—well downstream of where he planned to fill his drinking water skins later in the day—he talked Baby with Zarah. "Jaaaaaaaak," he said with slow exaggeration. "Jjjjjak!"

"Mak."

"Close enough." Jak felt warm inside. "I'm calling that your first word, I don't care what Dyan says."

"Awww, Pelft," said a hard voice out of Jak's vision. "Look at the cute little Landsy and its whelp."

By force of habit, Jak almost grabbed for bola holsters. Reminding himself that he was carrying no bolas and moreover didn't want to give any indication that he ever *had* carried them, he kept his hands away from his sides. Jamming a stupid smile onto his face, he looked up.

Two Outriders stood above him atop two small dunes. The one speaking was short and unshaven, with a badly bent nose; he stood closer to Jak and held a bola in his hand. Its counterweight was not extended, which was a good thing, because he tossed the little metallic ball casually up and down in one hand, catching it as if it were a toy.

The other Outrider, Pelft, stood further away and had both thumbs hooked in his belt. He grinned, squinted through long-lashed eyes, and spat in the sand. Jak didn't see their horses, or any sign of anyone else from the System.

"Hello, Outrider Pelft," he said, buying time. "And Outrider ..."

"Neko."

"Neko." Jak nodded at what he was doing with his hands. "I'm just cleaning my daughter's soiled swaddling."

"Ugly kid," Outrider Neko grunted.

Jak stood, holding the soiled diaper. He bit back hard responses to the Outrider's words. Of course it was unfair for a man with a face that ugly to comment on the beauty of a baby who had happened to be born with a birthmark. Of course it took a brutality and a smallness of soul for an adult man to mock an infant.

But that wasn't what was really happening. What was really happening was that Outrider Neko was mocking Jak, and Jak's baby. A pair of Landsies. And presumably—hopefully—Neko believed Jak was just some ordinary Landsman farmer, not even as smart as the young woman or young man Neko himself had once murdered in the Cull.

Neko must feel infinitely superior.

He must feel powerful, powerful enough to mask the gaping hole of guilt in his soul.

"Yeah." Jak forced himself to chuckle. "Well, you should see her older sister."

Neko guffawed so hard he almost missed the catch on his bola.

"You think you might show us this older sister?" Pelft asked slowly.

Uh oh. Think, think. Was this just the lewd and bullying demand of a lawless Outrider who felt entitled to make sexual use of a Landsman as he saw fit? Jak had known such, though they didn't all behave that way.

That would be ugly, but even worse was the possibility that Outriders Pelft and Neko didn't believe Jak; that they knew exactly who he was. That they knew there was no older sister for Jak to present to them.

On the one hand, Jak was grateful he had abandoned all their equipment manufactured by the System. On the other hand, he would have given a lot for an armed bola in one hand.

"She's spent the summer in Marsick," Jak lied. "With a shepherd there, name of Narl. We haven't seen her back yet." As he mentioned Narl, Aleena's bullying Goodman, he wished he knew some other shepherd's name to use. On the one hand, if the Outriders were familiar with Marsick, which they might be, he wanted to mention a real person. On the other hand, if they knew who Jak was and they were looking for him, the name Narl might be a giveaway.

Too late now.

Pelft arched one eyebrow and narrowed his squint even further. Neko stopped tossing his bola.

"That right?" Neko said. "Because I have another theory. I think you don't have any daughters. You're too young. Which means that baby's someone else's."

Jak forced himself to laugh. "You think I steal babies and run out into the desert to hide? You have a strange idea of Landsmen, Outrider Neko."

"The thing is, you kind of match the description of a Landsman we're looking for. His name is Jak. Jak, son of Rosyn."

"Sounds notorious," Jak said, struggling to keep any sign of his internal struggle off his face. "What did he do?"

Neko narrowed his eyes. "He sneaked into the System and stole a baby there."

Outrider Neko's description of Jak's act actually made Jak happier that he had Baby Zarah. It made her presence feel like an act of revenge—for all the children the System had taken from Ratsnay Station, Ratsnay Station had finally crept in and stolen one of the System's back.

Even if Zarah was Wrongborn. Even if her life in the System would have been a sterile and pointless life of trimming hedges and digging ditches.

Even if Jak's possession of the baby got him killed.

"I'm glad I only kind of match that fellow's description," Jak said. "I'd hate for you to take my baby over a misunderstanding."

"The only thing really missing," Pelft said, "is we understand Jak is traveling with a woman. An outlaw named Dyan."

Jak shifted to one side, taking a step away from Baby Zarah, who was fussing. If a bola hit him and he exploded suddenly into blood, he didn't want her to get soaked. The ludicrousness of his own care struck him and he giggled. He also tightened his grip on the soggy, foul swaddling cloth.

It was a terrible weapon, but it was all he had.

"Could have sworn I heard you talking to someone," Pelft said.

"Just talking to the baby," Jak lied. "We're alone."

Pelft nodded. "Even if you are alone, you have to figure I'd just as soon kill you and not take the chance we're missing the man we're looking for."

Jak pawed at the sand with his feet. He wished he were armed. He hoped Dyan was far away.

"It's hard to tell one person's footprints from another in sand like this," Outrider Neko said. "But if you're alone, you sure left a lot of footprints."

"Not to mention the fact that you have two horses and two saddles," Pelft added. "Are you going to tell us the baby was riding the second?"

A sudden loud *crack* ripped the sky open. It sounded like thunder and Jak almost fell in the lake, staggering back.

Outrider Neko grunted and dropped to his knees. A red blossom of blood appeared in his side. He looked down at himself, astonished.

A second *crack*, and a third.

Neko fell into the sand.

"Blazes!" Outrider Pelft dropped to all fours and whipped a bola from his holster, holding it ready and to the side. He stared over the dune to find the source of Neko's sudden death, but the sand blocked his view.

The sand didn't block Jak's view. He turned his head and saw Dyan, kneeling behind another rise of sand and holding a strange object to her shoulder. It was a knobby black assembly of metal resembling nothing he had ever seen. It had handles on it of a couple of different shapes, and the end against Dyan's shoulder looked like a triangular weight; the far terminus ended in a point.

Dyan aimed the point in the direction of Outrider Pelft and the sky cracked again. A spurt of flame jumped from the pointed end of the thing at her shoulder, and sand a few inches to one side of the Outrider sprang into the air.

"Blazes!" Pelft cursed again, but he couldn't see Dyan.

It was the gun, Jak realized.

So guns were real. And they were weapons, and they were lethal. Jak looked at the stiffening face of Outrider Neko with satisfaction.

Dyan was armed. On the other hand, so was Outrider Pelft. And if he hit Dyan first, his bola would kill her just as surely as her gun could kill him.

Jak raced up the dune towards Neko's corpse. It was a hard slog, with the sand shifting down under his feet and pulling him back toward the lake, but he kept one eye on Pelft and the other on the metallic ball inches from Outrider Neko's dead hand.

His bola.

"Stay where you are!" Pelft yelled at him.

Jak kept running.

Pelft turned to Jak, a look of irritation on his face. Before he could raise his arm and throw the bola—

Jak hurled the filthy swaddling cloth.

The Outrider wasn't expecting it, and the dirty rag struck him in the neck and chin. "Filthy Landsy!" he shouted, flinching uselessly to one side.

That flinch was all Jak needed. It gave him the time to drop to his knees and grab the fallen bola.

Pelft sneered at him still, one last dismissive look that said the Outrider didn't think Jak could do anything with the bola, anyway. Jak was just a Landsy, and would more than likely slice himself in half in the effort to use the System's weapon. Jak had seen such accidental deaths himself.

With calm motions, not quite as practiced as he would have liked, Jak took the bola, armed it, and swung.

Outrider Pelft's last act was to widen his eyes in surprise, the instant before his comrade's monofilament bola struck him.

Pelft and Jak hit the ground at the same time, but Jak was alive and Pelft hit in two pieces. Cold relief shot through Jak's veins.

"Jak!" Dyan shouted.

"Yeah," Jak muttered, and then forced himself to raise his voice. "Here! I'm fine! The Outriders are both down, don't ... don't gun me!"

"*Shoot*, I think." Dyan made the slow climb across the dunes to join Jak and sat next to him, cradling the gun in her arms with the dangerous end pointed at the sky. At least, that was the dangerous end Jak *knew about*.

Jak rolled over on his back and they both looked down at Baby Zarah. She was crying—when had she started crying? during the encounter?—but she looked unhurt.

"Shoot, then."

"When did you learn to throw a soiled swaddling rag with such accuracy?"

Jak laughed, a nervous explosion that released a knot in his chest. "Native talent. When did you learn to shoot the gun?"

"I saw it in my ... vision ... yesterday." Dyan's eyes seemed to focus on the distant horizon. "But really, it isn't hard. You just point, and then depress this little switch here." She demonstrated, without actually shooting.

Jak looked at the switch. His mind reeled with the possibilities.

"That's really excellent," he said.

"Is it?" Dyan looked at Jak with cold eyes. "It's just another way to kill, as far as I can tell. Has killing become an excellent thing?"

"They would have killed all three of us if you hadn't ... shot ... the Outrider."

"I don't regret this particular death," Dyan said. "I just regret all the death in general. At least this gives us a weapon we can be reasonably comfortable the System isn't using to follow or record us."

Jak sprang to his feet. "It's much more! Don't you see? Guns will even the odds."

"Sure," Dyan said. "Just as if we'd stolen a bunch of bolas."

"No." Jak shook his head. "Don't you understand? The System's weapons are hard to use. They take training. That makes it difficult and dangerous to be armed, but this thing, this gun, is easy to use. So anybody can be dangerous."

Dyan furrowed her brow. "Yes," she said slowly.

"Give anybody one of these things, and he can shoot and kill an Outrider on even terms, without all the Outrider's training. Don't you get it? The System is vulnerable! Give these to a few hundred Landsmen, and the System is done collecting the harvest every year."

Dyan said nothing.

A torrent of questions tumbled out of Jak. "How far do you think it can shoot? Do you think it can kill with just one blow, or do you think multiple blows will generally be required? More than one *shot*, I mean. How accurate do you think you can be? And how fast can you shoot?"

Dyan put a hand on Jak's arm. "Stop," she said. "You don't understand."

"Oh, I think I *do*. The Cull is done forever."

"First of all," Dyan said, "the gun requires something inside it called *bullets*. It can shoot once for each bullet loaded into it."

Jak frowned. "How many bullets do we have?"

Dyan shrugged. "Dozens. I haven't counted. Maybe a few hundred. Not more than that. And besides, we only have four guns."

"So we go back and get more."

"I don't know if there *are* more," Dyan said. "But if there are, I don't think I'm meant to have them. I think this is Mountain Home's gift to us. These four guns, and a couple of boxes of bullets."

"How are we going to do anything with just that?" Jak sat down.

"We can't do a lot," Dyan said. "But we can protect ourselves and flee."

Jak looked at her sharply, frustration and disappointment on his face.

"What exactly do you think we're going to do?" Dyan asked.

Jak tried to keep his voice calm. "I think *I* am going to keep a promise I made to someone. I hope *you* are going to help me."

CHAPTER EIGHTEEN

They risked taking the Outriders' weapons with them this time, but that was all. Not even the holsters, they decided after a long conversation by the side of the lake. Even the bolas and the whip represented a risk, but Dyan agreed with Jak that they represented the least risk they could think of, and if they were going to sneak into the System undetected, Jak didn't have a plan that didn't require either Systemoid clothing or a monofilament weapon.

Besides, for all the obvious advantages the guns provided, they were noisy. Jak didn't want to waste bullets, and he didn't want to attract attention.

That decided, they heaved the two dead Outriders onto the backs of the horses they found picketed at the edge of the dunes. Jak needed Dyan's help to get Neko's corpse into the saddle, but he insisted on handling Pelft alone.

In the first place, because he could; his bola throw had sliced Pelft in two right above his navel, so the Outrider's halves were of manageable size. In the second place, because separately putting a pair of legs and then a limp-armed torso into the saddle of a skittish, protesting horse was an ugly and uncomfortable job. If it had to be done, he wanted to be the one who did it.

His mess, he'd clean it up.

Then they tied them in place. They used cord from the Outriders' saddlebags—by now, he and Dyan could pretty accurately predict what gear the Outriders had. In the case of Outrider Pelft, Jak also used a microfiber cloth to wrap the dead man's torso and legs together in a gruesome bundle.

He felt bad for the horse, but it had to be done.

Then they shooed the animals out into the desert, eastward, away from the System and along the Snaik River.

"Do you think the horses are trained?" he asked Dyan as they watched the animals canter away.

She squinted at him. "To do what? Untie the knots?"

Jak laughed. It was a welcome relief from the sick knot of tension he felt inside. "To go back to the System. To the Camp, I guess."

Dyan shrugged. "It's all guesses and fear, isn't it? We fear we may be recorded or tracked, we guess the horses won't go back to the System. We take our best decision based on our guesses and our fears."

Jak had Baby Zarah in the sling, so his hands were free. He reached over and took Dyan's hand in his. "Not just fears."

"No?"

"No. Sometimes we take our best guesses based on our hopes."

Something like a smile cracked Dyan's face. "Yes," she agreed. "That's a good reminder. Thank you."

*   *   *

They crossed the river before turning east themselves. They rode at night, and Jak reassured Dyan that they were skirting far enough to the south of Ratsnay Station that defensive patrols couldn't accidentally stumble across them. This was true, although of course hunters could range much further abroad than watchmen, so Jak kept a careful eye out for other people.

Jak preferred his people to think he was dead. It would be safer for them to believe that than to know the truth.

They saw no one. In the early hours before dawn, from a cold camp on the mountains east of Ratsnay Station, they looked down and watched its fires as a dim red glow in the valley.

They hid through the day in a brush-tangled, waterless ravine, watching jackrabbits, deer, and once a wild cat stare back at them in between short, restless naps.

Their second night of traveling brought them to the hills at the edge of the Jawtooths and they camped on a promontory overlooking the Treasure Valley. After he'd laid out their bedrolls, Jak looked around and found Dyan missing. A few minutes' walk found her, sitting on a knee-high boulder and staring north at the System.

Where Ratsnay Station at night had been a few red fires, the System was a spangle of bright lights.

"It's almost like looking down at the stars, isn't it?" he said.

She started, surprised out of some solitary reverie. "I hadn't seen it that way. What do you see in those stars, then? Some marker to light our path?"

"Nah." Jak grinned, though in the darkness he doubted she could tell. "I see a monster. A big slimy thing with many tentacles. It's been eating the sacrificed young people of Ratsnay Station for years, and it doesn't know the Summer Son is about to come tie its tentacles in a knot and drop it in the deepest parts of the ocean."

Dyan laughed, but she didn't come to bed. Jak drifted off to sleep with the sky beginning to turn blue in the east and Baby Zarah breathing deeply on the bedroll beside him.

Once darkness had fallen again the next night, they set out. This time, they let their horses go and hid most of the rest of their gear. They carried the monofilament weapons in their pockets; Dyan had the bag of guns slung over her shoulder, and Jak wore Baby Zarah in the sling.

Jak's plan was simple. He worried about Guardsmen on the wall, and about Outriders on patrol, but in the darkness they just walked down to the Buza River and stepped into it. A clouded night sky sheltered them from unfriendly eyes, and they drifted with the river to where it passed under the wall.

As Jak had guessed, a row of iron bars blocked access to the interior of the System to anything bigger than a squirrel. But it was a simple matter to wade up to the bars, slice through two of them with Outrider Pelft's bola, lay the bars as gently as he could down in the water, and then step underneath the wall.

Unnoticed, undisguised, they were back inside the System.

*　　　*　　　*

The morning found Jak and Dyan crouched in trees across the river from Whitwark Bothy. They were in a spot as far from footpaths and other sources of likely traffic as Jak could find; concealed within a cluster of neatly-trimmed bushes but able to look out.

Jak watched the Gardeners come out of the Bothy in their brown uniforms. They ate standing around a table in front of the Bothy, some moving and talking as they continued to wake up, others slugging each other vigorously in the upper arm to get their blood moving.

The Gardeners of Whitwark Bothy picked the tables clean as efficiently as vultures, and much more quickly. When they had taken tools and filed upstream along a footpath, Dyan made to stand up.

Jak grabbed her elbow. "Wait."

A few minutes later, Gardeners from another Bothy appeared. They lifted the tables and carried them away, two to a table.

Jak nodded, then followed Dyan as she slipped down to the walkway over the top of the weir.

He felt naked, racing over the river. Baby Zarah's presence only made him feel more conspicuous—even if he managed to talk someone into believing he was a Gardener momentarily out of uniform, he couldn't possibly explain why he had a baby in his arms.

This was the moment of maximum exposure and risk.

It passed, though. In moments they were in the shadow of the Bothy, pushing upon the nearest door.

It was only once they were inside and Jak had let out a shuddering gasp that he realized he had raced there without breathing.

He slipped Baby Zarah onto the nearest bunk. She gurgled. "You should wait here," Jak suggested. He rifled through the occupants' belongings and found a set of brown Gardener clothing that looked as if it would fit him. Shucking off the articles he'd bought from Orvyl Rich in Marsick, he dressed himself as a Gardener. "You, too," he added, pointing at other unused clothing. "If you get caught by someone, you can bluff, but only if you don't look like a Landsy."

Dyan began changing her clothing. "I'll keep Zarah," she said. "And the guns, of course."

Jak nodded. "I'll carry the bolas in my pockets. Just in case."

"I'll just wait here?" Dyan's tone suggested she didn't think that was a great idea.

"I think it's safest."

"But not safest for you."

Jak ignored the comment. "I'll try to bring Headman Anji back here, so we can talk." Jak looked down at Zarah on the cot. "I don't know what to do about the baby."

"I'll lie," Dyan said simply. "I'll tell anyone who asks that the Healers have asked me to deliver this Wrongborn baby to one of the Bothies."

Jak, heading for the door, hesitated. "Will it work?"

Dyan shrugged. "It will buy time."

Jak nodded. "Stay out of sight."

He grabbed a long-handled hoe from a rack of Gardeners' tools in one of the Bothy's chambers and headed up the bank of the Buza River. The Bothies kept him generally out of sight of the highway, but still Jak kept his eyes fixed firmly on his feet and his face pointed away from the road. If he ran into Shad or Cheela, or anyone else who might know him—though it seemed that most Systemoids who met him and could remember his face died shortly thereafter—his plan would end.

Probably in sudden death.

After twenty minutes' walk Jak came across the Gardeners of Whitwark Bothy. He ran into Tulit first; the narrow-faced man's sour eyes skimmed over Jak at first, turning back to the wall of rock he was shoring up on the riverbank, but then jumped back and stared.

Tulit had known Jak as a Mechanical.

"Good morning, Tulit." Jak smiled his friendliest smile and got a scowl in return. "Can you tell me where Headman Anji is working?"

Tulit sucked at his teeth slowly and then spat. "Mechanical Jass." It wasn't a greeting, or even an acknowledgement. Was it a challenge? The scar across the man's eyebrows seemed to glow a bright red, but now that Jak knew it meant the Gardener was Wrongborn, it almost seemed like a badge of honor.

Should Jak reveal himself to Tulit? No, he decided. He just wasn't ready yet. "Yes. There's more I want to tell you, but I need to talk to Headman Anji first."

"Headman's up there." Tulit pointed upriver with his nose at a clump of trees and earth protruding out into the river. Anji stood in water up to the middle of her thighs, levering up a fallen log with a pole while other Gardeners tied a rope around it.

"Thanks." Without looking back, Jak walked to where Anji worked.

She watched him approach. An expression of wariness filled her face momentarily, but then she dropped a shield of polite obliviousness down over it.

"Headman," Jak called. He noticed other Gardeners watching him. How many of them recognized him as the Mechanical they'd seen a week earlier? "May I have a word with you?"

Anji handed her pole to a burly Gardener with clumps of cauliflower for ears and sloshed to the riverbank. Jak offered her his hand and she ignored it, climbing out under her own power.

"Come over here," she said, a bit more loudly than she needed to. "Let's not distract the others at their labor." Jak followed.

A stone's throw from where the people of Whitwark Bothy worked stood a bower. Vines ran over its latticed walls and ceiling, and Anji led Jak inside. Ignoring the seats lining the bower's walls, she stood in the center and folded her arms across her chest.

"You came to tell me something, so I guess you'd better do it. Then you can give Leita back her clothing and be on your way."

Jak looked down at his clothing. "How do you know this belongs to Leita?"

Anji's face was expressionless. "Stitch in the sleeve. I put it there after she cut it on a scythe. I'll just hope no one remembers they saw you before, only you were dressed as a Mechanical."

"Ah … too late," Jak said.

She arched her eyebrows.

"Tulit. At least Tulit saw me."

"Tell me why I shouldn't just turn you in. Call the nearest Guardsman or Outrider and have you taken to the Prison." Headman Anji's nostrils flared. "It's the only safe course for me. The only safe course for the people of my Bothy."

Jak's heart raced. Had he misjudged her? Was his plan a mistake from the beginning?

Or did she just need a token?

He took one of the bolas from his pocket and held it out. Taking the weapon in her hand, she frowned.

"You claimed you were here to rescue someone," Anji said. She still held the bola in front of her.

"I did it. She's in one of the rooms in your Bothy."

"Blast." But Anji's voice was softening.

"Now I'm here to rescue you. As I promised."

"Madness."

"No." Jak shook his head. "I have a plan. And I have a weapon."

"*I* have your weapon." Anji sneered, shaking the bola to remind him. "And you'd need a lot more weapons than this to do any good. The System has hundreds of Guardsmen, hundreds more Outriders, and thousands of people who are armed with weapons just like these and know how to use them. If you armed every Gardener in every Bothy, we'd never be able to overthrow the System. Even if we were able to fight with these without hurting ourselves." She put the bola in her own pocket. "The best thing you can do is run right now. I'll give you five minutes before I raise the alarm."

"That isn't the weapon," Jak said. "I have something new. Well, no, something very old. But useful. Perfect. Just the thing we need."

"We? *We?* There is no *we*, Landsman. There is me, Headman of Whitwark Bothy, trying my best to keep my Gardeners contented, safe, and productive. And there is you, trespasser, criminal, rebel, trying to cause trouble."

"Let's say it were possible, though," Jak said. "Let's say I could show you it was possible. Would you be interested? Would you want to leave?"

Headman Anji sighed and looked down at her feet. "You know I would."

A new voice broke into the conversation. "Well, that is profoundly disappointing to hear."

Jak spun around. At the edge of the bower, whip in his hand, stood the man in the red cape whom Jak had seen casually execute two Gardeners and force Anji to punish one of them herself. The Overseer.

Jak couldn't tell if the whip was of the monofilament executing kind, or the electric pain-causing kind.

"It's not what you think," Jak said.

"It's exactly what I think," the Overseer said.

He raised the whip over his head to strike.

CHAPTER NINETEEN

T here's something you should know," Jak said.

The Overseer struck him. Thank the Mother, it was an electric whip. Still, being hit by the whip hurt—and not just where the blow landed, on Jak's shoulder, but all over. His muscles jerked involuntarily in a kind of spastic dance. He barely kept his feet.

"Turn around," the Overseer said.

Anji took a step back.

"Don't you leave," the Overseer warned her.

She stopped, put her hands in her pockets.

"Wait," Jak said.

The Overseer whipped him again.

This time both knees jolted forward and Jak tumbled to the ground. He banged his head on one of the bower's benches and his vision swooned.

He wanted to grab the other bola in his pocket, but he couldn't make his hands do what he wanted them to do.

"I-I-I-I'm n-not alone." His teeth chattered. It was a betrayal and he knew it, but he had nothing else to try. If he stopped the whipping, maybe he could get control of himself enough to get at his weapon.

"No?" The Overseer seemed only mildly interested. He whipped Jak again, and this time Jak's back arched, slamming the back of his head into the ground. The pain sizzled and cut him, it hurt, but it wasn't the worst pain he'd ever had. But losing control of own body was humiliating.

The Overseer hit him again, and then stopped.

"Oh, how interesting." The Overseer stepped forward and stooped down to touch Jak. No, to touch the ground near him, but it was hard to tell the difference because Jak's vision was fading. What did the Overseer want?

And then his vision returned and Jak saw what had happened. The Overseer held a bola. Jak's bola. It must have fallen from his pocket, and the Overseer had seen it.

Jak was defenseless.

"So." The Overseer flashed the bola to Headman Anji, and then to Jak, and then tucked it into a pocket in his cape. "We have insurrection. Theft. What else? Murder? How did you come by this weapon, Gardener?"

Jak wanted a lie, but none came to him.

The Overseer whipped him again, across the chest. Jak heard screaming and realized the sound was coming from him.

"Out-outriders!" he chattered when he regained control of his jaw. "Outriders have invited me to come with them. To Marsick!" It was the first name that came to mind. He needed to practice lying about other places. "And they asked me to invite Headman Anji."

The Overseer hesitated. "You're a bad liar, Gardener."

"No, really." It was a stupid lie, but Jak had said it, and he pushed forward. "Headman Anji didn't believe me either, but this is what I was telling her. I need someone to come with me on a task for the System. For the Outriders. Outrider Shipto and his team." He hoped the made-up detail would add verisimilitude. "To Marsick." The jittering of his fingers was slowing. "This is what I meant about leaving the System."

The Overseer laughed. He whipped Jak again and Jak's limbs all shot straight out.

"Stop it," Headman Anji said.

The Overseer turned to look at her.

The Headman stood with her feet planted resolutely apart. She looked ready to wrestle a bull, but in her hand and over her head she held the bola she had taken from Jak.

The Overseer laughed again. "Really, Anji? I don't think you know how to use that, and it can be a … tricky weapon."

Anji's mouth was flat. "I figure it's even odds whether you get cut in half or I do. I'm okay with either outcome."

Jak realized a crowd had gathered. The Gardeners of Whitwark Bothy surrounded the bower, but none of them intervened. Some of them clenched and unclenched fists around gardening tools, but mostly they just leaned on their rakes and shovels and watched.

If Anji threw the bola, she might kill or mutilate several people.

"You hate the System so much?"

Anji was slow to answer. "I don't mind the work," she said. "I don't mind having to wrestle younger, lazier workers to get back to their jobs. And I'm even grateful for the food and shelter, I suppose."

"But?"

"But the price is just too high."

At the moment, when Headman Anji said the word *high*, the Overseer snapped his whip at her. She hurled the bola, but didn't arm it properly, so the counterweight never extended and the bola remained in the shape of a ball, uselessly bouncing into the crowd of watching Gardeners.

The Overseer didn't miss. The lash of his whip struck Headman Anji across the face. She dropped to the ground, conscious but twitching.

The Overseer stepped forward and stood over her. "So, here we are."

Jak struggled to rise to all fours and the Overseer saw him. Without stepping away from the Headman, he cracked his whip three times more, striking Jak once in the neck and once in the chest and knocking him back to the ground, and with his third blow sending another jolt of power into the Headman.

Jak and Anji both lay on the ground and twitched.

Jak struggled to get breath into his lungs. This was defeat. He had come back to keep his promise. To offer the Headman and her people a way out. Instead, he'd brought her to the dirt.

With a soft *thud*, the Overseer dropped his whip.

Then he drew his sword and activated it.

Jak heard the hum of the vibro-blade and saw the faint distortion of the weapon's outline. The blade would cut through steel or stone now, just as surely as one of the monofilament weapons. The Overseer held the sword lightly, casually, but he pointed its tip at Headman Anji's face.

The Gardeners still held their positions. Some looked away in sorrow, others looked down in shame. A few stared with open eyes and grinding teeth, and Jak thought those wore expressions of rage.

Tulit, and a few others, looked happy. Or hungry. Or delighted.

There was some disturbance at the back of the crowd. Were some of the Gardeners leaving?

The Overseer looked at Jak.

"You aren't here recruiting for some trip to the Wahai with Outriders," he said slowly.

"No," Jak agreed. He wouldn't give up Dyan, he promised himself. If he and Headman Anji both had to die, so be it. He wouldn't betray Dyan and the baby she carried. *Their* baby.

"Now is the time to tell me what you're doing. And who you're with."

"I'm alone," Jak said.

"That's not what you told the Headman."

"I mean … there are others like me. Other Landsies. I'm here looking for Gardeners to come to Marsick because we're shorthanded. Because of the …" he almost said *the Cull*, "the Selection. I thought I might find my friends who had been selected and invite them to come back. But I can't find them. But if some of these people came instead, that would help us … bring in the harvest."

He couldn't tell whether his lie was clever or idiotic.

The Overseer shook his head, removing any doubt. "That's nonsense on its face. And if it were true, it's the kind of nonsense not worth lying for in the first place. Last chance to come clean, Landsy." He lowered his humming blade to within a hand's breadth of Headman Anji's face.

If he simply leaned forward, she'd be dead instantly.

Jak dug deep, but came up with nothing. He had no lie to tell, and he simply wouldn't tell the truth.

The Overseer smiled sadly and shrugged—

Boom!

The Overseer fell backward, his face disappearing in a sudden burst of blood. He struck the ground at full length and his sword, fumbled from his hands, slid effortlessly through his leg, pinning it to the dirt, and then switched off.

The Overseer twitched once or twice and then lay still.

In the aftermath of the loud report of the gun, Jak and all the Gardeners were silent. Slowly, they turned to look at where the sound had come from, and saw Dyan, standing in their midst. She was dressed as a Gardener, with the bag of guns and bullets over one shoulder and one gun in her hands, which she now lowered and pointed at the earth.

Baby Zarah, who lay in the grass at Dyan's side, started to cry.

The Gardeners stood still.

Jak couldn't quite manage to get to his feet, but he climbed onto all fours and then crawled over to where the Headman lay. Her eyes were closed and her face was spattered with blood, and for a moment Jak feared the Overseer's whip had done more damage than Jak had realized, but then Anji opened her eyes.

It was the Overseer's blood on her face.

Her gaze and Jak's met. The Headman's mouth was a serious line, but her eyes twinkled. "Well," she said shakily. "I'm committed now."

Jak took her by the arm and together they managed to stand. Jak laughed out loud. It was like climbing a tree that was climbing you at the same time, but it worked.

Anji took a deep breath and looked around. "Everyone's here," she said. She looked each of her people in the face. "And everyone's staying here, agreed?"

No one left. Anji turned to look back at Jak expectantly; she was handing control over to him, lending him her authority.

"We have to hide the body." Dyan had picked up the baby and was adjusting the sling on her shoulder.

Jak nodded his agreement. "Fortunately, we have shovels."

The bower stood on a sandy path running down to the river and up towards the highway. Jak looked around for witnesses and saw none; hopefully no one had seen the shooting and run away to report it, but Dyan was right, and moreover speed was important.

He spoke fast. "You five, stand over there and pretend to work. I don't care what you do, you're just blocking the view of anyone who happens to look down from the highway. You two, get up to the highway do the same. I don't know, rake gravel or something. If anyone asks about a loud noise, say you didn't hear it. You two, watch the river path. You three, dig a grave."

He pointed at the sandy path.

"Really?" Anji arched her eyebrows at him.

"The sand will make it quick," Jak explained. "Meanwhile, you three take those rakes and disturb the sand all along the rest of the path. Make it look like the whole path has been sanded with fresh sand. That will hide the fact that this sand here has been disturbed."

Tulit was in this final group of three. His eyes suggested he had something he wanted to say, but he kept his lips pressed firmly together as he picked up his rake and started disturbing sand as directed.

Jak tugged at the sword impaling the Overseer and pinning him to the ground. At first it resisted, but when he found the switch in the pommel and turned the vibrating function on, the sword came out effortlessly. Then Jak turned it off and resheathed it. Headman Anji picked up the Overseer by the shoulders while Jak grabbed his feet and together they laid the Headman in the quickly-excavated grave in the center of the sanded path. Jak tossed the man's whip in after him.

"You sure you don't want to take his weapons?" Anji asked.

"I'm not, actually," Jak said. "But it seems like the safest bet." He didn't explain his fears about being recorded or followed, but she nodded and accepted his word anyway.

"This is not the first corpse you've handled," she guessed.

"Holy Mother, no." Jak suddenly felt old and tired. Too many images of violence and death crowded into his mind and he tried to push them away. "At least this one is in one piece."

The Overseer's face had been ruined by the gun, though. Jak wasn't sure how the weapon worked, but it threw its bullets at a shockingly high speed, and if they came into contact with human flesh and bone, they devastated it.

The avatar had warned him.

"The casing," he said, remembering a word Dyan had taught him.

He took the bag of guns from Dyan's shoulder to lighten her load, then poked around in the grass until he found the little brass tube the gun ejected as it fired each bullet. Probably the Systemoids wouldn't realize what it was even if they stumbled across it, but he wanted to take no chances. When the time came, he wanted the guns to seem as mysterious and powerful as possible, and not just a piece of unfamiliar but understandable weapons technology.

The Gardeners, meanwhile, covered up the body. Anji herself stamped the sand flat over the Overseer's wrecked face, a look of grim satisfaction in her eyes as she did so. Then she took a rake and scratched the sand to the same rough, fresh-looking texture as the rest of the path.

"There," she said. "Until the river floods or the System tears out this pavilion to replace it with a new Bothy, our friend the Overseer has a comfortable place to rest."

"Let's hope," Dyan said, "the System wasn't watching the Overseer through his belt buckle or his whip or something else." She spoke softly, so no one but Jak and Headman Anji could hear.

Anji frowned, not understanding.

"We know some of the System's agents carry recording devices on their person," Jak said. "That's why I didn't take any of the Overseer's weapons. In case they could track my location or record what I said or did."

"Then I hope your plan is to act quickly," Anji said. "Just in case."

"My plan is to act *immediately*." Jak waved his arms to call back the Gardeners at the top of the path. Beyond them, a Collector's wagon and a pair of Outriders passed by slowly, not paying any apparent attention to the Gardeners.

So far, so good.

When the Gardeners had huddled around in a semicircle, Jak raised his voice slightly. "I'm getting out of here," he said. "I'm taking everyone who wants to come with me, but I won't force anyone. Would anybody prefer to stay in the System?"

There was silence for a moment, and then Anji spoke. "Some have already left." There was a note of urgency in her voice.

Jak looked at the faces around him and realized Tulit was one of the ones who had already opted out. Opted out, and possibly was now on his way to inform the System of the murder of its Overseer.

Well, Jak could hope that *wasn't* happening. But he had to act as if it *were*.

"I have a plan," he said. "I need black paint and chunks of wood to carve." He sighed. "And I guess someone better dig up the grave. We could use the vibro-blade."

CHAPTER TWENTY

F ear ate at Jak.
He didn't have much time. Tulit was running to find the nearest Overseer (were there more?) or Guardsman, and Jak had no idea how fast the System would react. He might have an hour. He might have minutes.

Anji barked at her people. "Wood! Now!"

When a few of them moved to obey and just dragged their feet aimlessly through the underbrush, Anji held her open hand out to Jak. "The sword, please."

Jak handed it over. "Be careful."

Headman Anji activated the Overseer's blade and promptly attacked the bower with it. In moments, the trellis roof collapsed, and Anji was yanking out beams and throwing them in Jak's direction.

"Okay, look." A group of Gardeners gathered around Jak with buckets of paint and brushes. Jak laid out one of their four precious guns on the grass. "We need to carve things shaped as much as possible like this."

One of the Gardeners, a young woman with dark skin, tightly curled hair, and a pronounced leftward curve to her spine, shook her head and pursed her lips. "That's a lot of detailed carving. Look at all those grooves, and the little notches and buttons. How much time do you think we have?"

"Assume we have none. Dyan and I will block out the rough shapes for you, but I need you to make them look as good as you can. As much as possible, I said. It won't be perfect. Add handles, make a hole in the end, paint them black at least."

"I can do that." The young woman pulled out a knife and started carving, confident and fast.

"Thanks. I'm Jak." Jak offered his real name as a gesture of solidarity, and extended his hand along with it.

"I'm Zo." She didn't look up. "I'll shake your hand when I've done my carving."

"You've got the idea!" Jak took his bola and went to work slicing the timbers from Headman Anji into the right basic shape and size. "Make two each, and it'll be enough!"

He hoped it would be enough.

Gardeners crowded around and carved. Dyan handed Baby Zarah off to a man with a shriveled left hand, a shock of white hair, and a face lined with age, and then she waded in with a second bola. The monofilament weapons had to be handled carefully, but they made it easy to cut the wood in seconds to approximately the right size.

"This paint will take an hour to fully dry," said one of the men as he pried the lid off a can. He was wiry and tall, like an antelope in his movements. Strikingly, his eyes were two different colors.

"Jak." Jak handed the man a carved fake gun.

"Taryl."

"Well then, Taryl, we're going to have to hope no one wonders why our hands are black."

His entire plan, simple and stupid as it might be, hinged on the guess that no one in the System had any idea what a gun was. Dyan hadn't. If the Systemoids didn't know, then he could catch them by surprise and play off their fears. Black hands might only add to the weapons' mystique.

And if his guess was wrong, and the Guardsmen or the Outriders knew very well what guns were, then they'd recognize the fakes and Jak and the Gardeners would most likely be dead in seconds.

They might be dead in seconds, anyway.

The first of the wooden guns were ready. Jak stepped back from carving and put his bola away. "We have four guns," he said to Dyan and Anji.

"Guns?" Anji asked.

Wasn't that a good sign? "Weapons," he said, pointing at the gun in the grass he'd used as a model. "Like the one Dyan used to kill the Overseer."

Anji nodded. "You're going to bluff."

"Yes. The three of us should each carry a real gun, and one more person you trust."

Anji shook her head. "No, to make the bluff stronger, you and I need to hold fake guns. And we need someone who looks like the least responsible, least trustworthy person to have and use a real gun. And preferably kill an Outrider the first time."

Jak considered her point, but only briefly; she was right. "I'll hold a fake. But I want you holding a real one, and Dyan, too. And tell me who else should."

"Zo and Taryl." Anji indicated the two Gardeners Jak had just met. "They're as good as anyone else, and you can see how much energy they've put into pitching in."

"Okay," Jak agreed. "Dyan, can you teach these three the basics? I'll check our little gun-craftery's output, and then we need a brief organizational meeting." He looked up and down river. The arrival of the System's agents had to be imminent.

Dyan showed Anji, Zo, and Taryl how to shoot the guns, and loaded bullets into each of their weapons. Jak surveyed the work accomplished.

Twelve fake guns.

Twelve carved knobbly bits of wood vaguely resembling guns, shining and wet from their new black paint jobs.

Jak took a deep breath. It would have to do.

He looked up and down the river. Still no sign of an Outrider or a Guardsman. How was that even possible?

Maybe it was deliberate.

Something about that thought nagged at the back of his mind, but it didn't catch and he didn't have time to chase it.

"Okay, everyone over here!" he called.

The Gardeners assembled around Jak. Even of the fake guns, Jak had enough to pretend to arm only about one person in ten. It would have to do. Counting and pointing, he selected eleven people who looked firm, competent, and resolute. He chose people with the kinds of faces he would expect to be armed.

"You will each pick up a gun as we march. Remember, hold them as if they were weapons." Jak picked up one of the fake guns himself and demonstrated how to hold it. "This end down here is the end from which lethal fire is supposed to come, so treat that end as if it's dangerous. Point it always forward, or at the sky, or an enemy."

"A Systemoid," muttered one of Jak's chosen eleven, and spat on the grass. That was interesting. Did the Gardeners not think of themselves as part of the System?

"We're going to come to a conflict. In fact, I'm going to provoke a conflict, but I'm going to try very hard to make sure the conflict is short and ends in our favor. Point your guns, but don't pretend to use them. If you fake an attack—the word for attacking with a gun is *shoot*, by the way, just like with a bow—if you shoot, but fire doesn't come from the weapon and your targets don't get hurt, you've spoiled the bluff."

"And what do we do if we're attacked?"

Jak shook his head. "Well, this fake gun is useless as a weapon. So unless someone comes close enough to be clubbed, I suggest you run away."

"I'm not sure I like the sound of this plan." This from a man with a heavy forehead and powerful arms.

"It isn't perfect," Jak admitted.

"But it's the only plan there is." Headman Anji stepped to Jak's side, holding her very real, loaded, deadly gun cradled in both arms. If she was even half as uncomfortable as Jak was, she must be terrified, but she did a great job of hiding it. She looked calm and confident.

She was the right person to be Headman of Whitwark Bothy. But more, the fact that she was stuck in the Bothy rather than, say, teaching children in a Creche or leading Outriders to hunt down renegades in the Jawtooths showed how broken the System was.

What was wrong with her? Why had she been identified as Wrongborn in the Cradle? It wasn't anything visible. Maybe she had something wrong with her internal organs, or an allergy. Were all the Crechelings physically perfect? How big did an ... irregularity ... have to be before it put a baby in the Wrongborn Cradle?

Jak shook the questions out of his head. Time for those later.

"It's the only plan there is," Headman Anji repeated. "And it's going to get us out of here."

"And then where will you go?" This was a new voice from the back of the crowd, and even though Jak recognized the voice, it took a moment for the Gardeners to part so Jak could see the face.

Tulit.

But hadn't he left?

"Where will you go?" Tulit repeated. "None of you knows the world beyond the System's walls."

"I know it," Jak said. He wanted to walk forward and club Tulit in the face with his wooden gun, but he stood still and tried to look persuasive instead. "There are farms, Tulit. Empty land to put new farms in. Places where you can grow your own food. Relax without being whipped for being lazy. Be free."

"Have children." Jak barely caught the murmured words, and it took him a moment to realize it was Headman Anji talking.

"Herd animals," Jak continued. "Trade. Live life without fear that someone will slice you to pieces for their own entertainment."

"Are you saying the Shoshan never slice anyone to pieces?"

"Funvids!" Anji snorted.

"Well," Jak said slowly, "no, people get killed, outside the System as well as inside. And sometimes, if you run afoul of the Basku or the Shoshan, yeah, they might hurt you. And there really are outlaws in the Wahai." He shook his head, remembering some of his own close scrapes with death. "And Ka-Yoss and Wallalla and I don't know what else. So there are dangers."

He looked over the heads of the Gardeners, still baffled the System hadn't yet reacted to the Overseer's death. Maybe this was evidence of Jak's paranoia, proof the Overseer's tools hadn't recorded the man's death and informed anyone of it.

"So I'm hearing that your offer is still a life of work and danger."

"Yes," Jak agreed. "I don't know any other kind."

"But different dangers!" Headman Anji practically shouted. "Dangers you *choose*, rather than dangers *imposed* on you by someone else. And a life of meaning! A life where you can build something for yourself, for your family, and not just keep the paths neat for the System."

Jak wanted to put his arm around the Headman, and he wasn't sure whether it was to console her or out of his own feeling of relief.

"Yeah," Tulit called, "but—"

At that moment, the Gardener with the heavy forehead punched Tulit in the nose. Tulit went down and lay in the grass, whimpering.

Jak took the blow as his cue. "If you want to stay, stay. Those who are leaving, follow me."

He organized them as they walked, putting Dyan and Anji at the two front corners of the column and Zo and Taryl at the back. He and the other eleven people carrying false guns were dispersed along the column with instructions to look and point the guns outward.

"Bother no one who doesn't bother you!" Jak cried. "Remember, if they don't know what guns are and haven't discovered the Overseer's death, they may think we're just traveling to cut down some trees."

Except for the baby, of course. Jak took Zarah and slung her from his shoulder. Gardeners didn't carry babies around with them, as far as he had ever seen. But he wasn't about to abandon his child now.

Setting aside his fears as best he could, Jak discussed his plan with Dyan, Anji, Zo, and Taryl. His proposal got raised eyebrows and a whistle or two, but ultimately won nods of assent.

Then he led the march, up the Buza River.

He headed for the gate nearest where he and Dyan had entered the System. One response the System might have was simply to wait until Jak and the Gardeners approached a gate and then shut it. But only a few hours had passed, and he was counting on the likelihood that no one had noticed or repaired the gap he and Dyan had made in the bars where the river flowed under the walls.

He planned to walk out, but if they had to wade, he would.

No one molested them. Very few people even noticed them. The System was used to seeing groups of Gardeners marching about with unknown tools in their hands; the effect of wearing the uniform, again.

The armed column of Gardeners walked along the river right through the center of the System, past the Cradle, the Garage, and the Prison, and then the column followed Jak out of the riverbed and walked toward the System's south-facing gate.

"Be ready," Jak said.

Everyone in earshot nodded. Dyan and Anji tightened their grips on their guns.

"I count two on top of the walls," Headman Anji said. "Two in front of the gate on horseback. Are you sure you don't want me to shoot one?" Jak couldn't tell whether the slight tremor in her voice came from trepidation or enthusiasm.

The sun was climbing down in the west, and other than the four Guardsmen, there was no one in sight. Mealtime.

"Nope." Jak leaned back to whisper to the next person in line. "When Dyan fires, point your gun at one of the two Guardsmen on top of the wall. Pass it on."

He heard the murmur of his instruction being passed back.

One of the Guardsmen rode forward. The Captain. As the Guardsman's eyes scanned the column in front of him and took in the fact that they were all Gardeners, he loosened his vibro-blade sword slightly in its sheath.

"You have written orders to show me that would take you out of the System?" the Guardsman gruffed. He was muscular, with a strong chin and nose, and his eyes flashed with confidence. Jak hated him immediately.

"Hello," Jak called back, waving his hand. "Now!"

"Now?" The Guardsman rested his hand on the hilt of his sword and frowned.

Boom! Boom! Boom!

The Guardsman's horse screamed and reared back in surprise, throwing its rider off. The Guardsman hit the ground, the impact throwing up spurts of bright red blood. Then he lay still.

Immediately, Dyan and Anji pointed their guns at the second horseman. Every other gun in the column but Jak's, real and fake, tilted up to point at the two men standing on the walls.

"Stop!" Jak stepped forward into the space between the column of Gardeners and the gate, careful not to position himself directly in front of Dyan's or Anji's gun. "Stop, no one else has to die!"

The mounted Guardsman controlled his horse with an effort. Spooked by the sound of the gun, the animal was trying to bolt. "Blazes!" the Guardsman bellowed. "Die! Die? Is Sholk dead? Sholk? Sholk!"

"Sholk's dead." To prove it, Jak stepped over to Sholk's corpse and kicked it in the temple.

"Who are you?" The living Guardsman's eyes blazed with fury.

Jak hadn't intended to introduce himself, but he felt some pride at being asked the question. Plus, the fact that Outriders Neko and Pelft had known him by name suggested the name *Jak* had become a name to conjure within the System. He straightened to his full height. "My name is Jak, son of Rosyn. I'm sorry I had to kill Sholk, but I needed you to understand we are armed with deadly weapons, to avoid more serious loss of life."

The Guardsman squinted. "What are those things?"

Jak considered. If they knew the name guns only as folklore, as Jak had as a boy, the word might strike fear into his enemies. On the other hand, someone in the System might actually know what a *gun* was. Since this man didn't recognize the guns, Jak decided to rely on fear and ignorance.

"You don't need to worry about what they are," he said. "All you need to know is that they're nasty weapons. But if you let us pass, we won't hurt anyone."

He could see in the Guardsman's eyes the calculations rattling inside the man's head. Jak's Gardeners seemed to have sixteen of these lethal weapons, whatever they were, or more than five for each armed Guardsman.

"Tell your men to drop their weapons on the ground," Jak said. "Swords and bolas, bows and whips if they have them."

A last fantasy of resistance flashed in the Guardsman's eyes and then died. "Drop your weapons!" he called to his men. "All of them!"

CHAPTER TWENTY-ONE

J|ak took the horses, too; including two picketed to one side, there were four of them.

A quick question confirmed his intuition that none of the Gardeners knew how to ride, so he and Dyan mounted. Jak kept his false gun, holding it across his saddle in front of him, but he kept one hand near the bola in his pocket.

He kept Zarah with him. Her crying quickly subsided to a low fussing mewl.

"We need a scout before and behind," he said to Anji and Dyan.

Anji said nothing, just handed the gun to the Gardener standing next to her. Then she climbed on the nearest horse.

Jak would have laughed out loud at the awkward sight of Whitwark Bothy's Headman levering herself up the stirrup with both hands and legs as the horse shied away and whickered a complaint, only he was no great rider himself and he knew how much courage was involved in her action.

Once she was in the saddle, she took back the gun. She gave the animal too much rein and it shied from side to side, swinging its long head to see how much it would get away with, but she had a fierce light in her eyes.

"I'll take the rear," she said.

"I'll ride with you," Jak said immediately. "Dyan?"

D.J. Butler

Dyan nodded and led out. Her horse's brisk trot quickly pulled her out ahead of the column crawling in her wake.

Jak and Anji turned back to the three Guardsmen, who stood with their fingers locked together behind their heads.

"Sholk, was it?" Jak asked.

"Sholk's the dead man," the Guardsman said, slitting his eyes. "Sholk's the reason you're all going to hang."

Jak chuckled. "Liar. If you had your way, you'd kill me on the spot. Slice me to pieces, stab me through the eye, wouldn't you?" He snorted. "I'd never live long enough to be hanged."

The Guardsman growled. "Landsy, are you?"

A faint alarm bell rang in the back of Jak's head, but the adrenalin rushing through him manifested itself as a manic need to be witty and he pushed on. "No, on second thought, you'll keep the five worst offenders to hang, publicly. That's what you do, isn't it? You have to show everyone who's in charge, all the time, so you kill people. So you'll hang me, if you can resist the urge to skewer me on the spot, and maybe the Headman here, and three others."

"Headman?" The Guardsman arched his eyebrows and turned to look at Anji.

"The rest of us you'll just slice to pieces. Hey, maybe you can use us for target practice. Or instead of sending your Creche-leavers all the way out in the desert to find victims, you can just deliver some right to their doorsteps. It would take some of the mystery out of the whole thing, I grant you, but it would be efficient."

The Guardsman grinned, a brutal look full of sweat and murder. "Oh, I think we'll manage to save you for something special."

Boom!

The Guardsman fell over backward, blood spurting from his neck.

Zarah shrieked.

Jak's brain was slow to process what was happening. Even before he could realize that Anji had shot the Guardsman, she had turned in the saddle to shoot the second. He took the blow in his stomach and fell facedown.

The third Guardsman turned to run. *Boom! Boom! Boom!* Anji's shooting hit him twice, once in the thigh and once between the shoulders.

Jak stared at Anji. Two of the Guardsmen lay still, but the one who'd been shot in the stomach was screaming.

"We didn't need to kill them," he said.

"We didn't," Anji agreed. "Until you started telling them who we were." She pointed at the last Guardsman. "Now he has to die, too." She raised the gun to her shoulder again.

"Wait!" Jak handed her his reins and climbed down off the horse. He had no one to hand Baby Zarah to, and she was howling and shaking, so it was a rough descent. "We only have a limited number of bullets."

Anji nodded. Jak armed his bola and sent it into the dirt right through the fallen Guardsman's neck.

For good measure, he took his bola to the bodies of the other three Guardsmen. Holding the bola and its counterweight in his two hands, he neatly severed each of their heads.

Then he wobbled on unsteady legs to the water. Standing in the shallows of the Buza River and pulling Zarah to one side to keep her clean, he vomited until he could vomit no more.

He was weak, but he managed to climb back in the saddle, even with the raging infant on his chest.

"I'm a terrible father," he muttered. He hoped the noise of the shooting hadn't permanently damaged Baby Zarah's hearing.

"Maybe," Anji said. "But I think there's a pretty good argument you're doing right by that child."

Jak smiled weakly. "You're right," he admitted to Anji, taking back his reins. "They'll figure out who we are eventually, but we don't need to make it any easier for them."

Anji nodded. "Now, show me how to make this horse go in the direction I want."

Jak shushed Zarah, but the baby would not be consoled. He laughed, cringing at the sour reek of vomit on his own breath. "It's not hard. But you have to pull the reins in tighter."

"It won't hurt the horse?" Anji did as Jak showed her, shortening the reins. Her horse shook its head once in protest and then calmed down.

"I don't think the horse likes it," Jak said. "But if you only did what the horse liked, you'd take off its saddle and bridle and let it run free."

It was Anji's turn to laugh. "In principle, I think I would prefer to let the horse run free. But right now, I need to go faster than a walk."

Jak took a long last look at the System. He had come here days earlier with Dyan, hoping to rescue her mother. Instead, Dyan's mother Zarah had died, and he and Dyan had come away with a blemish-faced Wrongborn baby they had named after the dead Magister. Now, standing in the System's gate, Jak saw and smelled corpses. The four dead Guardsmen struck him as a perfect summary of his experience with life in the System's shadow and what he knew of its inner workings: boundaries, restrictions, control, and murder.

His choices had been limited from birth, partly because everyone's choices are limited, but partly because the System had forced his hand repeatedly.

Still, when his hand had been forced, Jak had willingly killed.

So in the end, was he any different from the Systemoids?

Something … something about Zarah bothered him. Not the baby, the Magister. As Jak thought back through her final hours, it all felt wrong. Too convenient. Too … right.

Jak gave up trying to think it through. He was a hollow shell of a human being. Burned out, dried up. Jak felt like the sea of tall dead grass stretching out at his shoulders.

Baby Zarah continued to cry. Jak opened the sling a hand's breadth to look at her face; the Wrongborn child was howling at full volume, and he suspected she would cry louder until she was fed.

Jak laughed. In that moment, as he hadn't before, he knew why he and Dyan had taken the baby.

"Okay, Headman," he said. "I think the rest of our people have gotten enough of a head start now."

They rode slowly, keeping an eye over their shoulders for any sign of a response from the System. The sun was on the western horizon now, which turned the System's walls black and fearsome, but it also made the lights beginning to spark into view within them more striking.

There was life there, Jak knew, but it was hard and cold life.

"Don't call me *Headman*," Anji said after a few minutes of silence.

"You're the natural leader here," Jak said.

"Aren't *you*?"

Jak laughed. "I'm nobody. I'm just the person who survived when he wasn't supposed to."

"More than once. I'd say that's an impressive qualification for leadership."

"But these people have known you as their Headman."

Anji nodded. "All their lives, some of them. But it was the System that put me in charge of them."

"I see. You don't want to be the leader just because the System thought you should be."

"I don't want to be the leader *at all*. Leadership is a heavy burden." Jak heard a hint of a sob in Anji's voice. "But whoever is going to be leader, we should decide together. And we shouldn't call that person Headman."

"Agreed." Jak pondered. "And we should also agree rules for deciding who's going to be leader in the future."

"Once we get to safety," Anji said. "Until then, you and Dyan are leading us." She laughed suddenly. "Tulit was right. None of the rest of us has any idea where to go."

"I know a place," Jak said. He was thinking of Farkill, with its walls and, with a little luck, maybe additional troves of guns and bullets. "*We* know a place."

"There is one thing I would like very much, though," Anji said. "Something I've always wanted to do, and I've never been able. And I hope you'll let me do it now."

Jak looked back at the System. No lights at the gate, which suggested they still had not been discovered. Discovery was inevitable, but the longer the delay, the happier Jak was. "Sure," he said, distracted. "Tell me what you have in mind."

Anji's voice was soft. "I want to hold the baby."

Jak snapped his head around. The request surprised him, though once he heard it, it seemed obvious. Baby Zarah's crying was beginning to get louder.

"I'll make you a deal," he said. "If you trade me, I'll hold the gun for a few minutes and you can feed the baby."

In the last light of the day, Anji's eyes twinkled as she nodded.

It was an awkward transfer, but they managed to swap the gun and the baby in her sling, and then Jak handed over an avocado and took the reins of Anji's horse. "Her name is Zarah."

"Zarah." Anji dug into the avocado and fed a sliver to the baby. "She's perfect."

"Yeah," Jak said. "Kind of, she is."

"We need another new name," Anji said as she fed Zarah a second sliver. "We need a new name for the leader, but we also need a new name for the people. All the names we have are corrupt."

"Systemoid," Jak said. "Landsy."

"Gardener."

"Do you have an idea?" He suspected she did.

"We should name them after this child," Anji suggested. "The People of Zarah."

"That's an interesting suggestion," Jak said. "What makes you think of it?"

"This child is a free child. She was Wrongborn, but she will never know the fate of being Wrongborn. She won't dig ditches, nor be whipped for a mistake. She won't be forced to take another's life. She will never know the System and all its cruelty, not if I can help it."

"Zarah's folk," Jak said. "The Zaraites. The Zaru. The Zaran."

"I like Zaru," Anji, no longer Headman, said.

"We'll have to ask the others what they think."

Baby Zarah, unaware that a people was about to be named after her, had a full belly and turned her face away from more avocado. Anji put the child on her shoulder and patted her back until she burped. Then she loaded the child into her sling and took back her horse's reins.

"You don't want the gun?" Jak asked.

"I'd rather you hold it," Anji said. "I'm tired of death."

"I'm tired of death, too," Jak said. "I really hope death is tired of us."

"Somehow, I doubt it. Isn't that light in the gate we left?"

It was. They turned and rode to catch up with the People of Zarah.

*   *   *

They marched through the night.

Jak wished he hadn't sold the Outriders' gear to Orvyl Rich when he was in Marsick. One piece of equipment every Outrider carried was a pair of goggles that allowed its wearer to see heat sources, or on a different setting to see very well at night. With such goggles, Jak could look back and see a pursuing mass of Guardsmen or Outriders as a red blot on the land, unmistakable. He would know whether or not he was being hunted, and by how many people, and where his pursuers were.

Lacking that knowledge, he lived with fear and guesses.

And of course, if the People of Zarah were being pursued, their pursuers almost certainly included Outriders wearing such goggles. So if they were being followed, their pursuers knew just where they were.

Jak compensated by choosing rough trails. Once he and Dyan had switched positions, he led the people off the road. Crossing gullies and ruins, he deliberately chose every possible terrain that was easier for a person on foot than a mounted rider. It made his own ride challenging, especially since he was a mediocre horseman at best, but it also might slow the pursuit.

They rested only briefly, Jak driving people out of their rest before anyone could sleep more than a few minutes. They slowed down, but kept going, the column dragging out into a longer and longer string, through the next day and night. The horses didn't make it past noon of the first day, and had to be let go.

When the sun rose on the morning of the second day, Jak stood in the water of the Snaik River, looking back down river in the direction they'd come. In the blue shadows of morning, he saw no Outriders. He wished he could be sure there weren't any evading his gaze.

His head felt full of dust.

"We need rest," Dyan said.

"I doubt the Outriders will be resting." Jak took the baby from Anji, who had done as much carrying as he and Dyan had. She resisted giving Zarah up, just a little, until Jak smiled and patted her arm. Once the sling was off her shoulder, she straightened her back and cursed discreetly.

"The people need rest." This came from Tulit. He stood on the firm sandbank running along the edge of the river and he held a heavy stick in his hand.

"You're tired," Jak agreed. "We're all tired. But at night—if we're close to the Outriders at night, they have technology that makes us very easy to see. So we need to take advantage of the daylight and the river to get as far away from them as possible."

"Again?" Tulit thumped his stick into the palm of his hand. "For what? And for how long?"

"As long as it takes," Jak shot back.

"To escape," Dyan said. "To live a life not ruled by the System."

"That's right." Tulit pointed his stick at Jak. "But living a life ruled by *him* wouldn't be any better, I say."

Jak put his hand on his bola ... and then thought better of it.

He wanted to cut Tulit down, or shoot him. But that would make Jak no different from the Outriders and Guardsmen of the System.

"You're wrong, Tulit," he said. "But you're also free. If you want to go back ... or if you want to go somewhere else ... go ahead. Nobody will stop you."

Tulit paced in a short circle and looked around at the faces of the others who had once comprised Whitwark Bothy. "I say no rulers," he said. "No System. I say freedom." He pointed his stick upriver. "And I'm going that way. There was a canyon on the western side, just a few minutes' back. Anybody who wants to come with me is welcome." He snarled at Jak. "The first thing we're going to do is *sleep*."

Jak almost laughed out loud as Tulit turned and sloshed back into the river, heading off on his own. Did the Gardener think he had the skills he needed to live in the wilderness? Did he know how to get somewhere where food and shelter could be had?

But then others followed.

Not many. Jak counted a dozen people who turned their backs and trudged away. He saw fear on some of their faces, sorrow on some, and anger on others. He felt a hollow feeling in the pit of his stomach.

"Good luck!" Dyan called. "Mother go with you!"

The words sounded natural in her mouth.

Jak turned back to face those who had stayed. Already in his mind he was calling them the Zaru, though they had not agreed to it yet, or even been informed. Their faces showed fatigue, concern ...

... and hope.

"Okay," Jak said. "We need to figure out what we're going to do when the Outriders show up."

CHAPTER TWENTY-TWO

Jak set a trap within a trap.

Jak had his people walk up the canyon out of the Snaik, then march back down, then climb out again, to maximize the trail they left. He even tore a shred off his own stolen Gardener uniform and snagged it on a fallen tree.

"That's clumsy," Anji said, looking down the red rock cliff at the disturbed earth and grass. "And isn't it obvious, too? I mean, that looks like five hundred people marched up that canyon."

Jak finished laying out the third decoy. He'd shaped the decoys out of heaped-up sand, rocks, and sticks, and he'd dressed them in Gardener's uniforms—he and two of the other men were now stripped to breeches only, which felt good at first, but within a few hours their flesh would be roasting from their bodies.

But he kept moving. Every time Jak stopped moving, he had to fight sleep.

The decoys looked like human beings, lying on their bellies. And they held three of the fake guns. From even twenty feet away, Jak thought, they looked passably real.

From down in the canyon, he was sure they looked like Gardeners with guns, lying in wait.

"It *is* obvious," he agreed. "And if they fall for those tracks, we won't even see them. If they fail to notice the decoys here and just march up the canyon, they'll pass us by and the trap will fail."

Anji frowned.

"I'm counting on them giving me credit. Us. I'm counting on the Outriders treating us with a little respect. We escaped the System, after all."

"Only we haven't," Taryl said. "Not yet. Not really. Or we wouldn't be doing this."

"Okay, but we walked out and we got this far. So I think they'll expect us to be reasonably clever. I'm just counting on them not giving us more than a *little* credit. I'm counting on them thinking we're cunning, but not clever."

"In other words ..." Zo pointed at the four shallow pits Jak and his team had dug. "We hide in the pits. The Outriders see the clumsy trail, realize it's a trap, and so they sneak around to the top of the bluffs some other way—"

"There's another climb out just half an hour's walk downstream."

"Right," Zo continued. "So they take the other trail and sneak up on the ambush party, only to discover the ambush party isn't real. Fake people, like the fake guns."

"And then we spring from hiding," Taryl finished the story. "And with any luck, we don't have to fight, because we completely surprise them and they're at our mercy."

Jak frowned. "Well, probably not quite. I suspect they still don't know what the guns are."

"Have I mentioned I like the guns?" Taryl's eyes gleamed.

Jak chuckled. "Yes. But I made a mistake. Because of me," he carefully met Anji's gaze to emphasize his own responsibility, "we had to kill all the Guardsmen back at the south gate. But that means we didn't leave any witnesses to the power of our guns. So we're going to have to kill one of them again."

"Just one this time," Anji said.

"Just one," Dyan confirmed. She held Baby Zarah in her sling, and she was also armed with a whip and two bolas. The holsters and their belt looked strange over her brown Gardener's outfit. "We're going to kill one, then disarm the others and leave them stranded. That will give us enough of a head start to really get away."

Jak nodded, though in his heart he disagreed. He didn't see there being just one more death in the future. He didn't see there being anything but a bottomless pit of murder.

He was still going to try.

"But if I understand this correctly," Zo said, "and the Outriders really think you're an idiot—"

"They won't," Jak said.

"They might," Zo shot back.

"I'm counting on the fact that we've broken people out of their Old Pen and freed a bunch of ... freed Whitwark Bothy. They know me by name.".

"And if they know you by name and think you're an idiot, they're going to march up this canyon, and come right up on the heels on the rest of the Zaru and slaughter them as they march to this place Farkill." Zo was one of the first people to start really using the name *Zaru* after Jak had proposed it to them. Probably because it sounded a little like her own name. "Or as they sleep, which seems more likely."

"That's the risk," Jak said. "You're right. We'll post a lookout, so if the Outriders come up the canyon, we get warning here, and then we'll just have to sneak up on the Outriders from behind."

"It won't be as easy," Zo said.

"Yeah," Jak agreed. "That's why it's the *backup* plan."

"I'm a fast runner," Zo said. "That's why I'm pointing this out. I'd be a good lookout. I can outrun a horse."

Jak frowned. She couldn't be *that* fast, but he wasn't going to argue, especially since Zo's chest was puffed out with pride at her speed. "You also know how to shoot the gun. If you're the lookout and the plan works, the Outriders won't come up the canyon to your position and you won't be part of the ambush."

"You're forgetting the genius of guns," Dyan said. She stepped over to Zo and held out her hands, taking the gun from the other woman.

"Remind me," Jak said.

"They're easy to use. Who wants to learn to use one next?"

One of the Zaru, the heavy-browed man who had punched Tulit in the face back at the site of the Overseer's death, raised his hand. "Molek," he said to introduce himself before he was asked.

Dyan stepped aside with Molek, handing him the gun and going over the basics he would need to understand.

"Go." Jak nodded to Zo. "Hide at the top of the canyon. If you see Systemoids start coming up the canyon, stay down and out of sight, but run this way."

"And if I hear the guns shooting?"

Jak grinned. "Wait to see who's still alive. If the plan fails, you'll have to be the messenger who runs to report it to the others."

He was beginning to feel like a holy day roasting pig, but he kept his smile on as the young woman raced off over the rocks. She had taken her shoes off sometime during the march, or maybe they had worn off, but it didn't slow her down. He watched her run like an antelope until she disappeared in a knot of evergreens at the top of the canyon.

"That's it," Jak announced to the others. "Time to hide."

He wished he could creep to the edge of the canyon and look down to see what the Outriders did, rather than rely on guesses and messengers. The cliff here was treacherous, though; it bowed out before curving back in, so Jak couldn't get to anyplace where he could actually see the river, short of jumping off the cliff.

He'd tried.

So he took a false gun, reassured himself that the real bolas once in his pockets were now sitting on the ground within easy reach, and then climbed down into his pit.

"Remember!" he yelled one last word of advice. "Don't fall asleep."

It was necessary. They were all exhausted.

Then he and Taryl pulled the cover over the top of them. It was woven of branches and had dried sod stretched on top of it, bristling with yellow grass. The cover wouldn't pass the most casual inspection by a person standing next to it, but a person who wasn't actively inspecting the grass for an ambush would probably ride right past without noticing anything.

He was counting on the Outriders to do that.

He laughed.

"What do you find so funny?" Taryl asked. In the faint cracks of light filtering down through the cover, his face looked suspicious.

Jak shook his head. "I don't know. I'm counting on a lot of things happening just right. I'm counting on the Systemoids to have respect for my cunning, but not too much! Counting on them not to notice the blinds, or to realize before they get close that the decoys aren't human. Counting on them to react with fear to the guns. Counting on the System not to have sent too large a party after us."

Taryl nodded. "Counting on us not to miss. For that matter, counting on people like Molek and Anji and me not to take the guns and shoot you."

"I hadn't thought of that."

Taryl chuckled in the shadow.

"Anyway," Jak continued. "Just making plans and hoping for luck; it feels like it's all I can do."

"You know what's worse than having to plan and hope for luck, though?"

"Tell me."

"Not being allowed to plan. And knowing there isn't luck enough in the whole wide world to change your situation."

"Yeah," Jak agreed. "That *is* worse."

He felt better. They fell silent and waited.

They had a skin of water in the pit, and Jak resisted taking sips just to relieve boredom. The sun was blocked by the sod roof he'd pulled over his hiding hole, but the air in the pit was stale and dead. He sweated, Taryl sweated, and Jak longed for a breeze to cool them.

Every few minutes he'd poke the other man in the chest, to remind them both to stay awake. After the first few pokes, Taryl started poking him back.

Jak couldn't even crack a joke, for fear the Outriders were close by and undetected.

Eirig would have had a whole string of jokes to crack, huddled in this pit with a near stranger.

Silently, Jak brushed stinging tears away from his eyes and took a drink.

Taryl cocked a finger suddenly, pointing up and to his side and touching an ear with his other hand. Jak listened, and heard it: footsteps.

Not just feet, *boots*. Jak recognized the crunch of sand underfoot from his short time dressed as an Outrider, the crunch that only comes from the flat, wide, heavy sole of serious footgear. And from multiple feet, judging by the sound.

Jak nodded and tightened his grip on the false gun. The signal here was not to come from him, because his gun was false and useful only as a bluff.

If it was even *that* useful.

The signal was to come from Dyan.

Jak listened. Booted feet passed close by his hiding place. He realized he was also counting on the Outriders to not actually step on top of any of the covered pits—an Outrider disappearing into the ground would put a sudden stop to the planned ambush.

"Don't move!" An unknown voice barked.

Boom!

As planned, Jak threw off the cover. Taryl's gun was real, so it was important to get it deployed as soon as possible, just in case the ambush devolved into an actual fight. Jak pushed up at the woven lattice of branches with his fake gun and hurled the cover aside, dropping back into place at the lip of the pit with the fake pointed like a weapon.

Just in case, Jak and Taryl were one of the ambush teams who came from hiding facing away from the cliff, to look for any lingering rearguard of the Outrider party. Above them and all the way to the horizon lay nothing but red rock, sand, and the tenacious yellow-green scrub plants clinging to the tops of the canyon walls above the Snaik.

"Don't move!" This time the voice was Dyan's.

Spinning in opposite directions, Jak and Taryl both swung around to look at the site of the action. When he landed, Jak's elbows were planted right next to the bolas in the dirt and the ostensibly dangerous end of his fake weapon pointed toward six Outriders, standing a few paces from his decoys.

Five of them, rather, were standing. A sixth lay on the ground, clutching his chest. Blood flowed around his fingers.

"Or what?" one of the Outriders asked. Jak knew the voice, and when he focused on the face he almost dropped his gun in surprise.

It was Shad, the young Outrider who had been Dyan's Crechemate. She had wanted to be Love-Matched with him not very many weeks ago. Shad had his hands away from his holsters, but not far enough away for Jak's liking.

"Mother blast you, you Systemoid murderer!" Jak shouted. "If you say *capture or kill* even one time, I'll shoot you myself!"

Shad raised his hands a little higher.

"What are those things?" This question came from Cheela, who stood next to Shad. Jak's eye jumped to her forearm where it had been severed in the System's Old Pen, leaving her with only one hand and a surprisingly neat scar.

Not unlike Eirig had had.

Eirig, whom she had killed, though he had been unarmed and harmless.

For that matter, there were Zaru who had been designated Wrongborn at birth for the fact that they lacked a hand.

Something was different about Cheela's face, but Jak didn't have time to think about it.

"They're guns!" Jak yelled. "They're the death of the System!"

"Death to the System!" Taryl yelled at Jak's shoulder.

"Death to the System!" someone else cried, but then Dyan shushed the Zaru ambush party.

Jak regretted the shushing. He liked the sound of *Death to the System*.

"We're going to let you go." Jak kept his voice level. "We're just going to disarm you and send you back. We don't want to be followed."

A tall Outrider with stringy white hair and a drooping mustache snorted. "If you could have killed us, you'd have done it already," he grunted, and he went for his monofilament whip.

Boom!

The shot came from Anji's gun, not Dyan's. She hit the Outrider in his knee and he fell to the ground, screaming.

Anji's face showed not a flicker of emotion.

"Drop all your weapons," Dyan said.

This was the moment of truth. If they disarmed, the fight was over. Jak held his pose with his fake weapon, feeling beads of sweat trickle down his nose and between his bare shoulders like stinging insects.

Shad exhaled through clenched teeth, unbuckled his weapon belt, and dropped it to the dirt.

The other standing Outriders did the same, and then Jak clambered out of his hole to collect all their weapons. The Outrider with the ruined knee bit his own lip and glared, but he didn't resist and Jak disarmed him.

"Don't worry," Jak growled at him. "They'll fix you up in no time."

Jak saw Dyan staring. She had a faraway look in her face, as she sometimes did when she was thinking something complicated.

Or *feeling* something complicated.

Jak dropped the whips and bolas into a pile and then watched it as his party climbed out of their pits one at a time.

Dyan emerged last, and as she stood, she brushed dirt off her knees, turned to face the Outriders with her gun still pointed at them, and made an announcement. "Change of plan," she said.

Jak said nothing. He shot a glance at Anji and met her eyes, but he couldn't read Anji's expression. Who was really in charge here?

For the moment, Dyan.

"You don't have to kill us, Dyan," Shad said.

"True," she agreed. "Though I don't for a moment have the illusion you would spare my life if our situations were reversed. Jak's right about you. You say 'capture,' but you always kill."

Shad said nothing.

"Treat your wounded," Dyan said. "We're sending them back on their own horses. The other four of you will stay with us."

"The System won't care about hostages," Cheela said. "It's perfectly willing to sacrifice us if it must." Jak turned to her expecting an expression of twisted and animal hatred, and instead saw something else. Sadness. *Uncertainty*, maybe.

As if she could read Jak's thoughts, Cheela set her jaw and frowned.

"I am certain the System is willing to let you die," Dyan agreed. She looked Cheela in the face, and something passed between them that Jak couldn't read. "But maybe instead it will be willing to make a trade."

CHAPTER TWENTY-THREE

T he next morning, the Zaru gained new recruits.

Jak met them first. He was riding out along the canyon top with Zo, scouting out the road to Farkill. There was no obvious path on this side of the cliffs, so they were picking a route both sheltered and easy to travel.

Jak didn't plan to settle at Farkill. He had no idea how long they might stay there, but if nothing else they might be able to get more guns out of the avatar's secret chamber. Having a weapon anyone could be easily trained to use was fantastic, but having only four of them was a serious limitation—it meant every fight had to be a bluff, and Jak could only win by carefully springing ambushes or staging standoffs.

If every one of the Zaru ... would that be *every Zar?* Jak wondered; he'd never been part of naming anything as significant as a people before, and he rode a little straighter in the saddle asking himself questions like these. If every Zar had a gun, Jak would feel a lot more secure.

And more bullets. Jak wanted sacks and sacks of bullets.

Could he figure out how to manufacture guns? Might Dyan already know how, from the visionary briefing she'd received from the avatar of the Airfo Space? Or maybe they could get in touch with the avatar again, and it could show *Jak* a factvid on the subject. How hard could it be?

This was Zo's first ride on horseback and she bounced much more than she should, from energy or enthusiasm; she'd get sore and chafed. That would be fine, she'd learn.

Just as Farkill came into sight on the far side of the river, a woman stumbled into Jak's path. He hadn't seen her until she loomed up immediately in front of his horse, and he reined the animal in sharply, narrowly avoiding an incident.

The woman looked exhausted, but otherwise she didn't look like a refugee. She was dirty, but her clothing was neat and sturdy. It was traveling clothing, a cloak and good shoes, but it was the traveling clothing of a Goody from a decent town. She waved her arms, and Jak's heart raced.

He knew her.

"Goody Barrab!" Jak slipped down off his horse, tossing the reins to Zo. Zo nearly fell off the horse, but managed to keep both animals basically in line.

Jak grabbed Barrab by her forearms and found himself supporting her entire weight as she collapsed against him. She was frailer than he was used to seeing her, with a face shattered by care under her gray hair, drawn tightly back and braided behind her head. No wonder there—her son Hamish had been Selected along with Jak, and unlike Jak, Hamish had not survived the experience.

Except she shouldn't know about Hamish's death. Jak had been careful not to let word of his survival get back to Ratsnay Station. As far as Goody Barrab knew, her son was living as a Systemoid in Treasure Valley.

An Urbane.

"What are you doing out here?" Jak asked. Uselessly, he looked out beyond Farkill to the far side of the valley where Ratsnay Station lay, invisible to his eyes.

Barrab opened her eyes; she looked like a deer surprised by a hunter. "Jak?"

Jak was torn. The sight of Hamish's mother made him want to weep for the loss of Hamish; it also made him think of his home and his own mother, and he found an unexpected flood of tears welling up within him. On the other hand, he had been strict in avoiding contact with the people of his home, as a way to protect them. If the people of Ratsnay Station learned the truth about the Cull, he feared, the System would decide to eliminate them.

And now here was Goody Barrab.

"I'm alive," was all he could say. He managed not to shed any actual tears.

She stared into his face. "And my Hamish?"

He hesitated. "I'm sorry," he finally said. Part of him wanted to lie, but he couldn't bring himself to do it. He couldn't bring himself to support the murderous castle of falsehoods the System had built, but more importantly he couldn't lie to this woman he'd known all his life, and tell her Hamish was happily building machines in Buza System. "I'm sorry," he said again. "He's dead."

"Jak!"

This was a new voice, and one Jak knew very well. He turned and saw the depression from which Barrab had emerged, and from which nearly a dozen people now crawled. They were dressed in good traveling clothing and they carried heavy packs. And Jak knew them all.

They were people of Ratsnay Station.

And in the lead was Jak's mother Rosyn.

She fell on his neck and wept. Jak wept, and Goody Barrab wept as well; the three of them huddled in a knot of grief, shuddering with the sudden force of their collective sorrow.

"We heard," Goody Rosyn sobbed.

"Heard I was dead?" Jak asked.

"Heard that you *lived!*"

Jak held Goody Barrab tighter. She had known, he realized. She had known her son was dead, and had even known how he had died.

When the weeping had passed, Jak asked questions. Tulit and his friends, it turned out, had come to Ratsnay Station. The people of Ratsnay had taken them in for the night, and over the fire and in his cups, Tulit had told them the truth about the Selection. He had also spread the word that Jak lived, along with the fact that the other Selected youth had not survived.

Jak was too shocked to laugh, but not too shocked to appreciate the irony.

The twelve people who had left the Station in the middle of the night had all lost a child to the Cull in recent years. Jak's mother Rosyn had lost both her children.

Goodman Soren, Hamish's father, gripped Jak by the shoulder when he could finally get in past the women. "I hear you've killed some of those Systemoids," he said in a thick voice.

"As many as I could. I'm only sorry I couldn't save Hamish."

"He fought back?"

"Like a lion," Jak said.

Soren patted the long knife hanging at his belt. "So have I."

Jak pondered the possibilities. "Magister Stanton?"

"Pig food," Soren said.

Jak didn't ask for the details. The return to the main column was slow, since Jak was now traveling with a party that was mostly on foot. He put Rosyn and Barrab on his own horse and led it by hand along the rim of the canyon.

By the time they finally reached the camp, he was stumbling from fatigue and thirst. At the sound of the watchword, Jak looked up to see Dyan sitting on her horse above him, the midday sun shining behind her like a golden crown.

She smiled. "Rosyn," she said warmly. "Welcome to the People of Zarah."

*   *   *

Jak stood on a pillar of stone. It was natural, shaped by wind and rain, and he'd had to climb up Molek's shoulders to scrabble to the top of it. From a narrow base Jak could almost wrap his arms around, the pillar bulged out in an onion shape to provide a broad and almost flat spot to stand at its apex. He would have preferred to be standing atop an impregnable wall, but the nearest walls were Farkill's, and there was no way to reach them in time.

The pillar rose beside a narrow canyon cutting down to the north side of the Snaik. At the base of the pillar, a natural bridge of red rock shot across the top of the canyon, giving the arroyo a gate. Taryl lay on that natural bridge, out of sight of everyone but Jak and armed with one of the functioning guns. The sun set to Jak's left, behind the Wahai, and ahead of him he saw wagons trundling in his direction. Collectors' wagons. But where Jak was used to seeing Collectors' wagons loaded with bales of hay or sacks of grain, these held short wooden boxes. A string of horses followed the last wagon.

He had expected the wagons. Dyan had asked for them, sending the two wounded Outriders back to the System, with instructions to return to this meeting point. But Jak had expected the wagons to come accompanied by Guardsmen on horseback, aiming to kill him.

Capture or kill, he thought with a wry inner smile.

But he saw no Guardsmen.

Jak frowned. Each wagon was driven by one man. But even if each man were armed and dangerous, there were only eight of them. If this was a team of enforcers from the System, it seemed like an underpowered one.

Could there be Guardsmen hidden inside the boxes?

Zo, standing on a lower knob of rock beside Jak's pillar, looked down the length of her gun at the coming wagons. They still had only four guns. Jak would have liked fifty. Maybe tomorrow they could make it to Farkill, and maybe Farkill would reveal its secrets and more fully arm them.

On the other hand, if there were only eight drivers in the caravan, he had no need for fifty guns.

The wagons came to a stop. The driver of the first wagon lashed his reins in place and stood. His Collector's cloak opened, and under it he wore the white tunic and trousers marked with the System's emblem in black. Hanging from his belt was a gray sack.

Jak shivered, though the evening air was still warm.

A Cogitant. But not just *any* Cogitant. This Cogitant had a bird-like nose and small ears Jak recognized.

Yurvek.

Was it possible? Jak had seen the man's skull opened by a monofilament line, and his brains mingled with mechanical devices. How could he possibly have survived?

Or was it possible there were multiple Yurveks? Twins?

Or was it possible Yurvek was something other than a human being? Something created, and that could be created in multiple identical copies? He wanted to ask, but of course there was no way he could.

"Well?" Yurvek looked up at Jak.

Jak leaned forward, his hand carefully on his knee to keep his balance. "Are these the children?"

The Cogitant dropped from the driver's platform of his wagon and walked around the front of his team of horses. "The Wrongborn," he confirmed, nodding. "Where are my Outriders?"

"I'll need to see the babies first."

This was the deal Dyan had communicated back to the System. Anji had heard it at the same time Jak did and nodded grimly. The Zaru had offered to return their prisoners, but in return Dyan wanted the Wrongborn children.

All of them.

It wasn't a tactically sound trade. What Jak needed was more guns and more fighters, not more babies. But on a level Jak couldn't quite articulate, taking the Wrongborn babies was the right thing to do. Somehow, taking the Wrongborn babies was at the core of what he and Dyan had *become*.

The Cogitant nodded again, Jak raised his right arm in the agreed signal, and Anji emerged from behind a ridge of stone. As Jak sweated in nervous silence at the height of his pillar, the former Headman of Whitwark Bothy and four other Zaru climbed into the wagons and inspected the boxes. After three minutes of examination, Anji paced the length of each wagon, front to back and then side to side.

Then she raised her hand and waved back at Jak.

The wave meant there were babies, food, and clothing. It also meant the wagons were narrow enough to drive down the canyon. Jak and two of the other Zaru had carefully cleared the path, with whip and bola, of any boulders that would otherwise make it impassable.

Now Jak wore the belt and holsters, fully loaded with two bolas and a whip.

"You'll leave us the wagons," Jak called.

Yurvek shrugged. "We brought horses for the ride back."

Jak raised his left arm, which was a different signal. Molek rode slowly on horseback from a juniper grove to the Cogitant.

Molek held the end of a rope tied around the necks of the captive Outriders, who stumbled along behind his mount. Molek did his best, and even managed to look somewhat dignified clinging to his saddle.

Shad, at the front of the line of captives, stared up at Jak proudly. Behind him, the one-armed Outrider Cheela looked at her shuffling feet. Jak lowered his arm and smiled.

"Molek will lead your people north for an hour," Jak told the Cogitant, "and leave them there."

The Cogitant nodded and Molek continued his slow ride past the wagons.

"One more thing, Jak!" Yurvek yelled.

Jak's ears pricked up. "The only one more thing we need here is that you need to turn around and ride away!"

"The girl!" the Cogitant shouted. "Dyan! You don't need her, and we want her. Send her out!"

Jak laughed. He felt a cold knot of fear in his stomach, but he wasn't going to show it. "That's madness! Go home!"

The Cogitant said nothing. He slowly took the sack from his belt, opened it, and dropped something to the ground.

Anji sprang back.

Jak squinted, trying to make out what the object was. Yurvek stooped, picking up the object, and holding it up for Jak to see.

It was Tulit's severed head.

Jak thanked the Holy Mother he was so far away from the Cogitant. From where he stood, he could almost pretend he couldn't see Tulit's wide-eyed expression of surprise and the perfectly straight line of the cut that had removed his head from his body.

"Thanks!" Jak decided to bluff. "He was a troublemaker and we had to run him off. Wouldn't stop bothering the women, you know how it is."

"He was a troublemaker," the Cogitant agreed. "Troublemakers come to bad ends."

Jak frowned and shook his head. What was the Cogitant getting at? If he was making a threat, it wasn't very explicit.

Then Jak saw the smoke.

Over the Cogitant's shoulder, black smoke crept toward the sky. It wasn't the thin column of white smoke a campfire would send up, but a thick black cloud of smoke that moved slowly, as if it were greasy.

What would be burning out here that would send up such smoke? Then Jak understood what it was.

Ratsnay Station.

The Cogitant must have seen it in his face. "Why yes, Jak, son of Rosyn. Ratsnay Station is gone."

Jak's stomach turned.

"The Guardsmen will be here in minutes!" Yurvek tossed the empty sack to the ground. "You can't run with these wagons! Give us the outlaw and live! Do anything else, and you'll be Culled as you should have been in the first place!"

CHAPTER TWENTY-FOUR

T ake the wagons!" Jak yelled.

Anji stepped forward, but Cogitant Yurvek—or whoever he was—raised his hand and revealed that he was armed, at least with a bola.

Jak raised both his arms. This was a third signal.

Boom!

Taryl fired from his hidden spot atop the natural bridge and hit the Cogitant in the shoulder. Yurvek jerked backward, blood spurting down his arm.

Anji tackled the Cogitant.

Taryl must have realized he risked hitting Anji, because he didn't fire a second shot.

When they had time, and more guns, Jak intended to teach his Zaru to shoot accurately. In fact, he wanted to learn accuracy himself; it was only a guess, but he guessed with practice a shooter could probably kill from a mile away.

For now, when they practiced, they practiced to conserve bullets and aim for the big target: the chest. And mostly, they *practiced* without actually shooting bullets. That didn't leave the Zaru much room for clever use of the guns, like shooting a target in the hand or the foot.

Jak drew one of his own bolas and armed it.

The other drivers of the wagons reached into hidden niches around the sides of their vehicles—under benches, inside wheels, between boxes of weeping infants—and came out with weapons. Did all Collectors' wagons have such hidden compartments, or were these special? Five of the men rushed forward with whips, drawing back over their shoulders to attack. The other two had bows, and they aimed at Jak.

Well, that had been the plan. The reason Jak was on top of the pillar was precisely to attract attention.

"Blasted Systemoids!" he roared. He snapped his bola off at one of the archers and then dropped to a crouch on the pillar.

It was a poorly-aimed throw and it probably would have missed in any case. Still, the threat of being sliced in half sent Jak's target skittering to one side and completely spoiled his shot, sending his arrow nearly straight up.

The second archer had an unimpeded shot, and his arrow hit Jak in the thigh.

Jak grunted and fell sideways, nearly falling right off his perch. If he screamed, he risked distracting his own people. He gripped his thigh with both hands and willed himself to breathe through his teeth and be silent.

The arrow had missed his artery, at least. The arrowhead poked all the way through and out the back of Jak's leg. He could pull it out, but first he had to keep from getting shot a second time.

Anji knelt on the Cogitant's chest and punched him in the face repeatedly. Jak wanted to shout a warning as two of the Systemoids charged in her direction with whips, but he didn't need to. As the nearest turned to unleash his deadly microfilament, Taryl fired again. At the same moment, a second report told him Zo was firing from her place of cover, flat on her belly among the junipers.

Both shots hit the man with the whip, spinning him around and dropping him face-down in the dirt.

A second arrow rattled off the stone inches from Jak's head, bringing his attention fully back to the problem of the archers aiming at him. He rolled back on the stone, trying to find a depression to hide himself in and failing.

He looked down off the edge of the pillar, hearing more reports of the guns. He could just drop, but without someone to break his fall he was likely to break a leg instead.

He risked a look up, and his ear suddenly blossomed in a flower of pain. He'd only been grazed, he realized, but blood spattered the rock on which he lay, and he was afraid to touch his ear for fear of what he'd find.

He saw the two archers, sheltered behind one of the wagons and on the opposite side of it from Zo and Taryl. He didn't see Anji, and Yurvek seemed to be struggling to his feet. A second arrow whizzed over Jak's head, narrowly missing him.

And then, beyond the Systemoids, Jak glimpsed something much more troubling.

He didn't have time to count, but a mob was coming from the direction of Ratsnay Station. He was too far to see the details, but the colors suggested a combination of Outriders and Guardsmen, and by their pace, they would arrive in minutes.

Jak threw himself off the pillar.

The sky spun around him once in a blue flash and then the red sand hit him all along the length of his body, left shoulder first. Jak's resolve not to attract attention to himself shattered.

He screamed.

He couldn't stop, though. Even as the scream still hissed from his lips, Jak rolled and climbed to his knees. The long tail end of the arrow snapped with the movement, sending a jag of pain up along his leg and leaving the short tip and head behind.

One of the archers stepped to the side and took aim at Jak.

Jak scrambled left, but he was too far away from the pillar to get behind cover in time. Worse, he didn't think either Zo or Taryl could get a clean shot at the archer, with the wagon still in the way. Jak gritted his teeth to prepare for the pain—

—and a horse suddenly ran the archer down.

It was Molek! The heavy-faced man fell off his own horse with the impact and the horse galloped away riderless, but the archer was down. Where was the string of prisoners? Jak tried to press himself behind the pillar, seeing the dark red trail of his own blood on the rock with a sinking heart.

The foremost wagon lurched into motion. For a moment its movement hid the remaining archer and Jak looked into the driver's seat. He expected to see Yurvek and some new fiendish attack, but instead found the wagon was in Anji's hands, and she was driving it right into the canyon.

She was right.

"The plan!" Jak shouted. "Get the wagons down into the Snaik!" He didn't think anyone could hear him and he staggered forward, running toward the second wagon. At least for a moment Anji's wagon would shield him, and he looked about for any rock or trough big enough to hide him when the wagon had moved on.

Boom!

As the wagon pulled forward, the archer was exposed to Zo's more oblique angle, and she took the shot. Jak dropped to all fours—it felt like being shot in the leg all over again, but there was relief, too, in stopping his forward run. On all fours he could look under the wheels of Anji's wagon and see the archer.

Who lay still and bloody on the sand.

Yurvek? Jak looked around frantically and didn't see the man, so he tried to stand up again. The pain was too much and Jak collapsed.

"The wagons!" he croaked again. He needed to deal with his leg before he could do anything else, so he turned his attention to the arrow.

His fall and his attempts to run had torn the flesh around the arrow, but he still didn't see the thick, dark gush that would indicate an arterial hit. Jak gripped the arrow by the head and tugged at it.

He screamed, falling back and letting go of the arrow.

Dyan loomed over him. She was supposed to be down in the canyon with two of the guns, to watch for sneak attacks from other angles. "Hold still," she said.

"As if I have a choice," Jak grunted.

She yanked out the arrow in a single pull and Jak howled again. For a moment his vision blacked out, and when he could again see the bright blue sky, Dyan was wrapping a strip of cloth around his thigh. "Can you stand?"

He tried, leaning heavily on her, and got to his feet. "Let me try on my own," he said, and stepped away from her.

He managed not to fall, and flashed Dyan his most confident grin.

"I need to get one of the wagons," Dyan said.

"Go fast," Jak shot back.

Dyan ran forward and climbed into the last of the wagons' driver's seats. Jak surveyed the scene and spotted the four Outrider prisoners, roped to the rear of Dyan's wagon. The other wagons rumbled slowly down the canyon. Yurvek was nowhere in sight.

Jak hobbled a few steps up the base of the rock pillar to get a better look at the oncoming mob. With some relief, he saw that they were coming on in a straight line. But their sheer numbers struck terror into his heart.

He had planned to join Taryl and Zo in a rearguard defense and hold the Systemoids off long enough to let the People of Zarah escape. He hadn't counted on the number of fighters the System would send. The Zaru defense would be useless. They were outnumbered too badly, so badly he didn't think his bluffing tactic could possibly work a third time.

Dyan's wagon started into the canyon.

"Zo!" Jak waved and hobbled towards his Zaru. "Taryl!"

His shooters emerged from cover carefully, guns ready but pointed at the ground, eyes looking around for new threats.

Molek, a bow's shot away against a stretch of green scrub on a hump of gray rock, finally managed to get hold of his panicking horse.

"That's a lot of Guardsmen." Zo's eyes were fierce but her voice trembled.

"I'm ready to die," Taryl said.

What made Taryl so ready? The Gardeners didn't know the Holy Mother, or Redcap Rider, or the Summer Son. Though Jak had told a couple of stories over the campfires of the last few nights, they couldn't be enough to give this man the strength he was showing.

"I am, too," Jak said, and he meant it. "But not uselessly. If we're going to die, we're going to die as heroes."

That hatched a grin from Zo's face. "New plan?"

"New plan." Jak nodded. "You two, get down the canyon now. Stick with the wagons. Dyan will need defenders, because what I'm planning to do will only slow these Systemoids down."

"You sound like you won't be there with us." Taryl's expression was wary.

"Oh, I plan to live," Jak said. "But in case I don't make it, I need you two to be there for her. For the People of Zarah."

Zo looked troubled. "But—"

"Go!" Jak shot an arm in the direction of the canyon mouth and shouted.

Zo and Taryl stopped arguing. Guns still ready, they trotted down the canyon after the rest of the Zaru just as Molek reached Jak and reined in his horse.

"You ready to ride, Headman?"

Jak snorted. "I'm not the Headman."

"As far as I'm concerned, you are. Now get on this horse." Molek learned forward to reach out a helpful arm, nearly tipping himself over.

Jak shook his head. "I need your help for one minute, and then you need to ride down the canyon."

"And leave you?"

"Don't go all the way to the bottom. But ride far enough down to take shelter." Jak explained his plan.

Molek promptly slid down off the horse, tangling his reins in a gray-green shrub to keep the animal from riding off. Then he took the counterweight of Jak's whip and, following Jak's directions, stepped to the far side of the rock pillar. Raising their hands over their heads, the two men brought the invisible monofilament down at an angle through the rock, easing it carefully out the same way they eased it in. Inevitably, they sliced out several slivers of rock, which tumbled down into Jak's hair like a dusty red rain, but the pillar held its position.

It groaned as if it wanted to fall, but it stood.

"You're going to have to catch me," Jak reminded the other man, carefully returning the whip's counterweight into its handle. "Don't delay."

Molek nodded, mounted up, and rode into the canyon.

Jak hobbled behind a rock where he would be out of sight from the approaching force and knelt. At least, he tried to kneel, but a sharp pain in his leg dropped him flat to the earth.

He checked his bandage. Blood seeped through, but it was slow enough that it wouldn't stop him. Scrambling, he pressed himself up against the rock and watched.

He heard Molek gallop away down the canyon below him. He couldn't see Molek, and Molek couldn't see him, and the next sight Molek would have of Jak would be when Jak jumped down into the canyon, hoping to survive and be picked up.

Assuming both of them lived until then.

Minutes slid by like congealing cooking fat. Jak found his mouth dry as slick-rock pebbles. He was sweating, his skin felt like sand, and he desperately wanted to plunge his entire body into a stream of cool water.

Outriders arrived first. Jak watched as two women in long coats dismounted and examined the bodies of the dead while their two companions stood watch on horseback, bolas in their hands. They were all trackers, and there was no way they could avoid seeing where the wagons had gone, but when they followed the wheel tracks to the mouth of the canyon, invisible but for their broad-brimmed hats beyond the natural stone bridge, they stopped and waited.

Jak turned quietly in place, freeing his throwing arm and filling the palm of that hand with his bola. The chips he and Molek had cut out of the pillar gave him a target. He was reasonably sure he could hit it from where he was, so he turned his attention back to the Systemoids.

Guardsmen had arrived. There were twelve of them, and they had a hurried conversation with the Outriders. The result of the conversation was that two of the Outriders turned and rode back a few paces into a flat open space, turning their horses slowly to keep watch on all sides. The two trackers and all twelve Guardsmen urged their horses forward and into the canyon.

This was the moment. It hadn't been Jak's first plan, but it was the best plan he had now, in light of the size of the large force about to overtake him. The force, he reminded himself, that had burned to the ground his home, Ratsnay Station. The force that would now catch and murder his mother, Rosyn.

Except Jak was going to stop them.

He stood. He would be seen, but it didn't matter now. He armed the bola, as Dyan had taught him, swung his arm once, then threw.

The bola whipped through the pillar exactly where Jak wanted it to hit.

A divot of stone sprang forward out of the pillar with a loud *crack!* And then the pillar finally fell, groaning like a wounded giant feeling the release of finally lying down, and the mass of stone on which Jak had earlier stood now tumbled, shattering and splitting into a hundred smaller chunks of red rock, onto the natural bridge, and into the canyon around it.

Screams echoed from the canyon, and Jak grinned.

And then the bridge broke, too, and the screams abruptly stopped.

Red dust exploded into the air, throwing up a concealing cloud between Jak and the two Outriders. He turned to step toward the canyon—

—and something hit him hard on the back of his head.

CHAPTER TWENTY-FIVE

J ak awoke with a serious headache.

Above him was not a blue desert sky, but a smooth wall of pale concrete. Cool, mellow light came from strips punctuating the blank expanse.

He was in one of the System's buildings.

Jak turned his head and vomited.

He learned two things immediately. First, his stomach was empty, because although his body twisted and bucked in retching, nothing came up but thin bile.

And second, he was restrained.

Jak craned his neck to examine his bonds. Straps of a thick cloth like a thicker weave of the System's microfiber crossed his body and tied him down at his chest, waist, and knees. The straps were tight enough that he couldn't lift his body up. Additional straps at his wrists and ankles completed his binding.

Jak lay on a cool, flat surface. Turning his head as far as he could, he could see it was a slab of the same material as the ceiling.

"Welcome back."

Jak recognized the voice. "Yurvek."

Turning his head, Jak spotted Yurvek leaning against one wall. The Cogitant nodded and casually tossed a small object from one hand to the other.

D.J. Butler

"I killed you."

Yurvek shook his head. "I killed myself. But first you told me a secret. Do you remember?"

Jak said nothing.

"You admitted to me that you and your friend spied on Magister Zarah as she and her Creche-leavers approached Ratsnay Station to carry out the Cull in which you should have died. You spied on them before they arrived, and again on the night before the Cull itself."

It was the secret Jak had confided to Yurvek before the Cogitant's death. But couldn't the System have recorded Jak's words with some device hidden in the Cradle?

"Where's Dyan?" he asked.

Yurvek cocked his head to one side and met Jak's eyes. As always, the Cogitant's own eyes remained flat and expressionless, wrong. Jak thought about what he knew—that behind those eyes lay some kind of *device*, and within them shone a *light*—and shuddered.

"Dead."

A wave of nausea took Jak again. "You're a liar."

"All your friends. All the Gardeners who abandoned their Bothy and followed you into the wilderness. Dead. Sliced to pieces."

"Not hanged?" Jak's breath was hard to control and came in gasps.

Yurvek shrugged. "None of you is important enough to hang."

Jak laughed. "Now I know you're lying. You people *hate* Dyan. You'd *love* to make an example of her on that Gallows of yours."

Yurvek nodded. "You're right, Jak. The System lies. But it lies for the greater good."

"Whose greater good?"

Yurvek said nothing.

"So, what are you doing here?" Jak asked. "Just want to taunt me before you kill me?" He wanted to believe Dyan was still alive—Dyan, and Anji, and the others—but he couldn't believe anything Yurvek said, anyway.

"I don't *want* to kill you, Jak. Any more than I *hate* Dyan, or want to kill her."

"Oh, yes, I remember. This is the part where you compare me with grain to be harvested, or sheep to be culled from the herd."

Yurvek's face showed no emotion. "We see you have learned Magister-designate Dyan's lessons just as well as you have learned your own."

Jak spat. He meant to spit on the floor at Yurvek's feet, but he couldn't turn his head quite far enough, so the spittle ended up on his own shoulder. "Stanton's dead."

Yurvek nodded slowly. "We had to burn down Ratsnay Station to be sure there were no surviving witnesses."

Jak yanked uselessly at the straps on his wrists.

"Your people don't remember chess, do they, Jak?"

Jak said nothing. He didn't recognize the word.

"It's a game," the Cogitant said. He again tossed the object from hand to hand, but Jak didn't quite see what it was. "Chess is a game of two players. It is a game of strategy, with no room for the play of luck—chess has no cards, no dice, no throwing of fingers or the knucklebones of sheep. It is a game of complex moves, a game of pure decision played between two intellects."

"If you're inviting me to play, I'm going to have to decline," Jak muttered. "I'm all tied up right now."

"Before the Cataclysm," Yurvek continued, "the people who lived in this land created thinking machines."

If he'd been able, Jak would have sat up in surprise. As it was, he turned his head and looked more closely at the Cogitant. The Cogitant stepped closer, and he set the object he'd been fiddling with on the table beside Jak's head, and directly in Jak's line of sight.

It was a monofilament bola.

"Many of the early thinking machines and the experiments with them revolved around this game chess," Yurvek said. "Machines were built that could play the game, and they played humans. At first, the humans won."

Yurvek was himself, at least in part, a machine. Jak tried not to stare at the Cogitant and said nothing.

"Then there came a day when the humans lost. Not just one human, but the best humans ceased to be able to beat the thinking machines at chess."

"So what ... they quit playing?"

Yurvek still stood beside Jak's slab, but Jak now heard footsteps. He stayed focused on Yurvek.

"It's important to realize why the machines started winning, and then why the machines ceased to be able to lose. You see, chess is a game with no random elements."

"You said that already."

"It also has no *hidden* elements. There is very little opportunity to bluff. Victory therefore comes from out-thinking your opponent. From seeing the possibilities farther and farther into the future, from calculating successfully how far into the future your opponent is seeing, and from making moves that leave you more and more possible winning combinations, and fewer and fewer possible wins to your opponent."

"This is boring," Jak lied.

"And as they built thinking machines, humans told themselves a very particular story about the machines." Yurvek smiled, a humorless, lipless expression. "You can read it over and over in the books written before the Cataclysm. People believed the great advantage they would always have over their machines servitors was something they thought of as *intuition*."

Where was this going? Jak tried not to frown.

"Humans told themselves over and over again that a mystical ability to *guess correctly* would always let them win. They believed— they genuinely believed—humans would always defeat thinking machines because humans could make decisions that were on their surface irrational, but somehow correct. They believed the machines' strict rationality would allow them to be defeated by this magical power of intuition."

Jak finally did frown. "I don't know about *magical power*."

Yurvek ignored him. "Chess gave the lie to this foolish idea. What happened, you see, is the *machines* started to make moves that were on their surface irrational, but somehow correct. It turned out the machines had better intuition than human beings. What chess taught us was that what humans had called intuition reflected an ability, perhaps unconscious, to calculate all possible outcomes and play the odds, determining, even if unconsciously, that an apparently irrational move was in fact the strongest. And the case of chess proved, over and over, that machines are greatly superior to human beings."

"I don't know why you're telling me this."

Yurvek stepped back from Jak and clasped his hands in front of him. Jak took the opportunity to turn his head the other way and see who had made the footsteps he'd heard; standing opposite Yurvek, beside Jak's head and left shoulder, was a heavy woman in a Healer's uniform. Beside her was a shining steel cart with a number of implements laid out on it, including a series of very thin knife blades.

He looked back to Yurvek, a hard knot in the pit of his stomach.

"A funny thing happened to chess," the Cogitant said. "Humans and thinking machines began to play together in teams. The human would make strategic decisions, and would also decide each turn's move, but in both cases, on the basis of the thinking machine's long-term calculations and forecasts. The machines' intuition drove the moves of the human players."

"Until the humans became superfluous," Jak said. "I've heard this story before."

Yurvek fell silent and stared at Jak, furrowing his brow. "That is a very interesting thing to say, Jak, son of Rosyn."

"Yeah? That's my intuition, that is. Magical power."

Yurvek laughed. He almost seemed amused, but for his dead eyes. "Tell me where you heard a story about humans becoming superfluous."

Jak faltered. The System had destroyed Ratsnay Station to keep the secret of the Cull. What would it do to keep secret the strange history Jak and Dyan had learned in Farkill?

"You know," he finally said, trying and failing to shrug. "It's just the kind of thing that somehow survives out among the Landsies. Strange old memories you try to wipe out, but they keep coming back."

"Hmm." Yurvek didn't look convinced. "Were you bound for Satulak?"

The question came out of nowhere, but after it sank in it was followed by a wave of relief. Dyan wasn't dead; she had escaped and the System was trying to find her. Yurvek wanted Jak to tell him where they had been headed so Outriders could go capture the Zaru.

Jak managed not to laugh out loud. "Yeah," he said, "that's it. Didn't you know, Satulak is a magical garden where you can lie around all day and food will be magically produced for you with no price to pay?"

Yurvek nodded. "We'd heard the same thing."

"Is this the end of the story?" Jak asked. There was no way the Cogitant would kill him. They needed him to find Dyan. They wanted to make an example of her, and recapture all the Zaru, and stop them from telling people what they knew about the System and what they had done. His heart pounded, but a feeling of relief slowly filled Jak's body.

The Cogitant stepped back to Jak's slab and picked up the monofilament bola.

"The humans never became superfluous. The winning players, in life as in chess, were teams combining human and thinking machine players together and using both their talents."

"Yeah, but you just told me humans don't have any talents," Jak said. "You said human intuition was a myth."

"The fact that human intuition was a myth doesn't mean humans don't have talents." Yurvek armed the bola and pulled its counterweight an arm's length from the weapon. Jak tried not to stare at the apparently empty space in between. "Humans are very good at survival."

"We're adaptable," Jak said. "Magister Stanton liked to say so."

"Yes. Humans tenaciously survive the worst disasters. And to a surprising degree, their survival has to do with their powerful ability to breed."

Jak snorted. "I don't know what you have in mind, Yurvek," he said, "but I'm spoken for."

Yurvek chuckled, a slow, dry laugh. "Very good, Jak. The way humans reproduce, creating new generations not exactly matching either parent, allows the species to change over time. To become resistant to new parasites, to defeat new predators, to constantly change."

"We improve." Jak grinned.

Yurvek shook his head. "That doesn't follow," he said slowly. "New and successful generations may in fact be objectively inferior to their ancestors—they're simply better adapted to their ancestors' environment."

"Fine," Jak said. "And when do we get to the end of the story?" Now that he was confident he would be kept alive, he was almost looking forward to more conversations like this with Yurvek. The Cogitant said strange things, but they were at least interesting.

"Now," Yurvek said.

Then the Cogitant brought his monofilament line down through Jak's head.

ABOUT THE AUTHOR

D.J. Butler (Dave) is a novelist living in the Rocky Mountain northwest. His training is in law, and he worked as a securities lawyer at a major international firm and in-house at two multinational semiconductor manufacturers before taking up writing fiction.

Dave writes speculative fiction for all audiences. In addition to his steampunk, urban fantasy, and science fiction novels published with WordFire Press, look for *The Kidnap Plot* (Knopf) and *Witchy Eye* (Baen, March 2017).

Dave is a lover of language and languages, a guitarist and self-recorder, and a serious reader. He is married to a powerful and clever woman and together they have three devious children.

Read about Dave's writing projects at:

http://davidjohnbutler.com.

IF YOU LIKED ...

If you liked *Urbane*, you might also enjoy:

Crecheling
Dave Butler

Crystal Doors
Rebecca Moesta & Kevin J. Anderson

Beasts of Tabat
Cat Rambo

OTHER WORDFIRE PRESS TITLES BY D.J. BUTLER

City of the Saints

Rock Band Fights Evil

Hellhound on my Trail #1
Snake Handlin' Man #2
Crow Jane #3
Devil Sent the Rain #4
This World is not my World #5
The Good Son #6
Earth Angel #7

Our list of other WordFire Press authors and titles is always growing.
To find out more and to see our selection of titles, visit us at:

wordfirepress.com